LEARNING FOR LIFE
LONDON BOROUGH OF SUTTON LIBRARIES

RENEWALS   Please quote: date of return, your ticket number
and computer label number for each item.

NOTHING BUT THE TRUTH

Pauline Bell

Constable • London

Constable & Robinson Ltd
3 The Lanchesters
162 Fulham Palace Road
London W6 9ER
www.constablerobinson.com

First published in the UK by Constable,
an imprint of Constable & Robinson Ltd 2005

A copy of the British Library Cataloguing in Publication
Data is available from the British Library.

ISBN 1-84119-930-3

Printed and bound in the EU

For Charlotte and Alan

I am grateful for help offered by Ray Horner
in the minefield of insurance options

Prologue

In her high street bank in the centre of Leeds Lisa Prentice sat, biting her nails, until, at nine twenty precisely, she came to sit at Customer Service desk number 3. She had not needed Mrs Viner's warning that she must not let the bank down. This was her first chance to show her mettle since she had come to work here after leaving school ten months ago.

She had heeded all the advice Mrs Viner had given her the night before, rightly divining that 'advice' was her supervisor's euphemism for 'instructions to be followed to the letter'. It had gone against all her instincts of self-presentation to put on the low-heeled shoes and a skirt that reached below the knee – at just the level to make anyone's legs look like trees. She wore a demure blouse with what her mother called a Peter Pan collar and the dreadful, borrowed woollen cardigan with the bank's logo on the shoulder. At least, now she was off the counter for a few days, she didn't have to wear the tellers' horrible dark navy uniform.

Mrs Viner had come to her as she was clearing her counter the previous evening. Mr Carson still had this dreadful flu and, during the day, she had had to send home two more victims. Lisa knew. One of them had been her friend Jill.

For once, Mrs Viner had been almost friendly. 'Do you think that you could take over Mr Carson's desk for a day or two? You've done the basic training. It's mostly setting up new accounts that he deals with. All the information you need is on the computer. You're a bright girl. You can't go wrong, really.'

Lisa hadn't been so sure. You could easily go wrong if you didn't know where, in the computer's innards, the information was stored, or the magic words for calling up the right sites. Still, she had had no intention of letting this chance slip. Mrs Viner had stayed behind for a while, checking through her questions with her.

She rehearsed it all again as she took out the items she would need from Mr Carson's drawer. She would be glad now, less nervous, when business began and she was actually doing the job. She was determined, if she possibly could, to deal with everything herself and to refrain from calling on the help that Mrs Viner had personally offered if she should need it.

Four more minutes to go. As a distraction from her worries, she looked around her and upwards, enjoying the beauty of the bank itself. It was mid-Victorian, like most of the buildings around it, but very light because of its huge, curved glass roof. She admired its stained glass border with silver wreaths on rich dark red.

It was a pity, Lisa thought, lowering her gaze, that they hadn't done the chairs up in the same red. Scarlet was the only word to describe them. Just as unimpressive was the boring grey carpet with its extra dirty tracks leading from the revolving doors to the beginning of where the queue would very soon be snaking, between tapes in a path to the counter.

With their customary, squeaky protest, the main doors began to revolve. Lost in her own thoughts, Lisa had not noticed Mr Tanner doing his ritual unlocking. She made an unnecessary rearrangement of the items on Mr Carson's desk and tried to stay calm as, from the impatient surge of clients rushing in, four people detached themselves and made for her desk. Three men and a woman, she noticed.

The woman was sufficiently personable for the three men to stand back and allow her to head the queue. She was sensibly dressed for the cold March morning. Her narrow skirt barely skimmed her knees but her well-polished high boots reached up to meet it. She wore a white polo-necked sweater under a sheepskin jacket. Her brown curling hair was drawn back and tucked into a knitted beret a bit like the one Lisa's great aunt had made for her last Christmas. Her mother made her wear it when they went to visit, but only from the car to Aunt Lavinia's door. Lisa's mother was not unreasonable.

On this woman, though, the beret looked right. All the men in the queue were stealing glances at her. She was not young but she had style. Unfortunately, she also had big teeth that really spoilt her smile. Lisa felt sorry for her. Crooked teeth your dentist could sort out for you, but, if size were the problem, you would just have to live with it.

The woman was ignoring the interested glances and scrabbling in her handbag. It looked like a passport that she was taking out, together with an assortment of envelopes. In what Lisa considered a 'posh' accent, she made a request to open an account. 'Be pleasant,' Mrs Viner had told Lisa, so she smiled as she took the driving licence from the pile of papers and documents the woman had placed on the desk. She opened it. 'Good morning, Mrs Markey. Phyllida's quite an unusual first name. Is it a family one?'

'Yes.'

'Are you new to the district?'

'No.'

Well, if the woman didn't want to chat she didn't have to. Lisa tapped keys according to Mrs Viner's instructions and smiled again. 'I'll have to ask you a few questions. It seems like a lot of fuss but I need to establish that you are who you say you are and that the address you give me is where you really live.'

It occurred to Lisa that this was not quite the kind of pleasantness that Mrs Viner had had in mind, but her tongue ran nervously on. 'We just have to find you on the electoral roll.' She pressed the keys with unnecessary force to show her anxiety to oblige her customer. 'Here we are. Mr and Mrs Markey at 19, Boston Road.'

Mrs Markey seemed to know the drill better than Lisa did. She picked up the driving licence and an Inland Revenue coding notice from the pile on the desk for Lisa to examine. The licence dated from 1982 and therefore bore no photograph. Would this be a problem? Lisa decided that the supporting documents Mrs Markey had brought were ample compensation. Her face aching from her fixed smile, she asked, 'Do I have your permission to do a credit reference search?'

The woman indicated with a nod that she had no objection. Lisa applied herself once more to the keys, still pounding energetically. When she looked up, she saw that two of the three men had transferred to another queue. She hoped Mrs Viner was not going to take her to task for being too slow. Mrs Markey delved once more into her capacious bag, this time producing bank and building society statements, both sufficiently recent for their purposes. Lisa checked the information they gave with what was on her screen.

'That seems fine, but I'm afraid we're a suspicious lot. I have to ask you why, with a building society account and two accounts with a different bank, you now need another current account. Don't worry. It's just a standard question. You'd hardly believe it but we occasionally have people laundering their profits from drug dealing and so on by –'

The woman cut in sharply. 'I assure you I have no dealings with drugs in any shape or form. However, you may find my answer to your question – well, not quite creditable, if you'll excuse the pun.'

Lisa blinked. A pun was a joke. Had she missed something? She hoped she would understand the answer to her politely phrased question when it came.

'The other accounts I have access to are held jointly with my husband Donald. Now I've got a job – well, I'm self-employed – and I want to keep the money from it as mine, separate from what we share.'

Lisa was used to saving clients' faces. 'Of course. Then, when you buy him a present it's really from you and not just out of the housekeeping money.'

'I suppose so.' Obviously, this particular client did not require Lisa's efforts.

'Actually . . .'

'Yes?'

Lisa squared her shoulders. On another occasion Mrs Viner had told her not to be so diffident. 'You might be better with a small business account.'

The woman seemed to consider this. 'You could be right, but for the moment I'll wait, see how things pan out. I'm still – well, at the probationary stage, you might say. You could switch it for me later?'

'Oh, certainly.' Lisa hesitated. How could she get the details she needed in order to check things out with Mrs Markey's employer without giving her client the third degree? 'Is it interesting work?'

'Very, but it's freelance, mostly pieces for the *Yorkshire Evening Post*. It's going to depend what I find to report on and whether they like my stuff enough to keep thinking of me when they need someone. What goes into this account will be a bit hit and miss, at least to begin with.'

Lisa breathed a sigh of relief. This reply had made her next two questions unnecessary. The interrogation over, she relaxed. Guiding this obviously intelligent woman through the final stage of the necessary procedure would be easy. She began to look forward to the rest of her day. Her customer was beginning to dread the remainder of hers.

In a bank, still in Leeds but rather more off the beaten track, Tom Collins too sat at the Customer Service desk. The branch was a small one and Tom's customers, since he had taken up his present position, had problems, complaints and requests that were many and various. Fortunately, since it was a little-used branch, he was hardly overworked. There was talk of closing it but Tom was not worried. The time between talk and formal proposals, like the time between proposals and action, was always protracted and he would be retiring in eighteen months' time.

He slumped over his desk, his eyes resting on but not seeing the worn, marbled lino tiles and dusty pots of fabric plants that furnished the run-down building. There was no chair for a customer on the far side of his desk. He processed his clients swiftly from long practice and had no wish to keep them longer than their transactions made necessary.

He looked up as the door swung open and felt sufficient mild interest in the woman who entered to sit up straighter. He even felt no more than slight irritation when her purposeful strides brought her face to face with him. More lazy than lecherous, he nevertheless assessed her. Hard to guess her age, but well preserved, whatever it was. Her motley assortment of clothes was transformed by her general manner and bearing into an outfit that suited her. There was even a sort of outrageous chic about her old-fashioned knitted hat.

She wanted to open an account. Well, that suited him. The last client to stand at his desk had become almost apoplectic and demanded that his accounts here should all be closed. This woman even had the requisite documents ready for his perusal. Swiftly he complied with the majority of the bank's regulations, set up the account she required, considered briefly whether to extend their acquaintance, decided he couldn't be bothered and let her go. It was the awful teeth that swung it.

By early afternoon, the woman had completed her round of banks and had progressed to building societies. The one she had just entered was far less fancy than the rest and

12

not as warm. It was smaller, maybe a little too small to be safe, but she was not leaving now, not after all the trouble she'd had parking. The walls all round the room were grey-panelled, the ceiling, for variety, grey on white.

A loan sale was being advertised on huge posters, stuck in the windows and blocking much of the light. It was a modern building with flimsy grey internal doors, a row of intimidating grey machines and a grey checked carpet with a logo in dusty blue. The tables were grey. The personnel had grey hair and faces.

The woman took a grip on herself and pulled out her documents for the thirteenth time. She was tired and dispirited. After this there were still the Halifax and the Post Office basic account for the receipt of benefits. This was proving to be a long, long day.

Chapter One

The reunion for past pupils of Heath Lees High School in Cloughton, West Yorkshire, was to be held on the evening of the third Saturday in July. The original intimation of this event had come to the Mitchell family in the form of a hand-delivered note, pushed through their letter box one morning whilst Virginia was picking up the twins from nursery school.

Hi! Ginny, have you heard that Geoff Maynard will be retiring at the end of the summer term? The old pupils will be putting on a do for him – in the school hall, at his insistence, date still to be fixed. I know you never joined the Old Pupils' Association officially. You've kept in touch though, and several folk have suggested that you be co-opted on to the party committee. What about it? I'll ring you when you've had a chance to think about it. Cheers, Val.

Later, Virginia had shown the note to her husband and wondered aloud who might attend and how much they would all have changed.

He'd interrupted her, his tone horrified. 'You don't mean you're going?'

'You're not interested? I think I'd quite enjoy meeting up with everyone again.'

Benny had dropped the scrap of paper with its scribbled message on the table between them. 'Maynard's been at Heath Lees since the Dark Ages. We wouldn't know all the old codgers who'll turn up. You can please yourself, of course.'

She usually did, and with his full co-operation. She began to clear their supper dishes as she debated the matter. Yes, she would be there – and when he asked after all his old classmates he could whistle for answers. However, she hurriedly extricated herself from Valerie's plans for her. Four children aged between nine and three made a sufficient excuse. There was no need to say that the word committee was anathema to her.

Virginia had compromised, drawing up a very specific list of the contributions she was prepared to make and promising to publicize the event as widely as she could. As a start, she had rung her brother but Alex too was scathing and adamantly refused to return to Cloughton for the occasion. He was mystified by Virginia's wish to go back into her past. 'What has all that got to do with who we are now?' he'd demanded.

'But don't you want to give Mr Maynard a good send-off?'

'Don't give me that. This party has nothing to do with Maynard. It's just a chance for the committee to look important and organize us all. A lot of middle-aged men will come to tell lies about their phenomenal careers and the old biddies will bitch about each other. You'll believe half the stories they all tell and come away dissatisfied with the life that you used to be perfectly happy with.'

Virginia considered and decided that she half agreed with him. 'How good it will be to see so-and-so again' was not uppermost in her mind. She was certainly curious about what had happened to her former classmates and wondered how her own achievements would compare with theirs. Perhaps her menfolk were right. Still, as a mark of respect and gratitude to Mr Maynard, she would attend.

The official invitations were sent out and Virginia was amused at Benny's reaction. 'It says "Mr and Mrs" on the card, but the envelope's addressed to you. I'm not asked as an old pupil – just as your appendage.'

'Well, I've been the one who attended all the plays and concerts and gave to the bazaars and jumble sales.'

He usually tried to be fair. Now he nodded. 'That's true. And you wrote in to the *Clarion* about them when they were good.' But he didn't always succeed. Virginia grinned as he went on, 'Anyway, a fat lot of time I had for that sort of caper. They always came when I was in the middle of a tricky case.'

Virginia answered with a measured silence, part tactful, part politic, part disbelieving. She hadn't really expected Benny to attend the function. His school career had been inglorious. Few of his teachers had approved of him and could hardly be blamed for it. Benny admitted that he had regarded the seven periods of his school day as a series of battles with his long-suffering instructors, most of which he won. Maynard, though, had been one of the few staff who had recognized his academic potential and had encouraged him. He surely owed it to the old man to make a gesture at his retirement.

Benny's thoughts were obviously running along the same lines. 'I've already written to Maynard. Just a note saying I appreciated him sticking up for me and wishing him the best.'

Virginia was ashamed at feeling surprised and wasted no more time in trying to change his mind. As they got up to clear the supper dishes, he continued a muttered reinforcement of his standpoint. 'Alex is right. This do is just a peg to hang a lot of nosiness on. Wild horses won't drag me there!'

It was a decision which, professionally, he was soon to regret.

The evening in question turned out to be hot and sticky. In another Cloughton household Donald Markey, to whom such matters were of considerable importance, was having

16

to reconsider the garments he had planned to wear. What on earth, he demanded of his wife, was suitable wear for school if you weren't a pupil? He had recommended to his fellow members of Val's committee at least two local and good hotels as possible venues for the intended festivity, but had been ignored. The school itself had been Geoffrey Maynard's choice as the setting for this tribute from his past pupils.

To the oldest of them, he had been their junior geography master. To others, as his promotions followed, he was their year tutor, their head of sixth form, their deputy head or their headmaster. A bit of a stick-in-the-mud, old Maynard – thirty or so years working in the same building and now he was insisting that his leaving bash had to be there, even though his former pupils had declared themselves willing to foot the bill. Still, he'd been a good old sport, mildly asking for the best they could all muster and usually getting it.

So the suit that would have been just right for Cedar Court had been rejected in favour of Calvin Klein jeans and a Ben Sherman T-shirt. They were out of the question in this heat, though, and it would have to be a short-sleeved shirt and his thinnest slacks. And what on earth would Phyl wear?

He watched her now as she came back from the adjoining shower room and opened the doors at her end of the wall of wardrobe units. With her accustomed modesty, she had taken her undergarments into the shower room with her and was, presumably, wearing them. She had covered the rolls of flesh that were still on view with her dressing gown and must have been almost suffocating. He wondered whether she would resent his advice and sought to phrase it tactfully. He knew how to be diplomatic, was good at tact; he had to be.

She sighed, but the sound suggested impatience rather than depression. He was encouraged to whip off the draped gown and place his arms around her ample shoulders. 'Wear the purple for me. I love you in it.'

She neither encouraged nor repulsed the physical contact, but extended an arm to pull out the dress. She looked at him in the mirror. 'It's a bit formal compared with . . .' She waved a substantial arm to indicate his casually draped leanness.

'Who cares? Nicky won't be missing this opportunity to sport her finery, will she?' He was concerned that his wife should look right for her sake, rather than his own. Granted, she was not the sort of woman his former school friends would be expecting him to produce tonight but he had no wish to change her. He didn't need a trophy wife. He was content in his marriage to Phyllida and usually ready to indulge her. They suited each other. She had developed a sort of contentment since they were married – certainly since Zak was born. Having him had given her – not confidence exactly, perhaps fulfilment was the word.

He picked up the photograph of their son from her bedside table. He resembled his mother but there was no harm in that. There was no surplus flesh on the boy's fine-boned face, which was handsome in an ascetic way. He was blond and vulnerable-looking now but his hair would darken and become less wispy and his mouth would harden. He would probably grow up to look like Phyl's brother and that would do nicely.

Her head emerging from folds of the purple dress, Phyllida watched as he replaced the framed snapshot. He was annoyed with himself for reminding her of their running disagreement about the boy. He was not sure whether she was still sulking or now merely missing Zak. She said, 'I still think nine is far too young for boarding school.'

Donald turned away from the picture and repeated his usual argument that the boy needed more discipline than the local state junior school provided. Nevertheless, he had been a little surprised and very relieved when his son's letters began to arrive, full of excitement and enthusiasm for his new life.

When Phyl read them, he had expected to be let out of

the doghouse, but, inexplicably, the letters had made her even more upset and resentful of the arrangement. Usually he found his wife far more predictable than any of his other women. Even so he had better not forget that she was still a female and allowances had to be made for the capriciousness of all of them, even the amenable one he'd married.

He did up the long zip in the back of her dress for her, then gathered up his keys and wallet. She was going to do her face and he couldn't bear to watch the inexpert daubing she performed in order to 'make the best of herself'. If she really wanted to do that, she should lose at least three stones in weight and leave her pretty face alone. Phyl's bones were much better than Jane's or Nicky's. Her skin and hair would be too if only she knew how to make the most of them. She could have been stunning. She had all the ingredients collected but she never managed to follow the recipe.

Pleased with this conceit, he checked his own well-preserved person in the full-length mirror between the windows, winked at it complacently and went over to the door. 'I'll put the car away and so on whilst you finish off.'

Phyllida knew the job was already done, but she let him go. As Donald had guessed, the informality of the occasion had wrongfooted her. Her half of the wardrobe contained not a few long, dark, straight and suitable dresses, chosen by him for the formal dinners, theatre trips and concerts to which she more habitually, though not very frequently, accompanied him. Her casual clothes she chose because the colours cheered her up. It mattered little to her whether her neighbours and female friends were impressed by her appearance. In any case, there was no point in trying, since she knew she lacked the 'eye' to judge whether she had got it right.

The purple dress was a good choice for tonight. At least she could trust Donald for that. It was elegant but simple enough not to look too formal. It suited the weather too.

Donald understood her embarrassing problems with the heat. Her flesh insulated her too efficiently and yet needed a decent veiling even for her small degree of personal pride. Now she agonized over her legs. In tights they would cook. Uncovered, her huge thighs would sweat and chafe together till the skin was raw.

She scowled at her reflection, then reached into a drawer. Rather cook than bleed. After smoothing the nylon over her already damp flesh she opened the smaller bedroom window. This was the coolest room – it had had no direct sun since mid-morning – so the air that seeped in was warmer than that indoors. She left the window, though, deriving some psychological benefit from seeing it open.

Taking a step sideways to look into the mirror, she pulled her mouth into a gargoyle shape in an attempt to obtain a neat outline in plum-coloured lipstick, painted her eyelids blue and darkened her brows with a pencil. Not stopping to examine the total effect, she tidied the dressing table, then picked up her bag from the bed, pausing to look again at the photograph of Zak. She had thought that it was her own spoiling of him that had led to his removal from the house. There was nothing wrong with the area's little junior school. It occurred to her now that another reason for Zak's banishment might be his increasing awareness of his father's amorous adventures.

A car door slammed. Looking out of the window she saw Eric's Fiesta at the gate. Closing the casement she hurried downstairs to let their volunteer chauffeur in and to inspect his wife's outfit. Without jealousy, she admired Nicky's very short, very strappy summer dress and open sandals. With relief, she saw that Eric was wearing a formal suit.

Donald came into the hall behind her. She waited for his metamorphosis from taciturn husband to witty friend. His isolated and brief remarks to her would give place to ironic comment and caustic criticism that, in Eric and Nicky, would produce quiet chuckles and immoderate laughter

20

respectively. Only occasionally could she supply the stimulation with which most of their guests drew out the social Donald.

'Why is it,' he asked them, 'that, at school reunions, you always feel younger than everyone else looks?' Phyllida felt a faint doubt about the question's origin and hoped that, if Donald had stolen it, Eric would fail to recognize the source.

The conversation turned to who was likely to attend the reunion. Phyllida looked defensively at Nicky. 'I won't be the only one who is out of place tonight. You've brought Eric and Morris is bringing Valerie.'

Her tone was almost aggressive, and Nicky looked startled. Eric smiled. 'You mean the three of us might only have been invited because we're married to old pupils? I'm sure we'll be welcome.'

'Valerie will. She's organized all the food.' Phyllida realized she had embarrassed her guests and let her husband refloat the conversation.

'Morris said that seventy-odd folk have accepted. They've written to the five continents. It must have taken a year's supply of stamps and stationery. I wonder whether Sean Sefton will turn up.'

'Why ask about him in particular?' Nicky demanded. 'You weren't specially friendly with him, were you?'

Donald shook his head. 'Definitely not – though he's working for me at the moment. It's just that he was one of the very few in our year who didn't like Maynard.'

Nicky sniffed. 'As I remember it, Mr Maynard didn't care much for him either.'

Now Phyllida had something concrete to contribute to the conversation. 'We shan't see him. He's in Stirling on business this weekend.'

'How do you know him?'

'What's he doing these days?'

Phyllida answered Nicky rather than her husband. 'He's set himself up as a financial adviser.'

Nicky looked curiously at Phyllida. 'Are you one of his clients?'

Phyllida shrugged. 'Donald is. I happened to bump into Lorna Dyson and Val Tate in town last week and he stopped to speak to the three of us. In the end, we all four had coffee in Molloy's. Val was obsessed with the menus for tonight. We all had to give our views on whether the food should be hot or cold and whether it should be eaten sitting down or standing around, getting our fingers greasy. We all voted for sitting and hot, but none of us expected this kind of weather. It'll be completely wrong.'

Eric was sanguine. 'Can't see anything Val serves being less than delicious.'

'Will there be dancing?' Nicky looked hopeful.

Donald put his hand on his wife's arm. 'You hate dancing. Do you want me to make some excuse for you?'

Phyllida glared at him. 'I wouldn't miss it for the world. I dare say I can stand on the most crowded bit of floor and claim there isn't room for me to strut my stuff.' Nicky stifled a giggle. Phyllida continued with great dignity, 'Can you wait for me for another five minutes?'

'Surely.' Eric settled himself more deeply into the folds of his armchair. 'We're still a bit early. There wasn't as much traffic as I allowed for.'

Phyllida disappeared for precisely the five minutes she had requested. When she returned, she wore a garish dirndl skirt with a voluminous red T-shirt and dancing pumps. Her face shone quite literally, scrubbed clean of all its make-up but wearing a defiant smile. Donald groaned silently.

Virginia Mitchell had intended to arrive at the school half an hour or so ahead of the official start of operations. She felt slightly guilty for leaving so much of the preparation for it to Valerie and thought that she could at least be on hand to help with any small, last-minute crises.

She was unsurprised to find her family had other ideas. Michael had fallen on the garden steps, though fortunately he had needed consolation rather than hospital treatment. Sinead had knocked over a full glass of blackcurrant juice. Declan had been in questioning mode. 'What colour is a chameleon,' he had wanted to know, 'if it walks on a mirror?' Knowing that Benny would get his own back, Virginia had promised that his father would explain.

However, Caitlin, placid and practical in advance of her six years, had helped with the mopping of bloodied knee and stained carpet and Benny, for once, had managed to arrive home at precisely the time arranged. As he prepared and ate his meal, his elder daughter gave him a succinct account of the day's catastrophes and of the invaluable help she had given her mother.

Virginia had hurriedly showered and changed her clothes, reckoning that she could still offer Valerie and her cohorts ten minutes' assistance. She used the three-mile drive to the school to empty her mind of family matters and consider the evening ahead. Halfway up the hill on which Heath Lees was built, she took a left turn into Moorside Rise which would give her access to the school's back entrance. At a busy time, she would have had trouble at the top where the two pavements reached out into the road towards each other. It made a safer place for the residents to cross but it held up the traffic in a bottleneck. Now, though, it was clear and she drove without stopping past the houses with their peeling doors and littered gardens. At the brow of the hill she turned right into the school grounds and parked neatly in the space behind a row of bins where the smokers' club had used to meet – probably did still. Later, the main car park would be very crowded but, from here, she would be able to make her getaway when she was good and ready.

Finding all the back and side entrances to the main building locked, Virginia strolled round to the front. She noted that, since her schooldays, the spaces in the main car park had been neatly marked out, and that the gardens, only fairly tidy during her own time here, were now immaculate. Many of the school's pupils lived in the ill-kept housing estate through which she had just driven. Maynard had obviously run a tight ship, once he took charge here. Perhaps, after all, the smokers had been disbanded.

For old times' sake, she climbed the stone steps leading from the car park to the main road and considered the school from the place where she had first seen it every morning as she hurled herself off the school bus. On the whole it looked the same – the yellow sandstone surrounding wall, dirt-encrusted but overhung by trees that were older than the school. The stone of the main building it enclosed matched the wall. In Virginia's schooldays, the newer block had spoiled the picture. Now, in spite of clean air acts, it had become sufficiently scruffy to be assimilated into the general tidy shabbiness.

As she turned and hurried into the building, she noted that the school nameplate, permanently vandalized in her day, now bore the full title with all its letters present and correct. Another star for Maynard.

As soon as Virginia entered the main hall, her slight guilt disappeared. There was Val, in charge, in extremis seemingly but in her element. Her beautiful, slightly curling hair clung now to her perspiring neck and in the crevice between her two chins. Her acolytes scurried busily at her behest, whilst several youths, probably sixth formers, set up their disco equipment on the platform.

Maynard was in the middle of the hall looking slightly bewildered and Virginia paused for a moment, regarding him affectionately. He had dressed – as he had from time immemorial, except for the most formal of occasions – in sports jacket and baggy flannels with a crisp shirt but a rather chewed-looking tie. He stood in the same manner as ever, head slightly bowed, his left hand rumpling the unruly tufts of hair on his double crown. The hair had been black. Now it was greying and receding and cut closer to his head. She wondered if his pupils still copied the mannerism in mockery – when he was not looking, of course. She glanced at the platform and saw that they did.

It had been a mistake to look up. Before she could lower her lashes, Valerie caught her eye and her moment of contemplation was over. 'Could you just . . .' was the prelude to rather a long list of tasks. Val thanked her in advance for their completion and passed on to her next victim. Virginia spent ten minutes doing such of them as she considered necessary, then took out of her pocket the leaflet that she had picked up as she came in and studied the evening's programme.

As she read, she gave silent thanks that her husband had refused to be here. She had hoped for a school choir item, a short address from Maynard, a presentation, drinks, food and an early conclusion. In fact, the leaflet threatened, with heavy humour, the party games for which the retiring head had been notorious each Christmas. Virginia sighed. For years they had delighted first formers who now, gathered to indulge their former teacher, had conveniently forgotten the embarrassment the games had caused them in the third form – not to mention the boredom in the fifth when they were called on to assist with the jollifications laid on for their juniors.

Virginia resigned herself. She surveyed her fellow guests, recognizing some people at once, finding others vaguely familiar and some complete strangers. The men were outnumbered and most of them looked as though they regretted having decided to come.

Her inspection coming full circle, Virginia saw a neighbour, standing, his back towards her, at the next table. He was older than she was by some fifteen years and she had not realized that he too was an old pupil of Heath Lees. He was the last person with whom she wished to engage in conversation.

As she wondered how to escape from her corner without attracting his attention, another man bumped into him, quite literally, making him spill his drink. Apologies led to an exchange of news and views and finally to a football argument. From it, Virginia learned that the Cloughton team was negotiating a new signing for the following season, a goalkeeper from a second division side. She listened, wondering whether Declan would be interested, but Donald Markey soon diverted the flow of the conversation to the subject of his own present prowess, and thence to his sporting triumphs whilst still at school and his successes with his following of female fans.

'You had to share them with Morris,' his companion reminded him. Virginia supposed that the Morris mentioned was Val's husband. She liked him, and knew, from Val's fond boasting, that, long ago, he had swum for Yorkshire schools.

Donald confirmed this. He summarily dismissed that inferior sport, adding, 'I could always win Morris's girls away from him if I wanted.'

The tone of the conversation became more acrimonious. Virginia risked a glance over her shoulder at the two men who were providing her entertainment and noted that Donald's companion was wearing a clerical collar and an admonitory expression. 'As far as I remember, he let them go without resentment if they preferred what you had to offer. I don't think you'd have been able to help yourself to Valerie.'

Donald laughed unpleasantly. 'I'd hardly have wanted to.'

Trapped in her chair, Virginia was beginning to feel foolish. If she'd greeted her neighbour when she recognized him, she would have extricated herself by now from the kind of fatuous conversation she was overhearing. On the other hand, she was not sure that any of the other people she could see would prove any more stimulating. Alex's version of the evening was proving to be the accurate one. A lot of the women were overdressed in their efforts to make a good impression. The pair in front of her, with over-polite manners and superfluous aspirates, boasted about their offspring.

An exception to all the elegance was the woman who

now stood hesitantly in the doorway. As she gathered courage and came further into the hall, Virginia saw that her garments were not only rather shabby but actually less than clean. With a shock, she recognized Lorna Dyson, her partner in crime from the fourth form. Lorna had left school after GCSEs and their attempts to keep in touch had petered out.

She cast her mind back now and saw Lorna at fifteen, already goalkeeper of Heath Lees' First XI but otherwise scornful of school discipline, occasionally turning in brilliant work, but, more often, failing to do it at all. In her black moods, she had been in the habit of confiding and exaggerating her family problems. In the main, though, she had been cheerfully defiant towards all her elders and betters. What could have happened to turn her into this shabby, depressed-looking woman? Valerie seemed to have been looking out for Lorna. Now, she came forward and took her hands.

Virginia was about to get up and join them when Donald's companion interrupted the tedious recital of Markey conquests. 'So, which of them did you choose? Did you marry Nicky?' Feeling ashamed of herself, she stayed to listen. The woman who lived with Donald, presumably his wife, seemed a far cry from the glamorous girls the two men had been remembering.

'God, no! She was just a bit of fun. I didn't meet Phyllida, my wife, till I was up at Oxford.' Virginia blinked. She hadn't thought of Donald as an Oxbridge type.

Unwisely, his friend asked Donald what he was doing with himself now and brought down upon himself a torrent of self-important detail. '. . . but I'm just about to take up the sort of post I've always dreamed of . . .'

Virginia reached saturation point as the account reached its climax. She stood up, raised a hand to Donald in greeting and strode briskly off towards Valerie who was standing alone now and seemed to be upset. 'Geoff's having second thoughts about the games.'

Virginia grinned. 'Let's be thankful for small mercies.'

'But they're all printed out on the programme and some people are really looking forward to them.'

Virginia could see that one person at least certainly was. She tried to conceal her amusement. 'Well, some sort of compromise is called for. You shouldn't be entirely deprived of your fun after all your hard work. What about letting them talk till supper time?'

Valerie was reluctant to abandon her original plan. Virginia continued, desperately, 'When we've eaten and everyone's had plenty to drink you can have your game of Scavenging. By then, most people will be in the mood. If Maynard isn't he can go home early.'

Valerie looked bemused, then she shrugged her shoulders. 'OK. Like a drink?'

Virginia nodded. 'Yes, but I'm buying. In exchange you're telling me about someone called Nicky who nearly had the misfortune to marry Donald Markey.' The bargain sealed, Virginia selected a table as far away as possible from where she had been sitting and carried their glasses to it. 'By the way, where did Lorna go?' she asked, as they settled themselves.

Valerie's good-tempered features did their best to frown. 'To the cloakroom to freshen up. She doesn't look well, does she? It's hardly surprising considering the awful time she's been having.'

'I shouldn't get too worried. She was always a bit of a drama queen.'

Valerie looked surprised. 'It's not like you to be uncharitable.' Her tone was reproachful but Virginia was unrepentant. She remembered Lorna's endless complaints about her brother's being sent to a fee-paying school. In response to sympathetic questions, Lorna had reluctantly admitted that the schooling had been provided by the boy's godfather rather than his parents, and that it had been considered necessary because Colin was handicapped. Virginia had lost patience with the grumbling.

'She certainly doesn't look like the old Lorna,' she allowed now. 'I'll go and find her later. So, Nicky?'

'I haven't seen her for years until tonight. She was Nicolette Buisson at school. She came to Cloughton when Donald and Morris and company were in upper sixth. She's the one talking to Morris.'

Virginia was surprised. 'She doesn't look – well, as old as Morris.'

Now, even Valerie's tone was accusing. 'She's at least three years younger but she wasn't exactly shy. As a mere fourth former and a newcomer, she still had quite enough confidence to make eyes at the big boys. She was very pretty and having a French name and a French father made her a novelty. I think Morris rather fancied her but Donald cut him out. Coming from a swankier family, he could drive Nicky about and give her expensive presents.'

'She sounds a horror. Maybe they deserved each other. I'm glad Morris's taste improved.' Virginia sipped her wine and studied the woman Valerie indicated. Nicky was slim and still pretty, but not sufficiently young to carry off the strappy sundress she was wearing. She noticed that Valerie had already emptied her glass. 'The booze is good. They said at the bar that drinks were already paid for. How did we afford this?'

'We didn't. Geoff provided it.'

'Mr Maynard? Then, here's to him. Oh, who's the chap who's just managed to get away from Donald?'

Valerie followed Virginia's gaze. 'That's Neville Kyte.' Something about her tone prevented Virginia from asking anything further. Instead, she offered, 'Want some help serving supper?'

'No, it's all in hand. The caterers are behind the hatch and Geoff's sixth form trusties are to be waiters.'

'Splendid. By the way, did this gold-digger who rejected Morris find someone rich enough to suit her in the end, or is she approaching that serious-looking man with a pur- pose?' To Virginia, the man looked interesting, a refreshing change from the rest of the brash crowd around her. He had been sitting at the same table since he had come in just after Virginia. From time to time, various people had approached him and he had responded to their handshaking and spoken briefly to each.

'He's Nicky's husband. That's Eric Simpson. He's the man –'

'Oh yes, I saw it in the *Clarion*.'

But Valerie, having programmed herself to tell the story, was not to be diverted. 'He's written a book that's going to be made into a TV series –'

'And now he's a nine-days' wonder.' Determined not to be caught up in another tedious account, Virginia finished her own wine and put down her glass. 'I suppose we ought to postpone the rest of our chat and circulate a bit. You can find out what Nicky's done with her life besides marry a writer and I'll see if I can find Lorna.'

The evening was beginning to seem endless to Virginia. There was supper to get through before she could leave, never mind the dreaded game. There was nothing, she decided, quite so draining as being bored. Her busy day at home had nothing to do with her fatigue. There was not much that she found tedious, certainly not bringing up her children, however trying they might sometimes be. Adults behaving like children, though, were a different thing.

She sighed and went in search of her former friend. Starting with the nearest cloakroom, she found her there, weeping and refusing adamantly to go in to supper.

Virginia leaned against the white tiles, appreciating their coolness and approving of the graffiti-free doors. She tried to summon sufficient patience to deal with Lorna's complaints.

'I'm not hungry and I'm not feeling sociable. I was persuaded to come against my better judgement. Now I'm going home.'

Ever practical, Virginia merely asked, 'How are you going to get there?'

'The same way I came. I've got a little car. It's beaten up but it goes.'

Virginia gave her a hard look and decided she looked fit to drive. She was certainly upset, probably depressed but not overtly suicidal. There was reassurance in the fact that Lorna was returning her scrutiny. Hoping that Benny and the children would accommodate the arrangement, she invited Lorna to lunch the next day. Lorna accepted without any great show of enthusiasm, the two women exchanged addresses, Lorna washed her face and Virginia, jerked out of her lethargy by this more genuine exchange, went off to the dining room feeling more cheerful.

She remembered it as a bleak, chilly room but the party organizers had done their best, and here again the coolness was welcome. The wall of floor-to-ceiling windows was covered in balloons, sellotaped by their strings to the glass.

The seating plan at the door placed Virginia at a table with Geoffrey Maynard and Frances, his wife, in the far corner of the room. She wondered to what she owed this honour, especially when she found that Robert and Myrna Barnes, the headmaster elect and his wife, were also part of her octet.

The man whom Valerie had identified as Neville Kyte pulled back Virginia's chair for her before taking his seat beside her. On her other side sat a stick-thin, raw-nosed old man. Walking to the table had involved him in a complicated sequence of separate and deliberate movements, and folding himself on to the chair had obviously been an ordeal. Once established, however, he soon proved that the workings of his mind were in rather better fettle than his joints.

'Not on a diet, are you?' Virginia assured the old man that she was not. He beamed at her, revealing almost perfect teeth. 'Good. Good. Abstinence casts imputations on those who still enjoy.'

Maynard introduced the old man as his father, then worked round the table, making his guests known to each other. Reaching the empty eighth chair, he turned to Virginia. 'Where's Lorna?'

'She's had to leave.'

'I hope nothing's wrong.'

'I rather think there might be a problem. We haven't met for ages, so I'm not in the picture. I've invited her to lunch tomorrow to see what I can do . . .'

Maynard senior winked at her. 'Bet you were head girl before you left.'

'Only deputy, I'm afraid.'

The old man turned to his son. 'Bad mistake there, Geoffrey.' Before Maynard could defend himself, his father turned back to Virginia. 'Headmaster and headmaster elect for company, eh? Better mind our Ps and Qs. In high circles you have to listen more deferentially to nonsense.'

Virginia was beginning to enjoy herself.

Nicky Simpson's evening too was proving pleasanter than she had expected and most of what she had dreaded had not happened. Valerie had kept the supper simple. Nicky had found the soup revolting but she had swallowed a couple of spoonfuls to show willing. The chicken salad had not caused her to exceed her calorie allowance and other people had joined her in opting out of a pudding.

Maynard's speech had been boring but mercifully short. No one but Valerie Tate had wanted to play the silly game and so it had fizzled out after a few minutes. The dancing, therefore, scheduled for the last half-hour, had begun soon after the speeches finished. Half the guests were sitting out and, expecting Eric to join them, Nicky had looked for Donald. He should have been available. Phyllida had surely not been seriously intending to galumph about the floor in those awful clothes.

Eric, however, was in indulgent mode. He had taken her on to the floor where he had performed his usual two steps forward and two back, in time to the music, whatever the other dancers were doing. Nicky danced like a sylph, even with Eric as a partner, even in her sleep. Gyrating energetically around him, she had breath to make conversation, which offended no one, since it was mercifully drowned by the music.

'Donald wanted to make a splash with his Celica, but not as much as he wanted to drink. Maynard's whisky compensated him for arriving in our Fiesta.'

'He's not drunk much tonight.'

'Well, by his standards, maybe not. Of course, there are too many of his lady friends here tonight. He needs his wits about him if he's not going to let on to some of them about the others.'

Eric bobbed solemnly back and forth, matching the beat. 'I think anyone here who knows him at all knows him for what he is. None of his women thinks he's going to leave Phyllida and marry her. That isn't what they want anyway. They want his body, which you have to admit is superb.'

'I don't have to admit anything.' Her smile was enigmatic. 'Do you think Phyllida knows?'

'Of course. She probably knew before she married him. In an odd way, the two of them satisfy each other.'

The music stopped and Eric, rather breathless, was able to return to his table. He sat there, staring into space. Nicky leaned towards him. 'What are you thinking?'

'That it must have been a sticky little coffee party, the one Phyllida described,' he remarked as he fanned himself with his programme. 'Sean, Valerie and Phyllida are a very disparate trio. Perhaps the other girl was the catalyst. Lorna, was it?'

The music started up again. Nicky ignored it and answered the part of her husband's remark that she understood. 'That's the name of that scruffy girl who's been hanging round Val tonight. I saw her in the cloakroom earlier. She's an odd type to be here.'

'Oh? Was this such an exclusive school? All its past pupils successful and smart?'

'The ones who come back are.'

He smiled. 'The ones who've come to strut their stuff, to borrow an expression from Phyllida?'

Nicky laughed. 'Wasn't she odd tonight?'

'Yes, she's behaving rather strangely, even for her. Is she dancing as she promised?'

Nicky, who was still standing, looked about her. 'Well, she's in a crowd and moving about anyway. She probably calls that dancing.'

'Like I do, you mean? Perhaps for dancing Donald and I should exchange partners, then Phyllida and I would merely bump into each other, rather than into everyone else.'

Nicky seemed to take the suggestion seriously. 'We can't because Donald isn't with her. I can't see him anywhere.'

'Then he probably hasn't come back. He must be the tallest person here. He's easy enough to see.'

'And to hear. Anyway, back from where?'

Eric shrugged. 'He went out at the end of the meal. His phone rang and he probably couldn't hear his caller above the din.'

'Must have been a lady. He'll be back before the end with a wonderful cover story. Let's work out which female is missing. He isn't likely to have dragged someone up here who wasn't coming anyway.'

'I suppose not.' Eric fell silent, gazing into space again till Nicky grew impatient.

'Unless you're planning the next book that will make us even richer, come back to earth, will you? Penny for them.' She rolled one across the table to him.

He fumbled it and it fell to the floor where he left it. 'I was thinking that Phyllida wasn't the only person to be acting out of character tonight. Morris has been keeping a very low profile.'

'Maybe because he didn't want to do things Val's way.'

Eric shook his head. 'I think he's been generally subdued for some time. He doesn't come into the Shears much

34

these days and I've heard rumours that there's some trouble with the firm. If I was sure that that was the problem, and I could manage it without offending him, I'd like to help him out.'

'Financially, you mean?' Eric nodded. 'He wouldn't do it for us.'

'If our positions were reversed? Oh, I rather think he would.'

Nicky's mouth hardened and Eric wondered if her next question was meant seriously or whether it was just a ploy to divert him from his charitable intention. 'This Sean Sefton that Phyl mentioned, the financial whizz – you were talking as if you knew him.'

'Was I?'

'Well, saying he wouldn't mix in with Phyl and Val. Do you?'

'Know him? Yes. He's a very distant relative. I didn't realize he'd been at this school. What about him, anyway?'

'Well, should we be consulting him – or someone like him – now we're going to have to manage so much money?'

'Someone like him, possibly. I don't think it's advisable for a relative, however distant, to know too much about our personal business.'

'Right. Shall we get up and dance again? We're boring each other, stuck in this corner.'

As she made her way across the hall towards the door, Virginia Mitchell overheard this last fragment of their conversation and pondered on it. The Simpsons seemed to her an odd couple. The wife, she imagined, would be easily bored. The husband, dowdily dressed and looking older than his years, but probably much the more intelligent of the pair, had made an unexpected choice of wife. Perhaps Nicky was right and they did bore one another.

Much of her own evening had been amusing – certainly until Maynard senior, overtired and almost comatose, had submitted himself to a wheelchair to bear him away to his car. When he had gone, she had remained at their table for a while longer, studying the other five people, trying to see them through his eyes. She imagined the observations he would make on them in their absence the next day. People-watching. It was a fashionable term rather than a popular occupation, but it had saved the evening for her and provided material for when she started work again.

She had then chatted dutifully to several former class-mates, some of whom shared her concern for Lorna. Few had wanted to hear of her own experiences as a married student with an increasing tribe of children, as a police wife and as a budding journalist. The folk gathered here wanted an audience to admire them, or, in Lorna's case, to offer sympathy. Virginia had been happy to serve in both capacities. She was perfectly content with the way her life was developing and needed no one to bolster her self-respect. When a large crowd of younger guests began planning an adjournment to a nearby pub, she decided it was time to go home.

She breathed in gratefully as she opened the outer door and found that the sauna atmosphere she had arrived in had given way to a fresh coolness. She walked the long way round to the spot where she had parked her car. Dusk was considering whether to give way to darkness. Over the boundary wall, she could see a group of women, halfway down Moorside Rise, seated on dining chairs they had carried out of their houses and arranged in a bizarre half-circle on the pavement. They were chatting, drinking and smoking. Perhaps the rubbish dumps they had made of their gardens had become too malodorous for the social-izing to take place there.

Higher up the hill, at the bottleneck, a man lingered, possibly waiting for a friend. As she watched, he moved out on to the extension of the pavement that stuck out into the road, from where he could probably see further round the slight bend. His hand shielded his eyes against the weak blue light from a sodium lamp that would soon turn to its more illuminating dull orange. When he looked at his watch, then back down the road, Virginia recognized Donald Markey.

Suddenly, with its tortured engine screaming, drowning the cackling of the women, a small car appeared out of nowhere. It mounted the protruding area of pavement and struck Donald, throwing him into the air. Falling back, he hit the windscreen first, shattering it, and then the ground. The driver checked momentarily, then, jerking convulsively forward, drove over the body and sped away.

Virginia knew at once that Donald was dead. Mentally, she had heard ribs and spine crack, although she knew that the car engine had drowned that sound too. Only a few minutes ago, Donald had been chatting and laughing with Valerie. Only seconds ago he had been waiting for someone, probably a woman, to keep an appointment with him. Now, just feet away from her, over the wall, he lay immobile on the tarmac. She could not recognize this bloody mess as Donald, nor even as a man. The crumpled heap was just a ridiculous abstraction.

She forced herself to stride forward and climb the wall, oblivious to the damage to fingernails and linen trousers. Thankful that the women down the road seemed content with that vantage point, she made herself concentrate on the victim's pulse points and pupils. Blood flowed from too many wounds for her to try to staunch it. Only a clear-up job was needed here, a sanitizing of this already far from sanitary street.

Should she ring for help? Of course she should. She scrabbled in her pocket for her phone, then panicked. What could she tell anyone? She had looked at the victim, not at the driver, not at the car. She'd let the police down. She'd let Benny down. She'd betrayed Phyllida. Oh God! Phyllida! She tried to take hold of herself, began to count to ten.

On six, she was thinking logically again. Should she contact the station? Or go back into school and tell Donald's wife? She did neither. She rang her husband.

Chapter Two

Acting DCI Mitchell had enjoyed his evening on the whole. He took pleasure in his children's company and, once the battle over Declan's piano practice had been fought, and won by his father, the five of them had found plenty to do.

When the twins were safely asleep, he had taken Declan and Caitlin into the garden to improve on his wife's efforts of the day before. She had cut the grass to his satisfaction but he had been irritated by the odd sprigs and twigs that broke the line of the hedge. The two of them had argued about the garden many times. Virginia accused him of disciplining rather than caring for the plants, maintaining that a shrub should not look as though it were carved from a block of wood. She would notice that he had improved on her handiwork but she would not begin the squabble again – at least, not yet. All week, the garden had looked as she liked it by his default. Now, for a few days, until the recalcitrant regrowth appeared, it would give more pleasure to him.

Declan and Caitlin had entertained each other amicably, their complicated games unspoiled by the attempts of the twins to sabotage them. Declan had helped his sister to weed her own tiny flower bed. Now they were both on the climbing frame. His elder daughter turned energetic somersaults on the lower bar whilst Declan had climbed to the small platform at the top. He was there now, lost in his own thoughts. Mitchell wondered whether they were still centred on the chameleon and hoped not.

Determining to have strong words with his wife, he had suggested a Google search to answer Declan's question. Typing in 'chameleon', his fingers crossed for the spelling, he had printed out the two paragraphs that had appeared on the screen and handed them to the boy without reading them – a big mistake. Declan learned that chameleons make very interesting pets and that the website listed a great many books on their nature and their care. Mitchell, looking over his shoulder, discovered that the creature's lifespan was ten years, sometimes more. The accompanying photograph showed a fat, lizard-like little creature, brightly coloured and predominantly yellow. Mitchell had wondered whether the story that it changed colour to match its background were just a myth and hoped profoundly that there would be no campaign for the family circle to include a specimen.

His son, however, had been concerned with another problem. 'Will I,' he asked, as Mitchell took them indoors, 'have to go to boarding school like Zak Markey?'

Mitchell was startled. This had not been part of the family plan. 'Why? Do you want to go?'

Declan shrugged. 'I don't know what it's like. Zak said it's where clever boys go.' The child sounded anxious. He had seen his glowing school reports and, in any case, could hardly be unaware of his own intelligence.

Mitchell was relieved to observe a reluctance to accept this privilege that was beyond the family's financial resources. He grinned at his son. 'It's got more to do with being rich than being clever.'

This was not reassurance enough. 'Will we get rich?'

Mitchell laughed. 'It's not very likely – and, even if we did, you wouldn't have to go away to school unless you wanted to.' He dropped into the armchair beside the stool on which Declan was perched to indicate his willingness to pursue the subject.

Declan, his fears now allayed, had recognized his father's tacit admission that he had nothing urgent to do.

He grinned and placed his copy of *The Hobbit* on Mitchell's knee. 'Mum's got to chapter four.'

Mitchell objected to Tolkien. Fairy stories were fine, but they should be no more than half a dozen pages long and none of the fairies should have unpronounceable names. He saw with relief that it was already fifteen minutes past his elder children's bedtime. He pointed to the clock, then relented to the extent of allowing them to read themselves to sleep in their own rooms.

Duty done. It was time to reward himself now. He reached in the fridge for a couple of cans and tuned in to the remainder of the cricket highlights on Channel 4. There weren't any! In disgust, he watched the English batsmen treating the third day of a test match as a one-day frolic. When would they realize that these one-day games were not cricket? They should have a new name. The disastrous close-of-play score appeared in black and white, filling the screen. There was nothing else he fancied watching. He tried the radio, then Ginny's book, wondering how she made sense of it. Finally, he read the local paper from cover to cover. When the telephone rang, he welcomed the distraction and picked up the receiver.

'Benny?'

It sounded so unlike her voice that for a moment he wasn't sure. 'What's wrong?' There was silence. 'Ginny! Tell me what's happened.'

She did. A bald statement in a dozen words. He established that she was not physically hurt and wondered how soon he could find a substitute child minder so that he could go to fetch her. She was obviously in shock. That was hardly surprising. She had watched from a distance of ten feet as a speeding machine ripped into the body of – if not a friend, at least a close acquaintance.

Virginia spoke again. 'I wish I could have liked him, just a little bit.' Tears were not far away.

'Have you called HQ and the hospital?' Silence again. 'Don't worry. I'll do it. There'll be a squad car with you in a few minutes. There's bound to be one cruising that area on a Saturday night. I'll get my mother here, then I'll come.'

But Virginia was rallying. She was not taking in all that he was saying but the sound of his voice was restoring her scattered wits to her. She was listening to him, accepting his offer to summon official help. They wouldn't stop to question a request from him. Everything would happen faster. 'I'll wait for the ambulance and your folk. You'll want the scene preserving, won't you? There's an army of women down the street, just getting over their surprise and looking inquisitive. I'll do what I can about things until the car arrives. Oh! – and I'll try Val's mobile, get her to do something about Phyllida.'

She hesitated, then decided to put into words what was really worrying her. 'Benny, there's one other thing. I've got an image in my mind – just a silhouette, framed in the side window as the car shot past. The driver wasn't joy-riding, didn't toss Donald into the air because he'd got in the way. He was concentrating, leaning forward, intent. I think he did it on purpose.'

She cancelled her call, leaving Mitchell to make his more urgent one, and tried to decide what her priorities were. She had to keep the road clear and she had to make sure that Phyllida Markey heard about Donald's death from someone responsible and concerned for her.

She remembered that Nicky Simpson had followed her out through the foyer and into the main car park. Virginia thought she remembered the Simpsons and the Markeys arriving together. Nicky might have been a suitable messenger, but Virginia had the impression that Nicky had gone straight to her vehicle. If she had been leaving the school she would be miles away by now. If she'd been fetching something from the car she would be back in the hall. Think again. Praying that Valerie Tate would still have her phone switched on, Virginia punched in the number.

As she had expected, Valerie, although shocked, accepted her news calmly. Morris and Maynard, she prom-

41

ised, would organize the departure of all the remaining guests by way of the main gate and the direct road to the town centre. She herself would take charge of Phyllida until the police arrived. Thankful, Virginia turned to a consideration of how she might keep Moorside Rise free from traffic using only the slender authority of being a policeman's wife.

The hit-and-run that resulted in the death of Donald Markey was not the only motoring mishap to occur in Cloughton that evening. Halfway down the main road leading from Heath Lees High School to the town centre, a narrow cobbled track led off between two tall buildings down to the lowest part of the hollow that was once the centre of old Cloughton. This junction went quite un-noticed by the drivers who, by order of the police, had reluctantly left the excitement in Moorside Rise and driven at an unusually circumspect speed directly to their various homes.

In the days when supplies of raw wool from the sur-rounding farmsteads had been carried by mules into the central market square to be sold to the town's mill owners, this track had been considered a main road. The old mills lined up and lowering down on each side of it made it dark on even the brightest days. These buildings were now derelict, but so soundly had they been built that none of the bleak stone walls with their eyeless windows had fallen down, though their roofs had disintegrated. At night, what were probably the original Victorian lamp posts reproached the solitary sodium lamp that had made them redundant.

Now, the track, known locally as Old Lane, was chiefly used as a conveniently central yet secluded trysting place for Cloughton's lovers and lusters. Towards the bottom of the slope, where the lane turned right at an angle of roughly ninety degrees, the mills came to an end and it ran alongside a row of small terraced houses. In the resulting corner, a small grassy square boasted several shrubs and three trees. On this green patch the couples spread their jackets in summer and parked their cars in winter.

On this particular Saturday night a local squire and his lady had been availing themselves of the tiny copse with its sordidly littered grass. Daz knew that his Bev's father was apt to enforce his rules with his fist, particularly on Saturday nights. Consequently, as the dusk deepened, the two of them were returning to the small delivery van which Daz drove for a living. They noticed that another car, small and a metallic green in colour, was parked beside the lane, blocking their exit into it. As Daz contemplated a way out of this difficulty, without either spoiling another couple's pleasure or damaging his employer's vehicle, Bev was startled to see, through the glass of the driver window, a feebly waving white arm.

Coming closer, she made out, in the gloom, that the car's windscreen was shattered and its bonnet was snuggled round the base of a tree. She alerted Daz to the situation. 'Mebbe she's been raped,' she suggested hopefully.

Daz shrugged. 'You needn't sound so pleased about it. Any road, it's none of our business. You're already goin' to be late.'

'Oh, come on. She might be bleedin' to death.' Bev made towards the car with an enthusiasm that waned when Daz failed to follow her.

He did at least fish out a gold phone, studded with 'diamonds'. 'Get the proper folk if you want to be some use. Here.'

Bev took the proffered instrument before peering more closely through the window and then gingerly trying the handle of the front passenger door of the green car. It opened. She swallowed convulsively at the sight of the driver's bleeding left arm and face. 'She's cut 'ersen and her ankle's all swole up.'

Daz agreed to her call for an ambulance but when she suggested the police he shook his head vigorously. She knew this was on his own account but she was generous.

'Nah, mebbe not. The car's not stickin' out into the road much and she might 'ave 'ad a couple o' drinks. No need to get t'lass into bother. Poor cow's no oil paintin' even without all this blood an' mess. Probably needed to cheer 'ersen up.'

She stepped back, startled by a new voice from behind her. 'Excuse me. Is everyone all right?'

Bev glared at this young man with the posh accent who threatened to steal her role of valiant rescuer. 'I've done everything. The ambulance is coming. We don't need no help.' Her initial H and final consonants had been supplied in response to his cultivated delivery but grammar was beyond her.

The man justified himself against her accusing tone. 'My mother saw the accident from her bedroom window. She sent me out to find out what's going on.' He peered through the open car door. 'Is she a friend of yours?'

Bev shook her head. 'Never seen her before.'

'Are you two staying with her till the ambulance arrives?' Bev's narrow-eyed glare as she nodded had its effect. 'Right. I'll get back to Mother then.' He made off reluctantly with a nod towards the damaged car's coma-tose passenger. 'Hope she's OK.'

He walked back to the end-of-terrace house. The injured woman lay, unmoving, half supported by the driving seat but threatening to slide towards Bev now that the door no longer restrained her. Bev closed it, hurriedly but gently. She turned to Daz, her nose wrinkling. 'It's funny neither on us 'eard owt. Ah well, she isn't goin' to explain. Doesn't look as if she's feelin' very talkative.'

Daz grinned. 'We'll have to amuse ourselves till the medics come then.' He reached over and began undoing the buttons that Bev had recently refastened.

She smacked his hand. 'We can't with 'er 'ere!'

'She's not looking. I don't think she's even conscious.'

'But she's there. It's no good, Daz. I'm not in the mood no more. Anyway, if you want to save me a beltin' when

44

I get in, you can get that poncey phone out again and tell my dad what's keepin' us.'

Thus the two of them were keeping a chaste vigil when the paramedics came to collect Lorna Dyson and take her to the Cloughton Infirmary.

Virginia Mitchell usually woke at a child's slightest murmur. On Sunday morning, to Mitchell's astonishment, she slept through the seven o'clock eruption – when their offspring were allowed to emerge from their rooms to fill the rest of the house with their toys and noise.

Mitchell sidled out of bed and spirited the four of them downstairs, bribed into silence by the promise of sausage sandwiches for breakfast. A quick phone call to his mother confirmed his expectation that she and his father would be delighted to entertain their grandchildren until such time as Virginia wanted them back. Having delivered them and relieved himself of his domestic concerns, he happily turned his car in the direction of the police station.

Mitchell liked hunting killers and had been delighted by Superintendent Carroll's decision, taken late the previous evening, that the hit-and-run incident his wife had witnessed should provisionally be treated as murder. 'If we're wrong, so much the better.'

Mitchell had hastened to agree with his superior officer. 'In any event, it's at least manslaughter and the same work needs to be done.' He had accordingly sent the CID late crime car to assist the uniformed officers who had responded to his original call. Preservation of the crime scene would make or break this investigation.

His usual team went off duty at ten, so that Mitchell had rung not to the station sergeant's desk but to the station bar where he hoped one or more of them had lingered. He had been pleased to speak to his sergeant, who was his wife's good friend. Jennifer Taylor had agreed to his request to attend the incident after only one swearword and she had retracted even that once she understood the nature of Virginia's involvement.

Mitchell had therefore excused her from the briefing he had called for eight thirty on Sunday morning. He had been pleased, though not surprised, to find a detailed report of her findings on his desk this morning.

A glance at his watch sent him scurrying down to the incident room with the hastily scribbled sheets in his hand. There he found that someone had already acquired a photograph of Donald Markey and pinned it to the notice-board. It was being examined by DC Shakila Nazir. She turned and grinned at Mitchell. 'Bet he was a lady's man. I ask you! Dimples, perfect teeth, eyelashes you could sweep the floor with . . .'

'And a smug expression that tells you he's perfectly well aware of the effect they have.'

Mitchell was concerned by the bitter tone of his other DC's observation. Caroline, whom he must now remember to call not Webster but Jackson, would, until recently, have made the comment with a tolerant smile. He and Virginia had attended her wedding eight months ago. She had been temporarily released from hospital for the ceremony and no official photographs had been permitted. The unusually crass young reporter from the *Clarion* had therefore reproduced in words a picture of Caroline's sutured cheeks. They were still disfigured by livid scars which worried Mitchell less than his DC's scarred self-image.

'Is this a murder investigation?'

The question recalled him to matters in hand. 'For the moment.' Shakila nodded and subsided.

They all looked up as DC Clement slid through the door and into a chair. He squirmed under his chief inspector's silent scrutiny and muttered an apology. Picking up the two closely written sheets of A4 that he had brought with him, his mouth twitching at the corners, Mitchell began the morning briefing. 'I hope this isn't Jennifer's official report. At the moment though these two sheets comprise the file on last night's RTA. You will enjoy reading it in full in due course.'

He chuckled, then read them a sample. '"I found that the scene had been preserved by Mrs Virginia Mitchell's alternative method, using two borrowed clothes lines, a box of pegs and an assortment of white(ish) towels requested from the interested spectators."'

'Where did she get the energy to try to be funny, at that time of night and at the end of a late shift?' Caroline answered her own question: 'You called her at half-past ten? She'd been in the bar for half an hour? All is explained.'

Mitchell shrugged. 'Let's hope she found herself a driver then. Anyway, she's excused this session and the rest of us are here. Let's get on. The super's given us a few uniforms already, but, for now, quick lab results will be more use to us than extra men. We have some wild eyewitness statements from a group of gin-swilling tenants just down the street. The car was a white VW Golf or a grey Ford Fiesta or "one of those new-fangled things with a bar round the front". Of course, no one noted the registration – that includes Ginny, by the way. Someone will have to give her a grilling in the near future but I'd be grateful if it's not until after lunch. Oh! – and I'll warn you now. She's not much good on cars either.'

'Did the SOCOs think they'd found anything useful?' Clement asked.

Mitchell ran a finger down the second of Jennifer's sheets. 'A flake of paint with a pale green metallic top coat, stuck on one of the victim's shoes, and some glass on the road that might have been part of a headlight lens. Tracking down the paint will be fun. Every manufacturer will have a different poncey name for the shade. There was part of a black plastic moulding, maybe from a fog lamp. The skidmarks weren't helpful. Several bagfuls of stuff have gone off to the lab, including all Mr Markey's blood-stained clothes. We'll keep our fingers crossed.'

'When we've found the car,' Shakila volunteered, 'the

owner's going to say it was stolen before the incident. They always do.'

'Sometimes it's true.' Mitchell liked this new recruit to the Cloughton CID. Her first taste of detective work had come when her Urdu was needed in a case concerning a missing Asian girl. She had enjoyed her secondment and had achieved a permanent appointment as a detective by the straightforward method of muscling in on another major investigation, unasked and in her free time. She had made bad mistakes but, nevertheless, had proved her courage and intelligence. The ploy had worked.

Mitchell could identify with Shakila. What they had in common was that the very qualities that made them excellent detectives were the ones that got them into trouble with the force's hierarchy. Like him, Shakila went out on a limb, took her punishment, then settled down cheerfully to reoffend.

Mitchell turned to Clement. 'Adrian, you can go and see what the national computer can tell us about stolen green cars.'

'Wouldn't it be better to wait until . . .'

'Until we have a more accurate description of the vehicle? Well, you can always amend your list as the details come in.' Clement knew he was being punished for being late and said nothing. 'In the meantime, I think all you girls can do is see whether the residents of Moorside Rise want to revise their statements in the cold light of day. Don't ask suggestive questions, of course, but what I'd like to know in particular is whether anyone shared Ginny's impression that the killing was deliberate. Right, back here at one thirty.'

Clement looked worried. 'Could Shakila look for the stolen cars whilst I go with Caroline? I run on the school playing field most weeks and some of the lads from Moorside Rise come and laugh. Some even run with me till they're out of breath. Their mums wave to me on the bit of the track that passes the end of the tips they call back

48

gardens. I might just get something they wouldn't tell the girls . . .'

Mitchell put an end to the wordy persuasion with a monosyllabic 'No'. He waited for a petulant slam of his door, but Clement went out closing it quietly.

He understood the thinking behind Clement's offer. Only the previous week the *Cloughton Clarion* had carried a banner headline, 'More "Darkies" beaten up in Heath Lees'. The situation there was a complete reversal of that at the opposite end of the town where Shakila, together with most of the rest of the town's Asian population, had her home. There they beat up visiting whites.

He grinned to himself, remembering one of Virginia's recent remarks: 'You're beginning to talk about that team as if you were their boarding school housemaster.' Perhaps she was right. Shakila would have to fend for herself. Cloughton couldn't have 'no go' areas for members of his shift.

With a sigh, Mitchell turned to his permanent backlog of paperwork, hoping soon to be released from it by further developments in his present case. He made a feeble effort not to hope that this would become a murder investigation.

Virginia awoke just before nine. The sun was streaming through the window and she blessed Benny for keeping the children occupied so that she could enjoy this almost unprecedented lie-in. Then panic attacked as she remembered. Donald Markey was dead. Lorna was coming to lunch. There were no sounds of children. Benny had been given permission to initiate a provisional murder investigation and his day off was not going to happen.

She rolled over on to Benny's pillow to look at the clock, then fished for the paper that crackled under her cheek. Reassured that her children were safe she dropped the note into the bin, gave silent thanks to her mother-in-law, grabbed a bath sheet and made for the shower.

Downstairs again, she was delighted to discover that Benny had left a full jug of coffee on the kitchen work surface. She filled a mug and read his note as it heated. 'To wash down whatever you grab for breakfast. See you next century if I'm lucky but at least I'll phone.'

Virginia looked through the window as she drank the brew. The air was fresher and cooler and she saw that there had been rain during the night. Benny would be thankful that he had acted immediately on the scene in Moorside Rise before precious clues were washed away. She smiled to herself as she noted the results of his evening's work in the garden. The rain would soon have it looking shaggily friendly again and it seemed likely that it would be at least several days before he was free to make a further attack on it.

He had mentioned last night that Phyllida Markey had been taken in by the Tates. Wiping burnt toast crumbs from her mouth and fingers on a tea towel, Virginia went to the phone. Phyllida, Val reported, though obviously shocked, was bearing up well. She had refused to be sedated and was presently asleep in the spare room. Virginia sent best wishes and promised to visit later in the day, then turned her mind to her forthcoming guest.

Her usual ploy for lunch guests was to heat up a supermarket ready-meal. This was not meant as an insult to her visitor, she was at pains to point out. 'It's the favoured ones I don't cook for.' She rejected this plan today. Lorna could help with the cooking. It might not be one of her strengths – Virginia couldn't remember – but she was unlikely to be less expert than herself. If Lorna's hands were busy she would probably find it easier to talk.

A search inside the refrigerator produced a large chicken breast that would make a useful base for the sort of composite dish with which Virginia frequently startled her family. Her hands busy fishing out filler ingredients from her store cupboard, she wondered about the wisdom of the invitation she'd issued. She and Lorna had been fellow rebels in the fourth and fifth forms, her classmate reacting against what she saw as an unhappy home situation and herself against the restrictions of being a policeman's daughter. They had had little else in common and had not met, except briefly and by chance, since Lorna had left school without entering the sixth form.

Last night, however, Lorna had been so plainly and so deeply unhappy that Virginia had felt obliged to try to help. She was not sure that she could persuade Lorna to reveal all that was troubling her, nor whether she really wanted her to. She had had time now to remember Lorna's schoolgirl dramatizing of what had sometimes seemed to Virginia to be quite minor problems. Was she about to indulge a morning's negative and useless self-pity on Lorna's part?

She placed a collection of tins and packets on a tray and poured another mugful of Benny's coffee. There was no point in speculating till she had heard Lorna's story. Then she could decide whether she was able or willing to intervene. But she had a bad feeling that it was too late now to avoid involving herself in the troubles Lorna was bringing her.

She looked up as she heard the gate creak and saw the back view of her visitor, who was securing the catch. As the woman turned towards the back door Virginia had the impression that she was limping. She stepped back hurriedly so as not to be caught staring and opened the door before Lorna reached it.

As her guest stepped into the hall, her welcoming smile disappeared and she blinked at what she saw. Lorna's clothes were clean this morning, though not ironed. Her hair had been pushed untidily behind her ears but it had been freshly washed. Lorna had been squarely built and stocky even in her hockey-playing schooldays. Her T-shirt certainly had been acquired in her leaner days. It squashed her ample breasts and indicated her nipples as discs of crumpled cotton. The knee-length skirt was zipped half-way, its waistband inadequate to encircle Lorna's girth. The unfastened button stuck out, raising the hem of the skirt and revealing a triangle of billowy thigh.

Virginia shuddered and tried not to look. There was plenty to distract her. Lorna's cheeks were a mass of cuts, dominated by a huge swollen bruise on her temple. Her left arm was heavily bandaged and she had two further small dressings on her chin and neck. One ankle was encased in an elastic support.

Horrified, Virginia took Lorna's hands, the left one rather gingerly, and drew her inside. She made no immediate comment on the injuries, merely asking, 'Have you had any breakfast?' Lorna shook her head. 'Then the sooner lunch is on the table the better. Meanwhile you'll find Benny's coffee therapeutic.' She poured it before asking, 'Want to talk about what's happened to you?' She indicated the comfortable carver chair at the end of the table.

Lorna sank into it and drank, both her hands wrapped round the mug. 'My car was even more beat-up than I thought. I wrapped it round a tree. I was lucky, I suppose. Just a twisted ankle and a few cuts. This was a bit more serious.' She indicated her bandaged arm. 'Six stitches in that. I was too groggy to object to hospital last night but I discharged myself this morning. Beds are too precious to be wasted on minor injuries and, anyway, I was looking forward to having lunch with you.' Lorna paused but Virginia ignored her cue to protest at her friend's unselfish foolishness. She felt she was in a place she had been before.

After a minute, as though Virginia had asked, Lorna continued, 'It happened in Old Lane, where it turns the corner. The steering went peculiar.'

'Another car accident?'

Virginia's reply had obviously been unexpected. 'Another?'

Lorna seemed resentful that someone else's misfortune was about to eclipse her own. With compunction, Virginia wondered about the wisdom of passing on such shocking news whilst Lorna was still recovering from her own little trauma. But she would have to know, was sure to hear most of the gory details from someone before the day was out. So far as Virginia knew, Lorna was no more than an acquaintance of Donald, if she had even met him. Certainly, she was not likely to be overly distressed by news of his death. She related, as briefly and gently as possible, the incident she had witnessed the previous night, and its result.

The revelation had a more adverse effect than Virginia was prepared for. For a moment Lorna covered her face with her hands. Then, finding the movement painful, she dropped her injured arm and stood up abruptly, covering her mouth with her right hand. 'Excuse me. The bathroom?'

Mindful of Lorna's bound-up ankle, Virginia indicated the door to the lavatory at the end of the hall. 'Can I do anything for you?'

Lorna shook her head, limped into the tiny room and locked the door against her hostess's ministrations. Virginia shrugged and returned to the kitchen. If her visitor needed help she could call. She still doubted that Lorna was genuinely upset but she might be unwell, still suffering from the shock and injuries she had sustained. Or, considering her restless and uneasy manner since she had arrived, could it be that what Lorna needed was in her handbag, contained in a syringe?

As the silence from the little cloakroom continued, Virginia began to wonder if there could possibly be some connection between Donald's road accident and Lorna's own.

In spite of having retired to bed in the small hours of Sunday morning, Eric Simpson had been up and about since half-past six. Even during those hours he had slept badly, shocked by Donald Markey's death and worried by the fast-approaching deadline for finishing his next book.

It was well behind schedule, largely because all the publicity generated by the first had disrupted the organized timetable that had allowed him to move smoothly from his writing to his domestic duties and on to the lecturing that until recently had been his only source of income.

He knew that Nicky too had had a restless night. He had been aware, as he slid carefully out of bed, that her equally careful, deep and even breathing had been intended to convince him that she was asleep.

Fortified with strong coffee, he had set out the notes on his current chapter but inspiration to continue proved as elusive as sleep. Then he had prowled uneasily about the house, unable to settle to anything else. This beautiful house was another distraction. Dating from the turn of the century, it was expansive and gracious. Its architect had avoided the excesses of the Victorian era but adhered to its demand for space. Every detail of it gave him pause for pleasure.

The cramped and unpleasing proportions of his former dwelling had made him glad to escape from it into the realms of his imagination. Writing had been easy there and he had not been unhappy. Born in a house in one of the earliest council estates to very elderly parents, he had stayed with them when he became a working man. It had been a deliberate decision about which he had felt no bitterness. He bore against his parents only one grudge – for naming him Eric!

When his mother died, he nursed his father through his remaining eighteen months. During that period, he had purchased the house in which they had all been tenants and spent much of his income on making it convenient and attractive. He had succeeded to the extent that, when the old man died and Eric and Nicky married, she had agreed to live there with him.

One of the restful qualities Nicky had was that she usually knew what she wanted. She had taken pleasure for quite a while in living in the best house in the street, preferring to be queen in Hope Street to poor relation in

Parkside Lane. A bathroom upstairs and a cloakroom down, with a small conservatory taking up half the back yard, had rendered her content.

He had realized that, if and when children came along, her requirements would change. It had not happened and he had assumed without asking that she had taken measures to prevent it. He had had no strong feelings on the matter. When he had begun to write, he had even been quite pleased to be free from the responsibility of children.

With the enormous advance offered for this next book, Nicky had seen the chance to be queen of a bigger country. He had no illusions about his wife but his disillusion stopped far short of resentment. He loved her, accepted what she offered him and understood her far better than she knew. What he hadn't worked out was why she had married him. Had she suspected that she was pregnant by Donald Markey? There would be irony in that.

Since no work was being done, he decided to call her bluff and take her a breakfast tray. Deftly, he cut and toasted bread and scrambled eggs, allowing his mind, which had refused to produce material for his latest chapter, to sift through the events of the previous evening. He knew that Nicky had been offended when Phyllida had elected to go home with the Tates. She had reassured herself by blaming him. 'Phyl can't let her hair down with someone as po-faced as you.'

He had not been angry but nor had he accepted the responsibility she had cast on him. 'Someone as po-faced as I am would prefer your detachment, but Phyllida needs Valerie, who'll be practical and sympathetic.' He knew that Nicky, in her own way, was genuinely fond of Phyllida. Even while she shuddered at the flabby flesh, she saw through the embarrassment and awkwardness to the intelligent woman within.

At the same time, he was aware that Nicky was using her, aware that Phyllida's was old money and that she was comfortable with the luxuries that she had always enjoyed.

Eric thought that she had also been reasonably comfortable with her less than ideal husband. He and Phyl had more in common than being inexpert dancers.

He smiled as he took the Davenport teapot, part of the breakfast set that Phyllida and Donald had recently given them as a housewarming present. He measured into it a rounded teaspoonful of the jasmine tea that he suspected Nicky hated. She persevered with it because it was what Phyllida served at breakfast.

Nicky heard Eric's slow footsteps on the stairs and pulled herself up to a sitting position against her heap of pillows. She knew he would be carrying a tray, being careful not to spill. She hoped it would contain just tea. She couldn't face breakfast this morning, could hardly face Eric either. She knew she didn't deserve him. What was important right now was that he shouldn't know it.

What she really needed to know was how much he knew about her affair with Donald. Ought she to seem upset this morning? How much reaction would he expect to result from the death of the person Donald was supposed to be for her? More than an acquaintance but not quite a good friend. Eric at least knew that, years ago, the two of them had been accepted as a pair, spoken of in the same breath. Probably he suspected that they had been lovers. She'd have to play things by ear this morning. The dreadful jasmine tea would be difficult to swallow without any need for pretence. He'd observe her struggle with it and he would have to make of that whatever he could.

Her wakeful night had given her ample time to consider but no energy to make decisions. Was it too soon to have another go at Eric about getting some financial advice? She knew she'd have to be careful about this. Eric, in spite of his mild manner, was no pushover and, if she moved too soon or too far, he would dig in his heels and then there would be no moving him. Lucky old Phyl who'd always been in charge of the purse strings herself – not that she'd managed to get much joy out of it.

On the other hand, Eric respected professional people and listened to what they had to say. Surely someone whose business was money would advise him not to start giving it away to every lame duck he came across. Morris was the second person he'd suggested they should rescue. Perhaps she could make some sort of approach to this distant cousin of his herself.

The bedroom door opened and the tray appeared, followed by Eric. He gave her a chaste kiss on the cheek and laid his offering across her knees. She regarded the steaming heap of scrambled egg and discovered to her astonishment that she was ravenous.

The fluttering police tape that marked off the scene of the RTA in Moorside Rise marginally relieved the street's atmosphere of depression.

DCs Caroline Jackson and Shakila Nazir were surprised to find no one in at the first two houses they visited. They found the answer to the puzzle at number 6. There, the group of women who had sat out on the pavement to enjoy the evening warmth, along with their lager and gin, and had witnessed Donald Markey's demise, had reconvened to enjoy the excitement all over again.

Caroline was disappointed. 'They'll have pooled their ideas now, absorbed each other's impressions. Not one of them will give us an accurate account of what they saw.'

Shakila grinned. 'You reckon they would have anyway? We'll have it all mixed in with what the hysterical ones have imagined and the gory details of the nightmares they've all had. Let's break up the party.'

'Break it up? We're the entertainment they're expecting.' Caroline rapped sharply on the partly opened door. There was a moment's silence, then twitters of excitement as the ladies streamed out from the front room into the tiny hall.

There was another silence when they saw Shakila and the householder addressed herself pointedly to Caroline.

Both DCs stepped back as the party spilled out on to the step and everyone inspected again the marked-off area further up the hill. Children, more of them than the solitary PC on duty could control at once, threatened to breach the tapes. Leaving Caroline to ask the questions, Shakila turned and strode off up the slope towards them.

The women watched as she accosted two teenage boys and Caroline felt the group's surprise as the lads nodded, grabbed three of the smaller fry and marched them away into one of the gardens. Shakila followed for a few steps to check that she was being obeyed, then turned back to the rest. These, however, seeing how their leaders had fared, had retreated at least beyond touching distance of the tape. Caroline ignored a mutter behind her. 'There'll be trouble if that nigger touches our Glen.'

She bit her lip as another woman demanded, 'That bossy woman last night with the frizzy black hair, was she int' police?' There was an indignant tossing of heads.

'Tellin' us all what to do!'

'Wouldn't let us anywhere near to see owt. She 'ad a jolly good gawp 'erself, mind you.'

'Jumped over that wall to make sure she missed nowt.'

'Or to make sure that there was nothing she could do for the victim.'

The accuser, whose house they were in and whom Caroline had mentally tagged the Fat Controller, nodded towards her grudgingly. 'Well, maybe so.'

They all turned as another woman came in without knocking. 'Sorry.' She was breathless. 'Had to get my old dad up an' dressed and call our Sam up to mind him afore I could come.'

Caroline opened her mouth to say that they would have called on her in her own home. She shut it again as she realized the apology was addressed to the woman in whose mini-jungle they were standing.

Before the woman could be absorbed into the group, Caroline went up to her. She saw that she had been unintentionally intimidating when the woman, wiping her hands nervously on her flowered apron, muttered, 'Don't pick on me.'

Her tone more conciliatory, Caroline asked, 'Can you shut your eyes and see the accident again? Don't open them. Tell me everything as you see it, all the smallest details.'

The woman's aggression swiftly evaporated as she understood that she was the star of the show. Her version of events included a blue Fiesta. So far as Caroline remembered, Jennifer's report had not mentioned that model. She made a note to check whether any of these witnesses was a driver or married to a mechanic, or was, for any other reason, competent to recognize a particular car.

Her witness, eyes still obediently closed, was rather more charitable to Virginia, wondering whether she might have been an off-duty nurse. 'Silly bugger walked right on to t'most dangerous place, where t'pavement sticks out – as if he were goin' to thumb a lift.' She opened her eyes. 'I don't know. You try to get yer bloody kids to 'ave some road sense and then grown men carry on like that. Still, what 'appened to 'im'll teach 'em if nowt else does!'

This lady would apparently find a silver lining to every cloud. Caroline smiled at her as Shakila came up to join them and the other women moved away. 'Thank you, Pollyanna.'

The woman blinked. 'No, it's just Ann. At least the streets are a bit safer with all them tapes up and no cars getting past. Pity they can't be up permanent.'

The two officers spent the rest of the morning in Moorside Rise but learned little more. As they went back to their car, parked where Virginia had left hers the previous evening, the door of the house nearest the scene of the incident opened. A man came out, carrying a big garden fork. He ignored the DCs, the group of women and the bloodstained tarmac and began to turn over the earth alongside his garden path. This was manifestly a continuation of former labour. Caroline imagined the flower-filled plot that he might have had in mind himself and suddenly felt inordinately cheered. She saluted him, then turned to the solitary PC. 'Want me to ask the DCI for another man to help up here?'

The man shook his head. 'There's some coming later. In the meantime I've told 'em that DC Nazir might be back any time.'

When Lorna Dyson eventually emerged from the Mitchells' small cloakroom she seemed more relaxed and ready to talk, though Virginia did not consider that what they were having was normal conversation. Virginia chatted idly about her family and Lorna told a string of small jokes. By the time she reached each punchline, Virginia felt bewildered rather than entertained. Lorna laughed immoderately without seeming in the least amused.

No mention was made now of the brother that she had resented so much in her schooldays. Virginia preferred not to cloud the present issues with questions about him. She suggested they should each give a brief account of what had happened to her since they had finished school. Lorna volunteered that she lived alone in the flat that she had bought as soon as she started work.

'What work did you do?'

'I was a nurse – till Abby.'

Virginia handed her friend a tin of chopped tomatoes and all the still-edible salad and vegetables from her refrigerator. Then, trying not to sound like a lawyer engaged in cross-examination, she asked, 'Abby?'

'Abigail, my little girl.' Lorna paused to open the tin, then sucked away a bead of blood from the resulting cut on her finger. Virginia waited. 'She was so sweet when she was tiny. She had blonde hair and enormous blue eyes. I made such plans for her. In my mind, she grew up, one day into a famous actress, another into a university professor – you know? I wanted to give her every advantage, so that her life wouldn't be the failure and the mess that mine is.'

Virginia laughed. 'The cure for that is to have four. Then you don't have time to dream up plans for any particular one of them.' Immediately she thought better of this suggestion since Lorna did not appear to be married. It occurred to her that the little girl might benefit from exposure to the cheerful company of her own brood. 'You should bring her over. My family likes company and, with six of us around, it's always a party.' She saw that Lorna had hidden her face in her hands. 'What is it?'

There was no answer. 'Lorna!' Virginia was suddenly anxious. 'Are you sure it was wise for you to leave hospital?'

The reply came through Lorna's fingers. 'I'm all right. There's nothing wrong that needs hospital treatment.'

Virginia tried another approach. 'Who's looking after your little girl now?'

'Abby's dead.' Now the hands went down. The face was bleak, the voice tight. 'I knew there was something wrong from very early on. She didn't do any of the things that other people's babies were doing.' Lorna picked up Virginia's vegetable knife and attacked an onion with it, slashing viciously.

Virginia probed carefully. 'Was she a Down's child?'

'No! She was beautiful. She seemed perfect.'

Virginia sprinkled pasta into a pan of boiling water, then began to fry the chicken breast. If she looked only at the food, Lorna might find it easier to talk. If she thought about Lorna, then, just maybe, her hands would find it easier not to ruin the food. She was filled with remorse for her uncharitable attitude the previous evening to her former classmate. No wonder Valerie had reprimanded her. It was a wonder that she had not been more severe.

Lorna had begun to cry. 'These onions are strong.'

They were the mild Spanish kind that Virginia always used. She risked a glance over her shoulder. 'Stop rubbing

61

your eyes. Your fingers are covered in juice.' She pushed across a box of tissues and moved over to allow Lorna to wash her hands at the sink. 'Want to tell me how it happened?'

'She was born with TSC.'

'Which is?'

'Tuberous Sclerosis Complex. It's genetic so I won't be having the three others you suggested – though it might not be through me, of course.'

'It wouldn't be your fault either way. Go on.'

'It causes benign tumours to form in the organs – brain, eyes, kidneys, lungs . . . two main neurological symptoms . . . five different types of lesions . . .' Virginia was soon bewildered. Lorna's monotone continued, sounding to her like a recitation from a textbook. Then she remembered that her friend had been a nurse. If, God forbid, anything like this should happen to one of their own children, she supposed that she and Benny would consult books, doctors, the Internet and any other source of possible information and study it till they had it by heart. Lorna could even have learned these dreadful symptoms for an examination, never dreaming that they would occur in the flesh and devastate her life.

She had understood enough of what Lorna was saying to realize that the immediate cause of the tiny girl's death had been bleeding from abnormal blood vessels caused by tumours in her kidneys. Lorna's voice rose, full of resentment. 'Just over a year ago some work began in America with a drug called Rapamycin. The firm that was sponsoring it wanted volunteer patients to see if it would shrink renal tumours in humans like it does in rats. What would Abby have had to lose?'

Tentatively, Virginia asked about the child's father's view and now Lorna's became hysterical. She abandoned the onion as her excuse for tears and sobbed on Virginia's shoulder. Virginia, the least tactile of all women, tried not to shrink away. 'He could easily have afforded to send Abby to America. That drug might have saved her. All he offered to pay for was an abortion. It would have been a different story if it had been their little boy.' Perhaps aware of Virginia's discomfiture, Lorna broke away from her and sank on to a kitchen chair. 'Not that I want that poor little soul to go through what Abby went through.'

There was a sudden gleam of spite through the tears. 'Well, he's got his just deserts now and no mistake.'

Chapter Three

Virginia refrained from asking Lorna any questions about her young daughter's condition for fear of causing her further distress. Lorna had asked to be taken home soon after the two of them had finished lunch and Virginia had not pressed her to stay, knowing that she would rest better in her own bed and without the pressures of behaving as a guest.

On her return she had turned her back on the chaos in the kitchen and resorted to the Internet to find the information she needed to have any understanding of what Lorna and her child had suffered. She discovered that Lorna had by no means exaggerated. Glancing at the first printed sheet as it dropped from the machine, she read, '. . . collapse of the central nervous system, tumor growth and seizures . . . spontaneous bleeding of abnormal blood vessels compromise normal kidney function and lead to serious, life-threatening complications.'

Nothing like the agony Lorna must have gone through had ever been Virginia's lot. Throughout the previous two years she had watched her mother die of a wasting disease, but Hannah had lived a good life, borne her suffering heroically, and her daughter had admired her. Benny had done all he could for both of them.

She could not think how she would cope with losing one of her children, particularly if the unimaginable happened and Benny was not supportive. She didn't live exclusively for them. Indeed, she hoped to see them quickly become separate people, independent of their parents. Already, each had a distinct personality, aims and objectives, though none of the last-mentioned endured for very long. To believe one of them had died unnecessarily, through his father's neglect, would be inconceivably dreadful.

The useful article churning out of her printer did mention Rapamycin, the drug a desperate Lorna had pinned her hopes on. It appeared not to be the certain cure that Lorna believed it to be. Nevertheless, eminent-sounding neurologists allowed that it 'may provide hope for the first non-invasive treatment for TSC.'

Donald had denied his child that chance. Lorna might well have felt perfectly justified in arranging an equally horrific end for him. Still, there was nothing to suggest that she had done anything actually to make it happen. As long as that was the case, Virginia felt she had no option but to protect her from unnecessary suspicion and the unyielding workings of the police machine, which meant keeping this possible motive to herself.

Her musings were interrupted by a phone call from DS Jennifer Taylor. Was she now ready to answer their questions about the hit-and-run incident she had witnessed the previous evening? Virginia was startled by her friend's formal language and tone. She began to realize that the interview was going to be as difficult for Jennifer as for herself.

The car arrived less than five minutes after the call, which was not sufficient time for Virginia to deal with the devastation that resulted from her cooking. She explained it as nonchalantly as she could. 'A friend dropped in for coffee and stayed for lunch.'

She was not pleased to see Clement. Now there would be no chance to explain her dilemma to Jennifer, who might have understood it. She felt protective of Lorna, grieved for her little girl and regretted her own initial lack of charity. The least she could do now was to shield her as far as possible from unnecessary suspicion. She wished the inevitable interview could have taken place before she had been allowed so far into Lorna's confidence. She felt no resentment against her husband for sending a second officer, understanding perfectly that he had to adhere strictly to protocol in any dealings between the force and his own wife.

She settled them all round the kitchen table and saw Clement's surprised expression when the offer to make coffee came from Jennifer. She grinned at the sergeant. 'Don't bother. Benny made gallons before he left.' To Clement she added, 'I assure you, Benny's coffee warmed up is a great improvement on mine freshly made.'

She dawdled over filling three mugs from what remained in the jug, trying to decide what it was safe to tell. Shoving the mugs into the microwave oven, she switched it on. Clement and Jennifer graciously accepted the resulting brew and Virginia returned to the table with nothing decided. 'OK, what do you want to know?'

It was Clement who took charge. 'The CI wants the whole story. He's told us what the affair at the school was in aid of. If you'll take us through it all from your point of view, we'll butt in if necessary.'

'I'm not sure what to pick out, where to begin . . .'

'You're a detective's wife . . .'

She glared at him. 'No. Last night I was a hard-working mother having an evening off. I wasn't taking particular notice of anything. I didn't know that a rather pompous neighbour was breathing his last.'

'Sorry, I suppose you didn't. Can you start from when you went into school. Tell us what you did happen to observe, with any comments or opinions that occur to you. It's our job to pick out what is or isn't relevant.'

Virginia made a silent appeal to Jennifer, who refused to meet her eye. 'Well, Benny's already showed you where I parked. I wandered round the front of the building, then went into the foyer. I could see through the double doors that a few helpers were rushing about the hall. I only recognized Valerie – Mrs Tate – who'd organized every-thing. I stopped to admire the picture that was one of the school's leaving presents to Mr Maynard. Oh, and I peered into the cabinet that holds the house trophies. There weren't many with red ribbons. My house seems to be doing less well than when I was at school . . .' Now Jennifer looked up. Her expression warned Virginia to stop stalling. 'Donald was almost the first person I saw when I went into the hall.'

'You talked to him?'

'No. I didn't want to and, fortunately, he was busy with someone else . . .'

'Who?'

'A man I didn't know. Later Val told me his name was Kyte and he's a vicar. For the meal we sat at tables for eight and he was at my table.'

'Was the victim?'

Virginia shook her head. 'I don't know where he sat.' Wrinkling her nose as she tried to picture the seating arrangement, she listed her dinner companions.

Jennifer raised her head. 'That's only seven.'

'Yes. Someone called Lorna Dyson didn't show.'

'Did she come at all? Later on?'

'No, but she had been earlier. She went home.'

'Why?'

Virginia turned to answer Clement. 'She was upset about something.'

'Do you know what?'

Virginia squirmed. 'I asked her but she wouldn't tell me. We missed her and I went to look for her – ran her to earth in the cloakroom, crying. She said she wasn't upset about any one thing in particular. She was depressed, she hadn't been well and her job situation was dire. She didn't want to be sociable and wished she hadn't come.'

'So she went home?' Virginia nodded. 'You must know her quite well – if you missed her and went to look for her.'

Virginia did her best to explain the rather worn-out friendship. Then, deciding that Lorna might well mention their lunch together, she added, 'As a matter of fact it was Lorna who was here with me today.' Uneasily, she watched

Jennifer scribble a note, then rushed on. 'I can tell you a bit about Donald Markey. He was more than ten years older than me, so I didn't know him at school, but he lived round the corner and he considered Benny one of the few men it wasn't beneath his dignity to talk to.'

'You don't sound too keen on him.'

Virginia considered. 'He was entertaining but not very likeable. He seemed very friendly and generous, but he liked to confer obligations.' When Clement looked puzzled, she added, 'If he wanted you to do something inconvenient, he'd start by doing some small thing for you and then ask, so that you couldn't refuse.'

'A bit of a ladies' man from what we're hearing.'

'He liked them. Some of them liked him too. He was certainly a good-looking man of a certain type. He was suntanned and healthy-looking with thick curly hair – oh, and a dimple. That made old ladies like him.' Neither officer spoke and Virginia felt compelled to blunder on. 'He *was* very attractive. He had enormous self-confidence. It was almost a physical attribute. He was unhesitating in his movements and gestures . . . but . . .'

'But not your type?'

For the first time, Virginia smiled. 'I think the two of them had self-confidence in common – but I do prefer Benny.'

Jennifer took over the questions and Clement looked affronted. 'Did you overhear anything Mr Markey said to his vicar friend?'

Now Virginia relaxed and became fluent again. 'A good deal, before I moved away. He dropped in a mention of his student days at Oxford – which I hadn't known about – and how he met his wife with the aristocratic name. Then he went on in detail about his present job . . .'

'Which was?'

'Team manager for a telecommunications firm in Leeds. He was about to take up a new post, though. A big promotion, apparently.'

'So he was about to leave the district?'

Virginia shook her head. 'Not necessarily. I hadn't heard that they were moving. I got the impression it was with the same company. I don't know whether or not it has branches further afield. He said the appointment had been between him and one other man. He said, "We were old rivals, as you'll remember."'

'What did he mean?'

'How should I know? You'll have to ask the Reverend Neville Kyte.' She relented. 'I did wonder if it might have been Val's husband, Morris. He and Donald were big rivals at school. Donald's game was soccer. Morris was the Yorkshire schools' swimming champion in backstroke and butterfly. He was clever too, *and* popular with the girls. He's a nice man. He spent some time last night trying to draw Lorna out, I noticed.'

'What else did you notice him doing?'

'I'm not sure what he did afterwards. Val was everywhere, doing everything, but I hardly saw Morris at all after the meal. He was probably doing the boring, messy jobs that no one else wanted.'

'Was there a programme for the evening that would help us to pin down times?'

'There was one, but it was abandoned, much to most people's relief. Party games! Mr Maynard's speech was at nine.'

'Was it good?'

Virginia grinned. 'It brought a blush to not a few faces, but it was more amused nostalgia than shame. It was mercifully short – more so than the tribute to him from the head boy.' Looking up, she intercepted a glance between the two officers.

Jennifer asked, 'You said the headmaster-elect was invited, was sitting at your table, in fact. Was he a stranger?'

'Are you working out why whoever killed Donald chose last night to do it? Someone who only had the one opportunity?' When the two officers remained silent, Virginia continued, 'No, he was an old boy. Very insular school, isn't it? Though Robert Barnes has lived in Birmingham for a good many years.'

'What sort of impression did you get of him?'

Virginia shrugged. 'Sorry. I have to let you down again. He was a bit of a stuffed shirt. Old Mr Maynard was so much more entertaining that I left the Barneses to his son.'

'Did you notice Donald Markey leave the hall?'

Virginia shut her eyes, trying to see the scene again. 'Just a vague impression. It was quite well on in the evening, just before I decided I'd done my bit and could go . . .'

Jennifer raised a hand. 'Just a minute. Can we have slow motion and all the detail you can dredge up now?'

'Yes, but there's not much. I gathered my belongings and wove my way round the tables to the door.'

'You'd all stayed in the dining room after the meal?'

Virginia shook her head. 'No, we were back in the hall for the speeches so that people could get on with clearing the dining hall. There were little tables round the edge of the main hall too. Someone called Nicky Simpson followed me out. Val told me she was French but she sounded like a local.'

'You talked to her?'

'Only for a minute when she caught me up. She didn't say why she'd left the hall, just remarked that you didn't realize how stuffy it had been indoors until you got outside. She stood by that flower bed alongside the car park and watched me till I was out of sight.'

'Watched you carefully? As if she was waiting for you to be out of the way?'

'I don't know. I didn't turn round till I'd reached the corner. We waved to each other then. Her husband was a quiet little man. He seemed really out of his element. He sat in the same chair all night except for buying a drink now and then and going with all the rest into the dining room. He danced just the once with his wife.'

'Do you know him?'

'No, but I was interested in him. He's written a book that

I'd heard about.' There was a few seconds' silence, broken by Virginia voicing all their thoughts. 'Now we come to the vital bit. I'm ashamed to tell you that my impressions are no more accurate than someone's who wasn't born and bred in a police family. I wasn't specially efficient either. I panicked momentarily, I'm afraid. Of course I wish the hospital could have patched him up. For myself, though, I was relieved when I found that his injuries were too serious to treat. If that couple of minutes or so that I wasted in getting myself together might have given him a chance to survive . . .'

Her head jerked up suddenly. 'That is the truth, I hope, and not just a story the police have decided to humour me with? If a police wife and daughter can't jump to it in an emergency, how can we expect anyone else to?' She paused, biting her lip.

Jennifer's tone was cutting. 'I never expected melo-drama from you. Cut it out, Ginny. Benny says you don't think this hit-and-run was an accident. Tell us exactly what you saw and why you formed that opinion.'

'It's only . . .'

'An opinion? Yes. That's all I called it.'

Virginia had anticipated the question, had lain awake well into the early hours vainly trying to answer it. 'I was standing by the car, fishing in my coat pocket for the keys and just staring, without really looking, into the road.' She described observing, then recognizing Donald. 'It was quiet, except for the women. I could hear them talking, calling – not the words, just voices. I think Donald heard the car engine before I did. Thinking back, I believe he was stepping out to meet it, looking down the street for it – but that wasn't what occurred to me at the time. It was all very quick.' She stopped speaking, stared at her hands.

Jennifer prompted. 'Any details you remember about the car?'

'Benny says it was green. I saw it as a sort of shiny gold. The sodium lights were just coming on so they'd have

71

affected the colour it looked. I think the paint probably had a metallic finish.'

'And the driver?'

Tonelessly, Virginia repeated what she had told Mitchell already. No effort of her will either sharpened the picture or changed her conviction that the killing had been deliberate. 'The car checked and stopped, once Donald was hit. He went up in the air, hit the windscreen and broke it as he came down, then rolled off the bonnet on to the tarmac in front of the car. Then it started moving again.'

She paused and closed her eyes, concentrating hard. 'I think the engine had been running all the time. He – I thought it was a man but I wouldn't swear to it – drove over the . . . Donald . . . without attempting to go round. I suppose he could have been in shock. I don't think he was drunk or drugged. He wasn't swerving about. He mounted the jutting-out bit of pavement, granted, but I think that's what he meant to do.' Her eyes still closed, she saw again Donald's ghastly grimace. It had been a shock to discover that the shattered jaw was toothless. The broken fragments of his dentures lay around his face, telling his closely guarded secret – that the perfect smile had been someone else's work of art, undetectable and expensive. Suddenly, although she still could not like him, this posthumous humiliation, which he would have felt so keenly, made him vulnerable and she felt a genuine pity for the vain and silly man, a sincere regret that he had come to such an end.

She was grateful when Jennifer lightened the mood and her tone. 'How on earth did you get the group of women to keep off the vital bit of road?'

Virginia managed a smile. 'I called the mouthiest one to come and help me. Once the others had lost their leader they went back to being interested spectators. When they saw how much blood there was they kept their distance of their own accord. Then a man came out of the house nearest to where Donald was lying and he started bellowing at them. I calmed them down and told the women how important their evidence would be. I tried to make mental notes on what they said but they were all yelling and in wild disagreement with one another.'

Jennifer nodded to Clement who came out of his sulk to ask, 'Did you pick up anything useful when the police had taken charge and you went back into school?'

Virginia shrugged. 'Almost everyone who'd been there when I left was still there. No one seemed grief-stricken at Donald's death, though they were shocked at the manner of it – except Phyllida, of course. Having the police question them was the most exciting thing that was ever likely to happen to most of them.'

When the two detectives left, Clement took the driving seat of the squad car without invitation. Undeterred by Jennifer's being his senior and disapproving officer, he addressed her furiously. 'You cow!'

Jennifer was lenient as a penance for misunderstanding his anger. 'It was the only way to do it. If I'd sympathized and made her cry in front of us she would never have forgiven me.'

Clement gave a grudging nod. 'Where to now?'

'To little friend Lorna, I think. Let's see if we can find out what Ginny wasn't willing to tell us about her.'

The overnight rain, which had made the morning cooler and fresher, had quickly evaporated and the sun had begun to burn down so that the heat matched that of the day before. Through it, DC Caroline Jackson was making her way to the Markeys' house, round the corner from and rather grander than the Mitchells'. Phyllida had insisted that they meet her in her own home. Caroline was pleased, though rather surprised, that the newly bereaved woman had chosen to talk to the police without the support of the friends who had taken her in.

The house, though big and imposing, was not ostentatious. The garden was neat and large, green rather than flowery, certainly not elaborate. The paint on the window frames sparkled white and the curtains hung, simple and straight. Phyllida Markey was very much mistress of it all as she invited Caroline in. She was neatly dressed in a well-cut, floor-length skirt, as narrow as her girth allowed. Over it, the printed cotton tunic was not offensively bright but by no means funereal. The fair hair was shining clean, thick and curly but pinned back unevenly, as though without benefit of mirror. She showed no sign of recent tears.

Her expression solemn and composed, she led Caroline down a thickly carpeted hall into a sitting room, huge, light and gracious. Caroline's commiserations were simple and standard but none the less sincere. They were acknowledged with a dignified nod. There was no offer of refreshment and no attempt to treat the meeting as a social occasion.

Caroline carefully reassessed her mission before she spoke again. Part of her brief had been to explain the role of the family liaison officer and the help that he or she could offer. She had the impression that this lady was likely, politely, to send PC Clark to help someone more in need of her services. Instead she asked, 'I would like your permission for some of our officers to make an examination of your house.'

Phyllida Markey was both reluctant and curious. When, to parry her questions, Caroline assured her that she would be allowed to be present during the process, she was gracious. 'That won't be necessary. I'm sure that none of your officers would either spoil or steal my belongings, but I shall have to be given a good reason before I can sanction such interference.'

Caroline stifled a sigh. 'We shall be looking for anything that might indicate a person who wanted your husband to die.'

There was silence for some seconds as Phyllida considered all the implications of Caroline's statement. Then she asked, 'You think the driver might have been me?'

'You're one of the people we're currently ruling out. Mr Maynard's guests are queuing up to assure us that one or other of them was with you throughout the evening.' Caroline paused but her witness continued to regard her attentively, so that she felt obliged to continue. 'We've been in trouble too often, both with our senior officers and with members of the public, not to treat any unexplained death very seriously.' She had the distinct impression that it was Phyllida Markey who was controlling the situation.

'As if it was a crime and not an accident?'

'Hit-and-run is a crime, so we're certainly investigating one and we'll keep on with it until we've found that driver for you. What I meant was that we have to assume that the driver might have been acting deliberately until we have some evidence to the contrary.'

Phyllida nodded once, then sat as though deliberating on the information. When the silence had continued for an uncomfortable time, Caroline said, 'You don't appear to have any children.'

'Don't I?'

Caroline too could be laconic. 'Where are they?' Then, fearing she had antagonized her witness, she apologized. 'I expected that, if there were any, they would have been at the Tates' house with you.'

'Zak is at boarding school. I've sent for him.' The last sentence was offered with her first smile. Phyllida Markey continued to interview Caroline for a further fifteen minutes before dismissing her. Caroline blamed the enervating heat.

Telephoning her mother-in-law to arrange to collect her children, Virginia discovered that they had been taken by their grandfather to York for the day. She was free, therefore, to make her obligatory but also genuine commiserations to Phyllida Markey.

She was not pleased, having driven across town, to discover that she would have found her neighbour by walking just round the corner from her own home.

'You couldn't have had your little talk with her though,'

Valerie Tate pointed out, happily rushing to prepare refreshments for an always-welcome guest.

Virginia, who had had no intention of inflicting 'little talks' on anyone, frantically sought an excuse for avoiding an afternoon of Valerie's effusive gossip and advice. Then, finding she was losing the battle, she made the best of the situation and began to see that she could turn it to her own advantage. Perhaps she would learn a little more about what Lorna had been up to recently. Valerie was hard to turn off but easy to steer.

Having heard her friend's inevitable iterations on how shocking was the previous evening's 'happening', Virginia distracted her with congratulations on her organization of the total event.

'The games went wrong.'

'No they didn't. You realized they weren't appropriate for the people who turned up and were adaptable enough to switch plans.'

'For the second time! Till a couple of weeks ago I was planning that the entertainment should be country dancing. Morris and I could have demonstrated lots of them.' Virginia shuddered. 'I thought it would be a novelty for them and a bit of much-needed exercise for some. The committee threw it out when they heard. Even Morris voted against it.'

Virginia grinned. 'Ah, well, we women have to know when we're beaten. How did our famous visitor enjoy himself? He doesn't strike me as much of a dancer.'

'Eric, you mean? I didn't really talk to him last night. I've worked for him, you know.' Virginia remembered that Valerie did desktop publishing. 'I get his stuff ready for whoever he's sending it to – lectures and papers and such for learned journals.'

Virginia was genuinely interested. 'Did you help with the book that's making him famous?'

Valerie nodded. 'He scribbled it on file paper in spare moments. I prepared it for sending to various publishing houses. I'm glad it's succeeded. He deserves it. He's going on lecturing, you know, even though he's made a packet on the first book and got a huge advance for this new one.'

'What's it about?'

Valerie shook her head. 'He's done some of the typing himself. As far as I can gather from my parts, it's about a man on a journey but everything has a weird psychological double meaning.'

'I hope his lectures don't.'

Valerie raised her substantial shoulders. 'I wouldn't know. I can't understand a word of the ones I've worked on. I think his students like him, though. He's a bright chap. Well, in some ways he is. Not very sharp about some things, though. I can't understand how he hasn't realized about Donald carrying on all these years with Nicky.'

'You mean those two have been seeing each other ever since schooldays?'

'On and off, yes.'

'Then, perhaps Eric does know and keeps his mouth shut.'

Valerie shook her head as she poured tea, managing not to spill it. 'No. He wouldn't have stood for it. He's a big churchman, very moral. I think Nicky was beginning to get scared that he'd find out. She's certainly been cooling off a bit recently for some reason. In fact, last night I saw Donald go over and offer her a drink. She refused and went back to sit with Eric.'

'Why wasn't she scared before?'

Valerie laughed. 'Eric wasn't rich before.'

She chattered on whilst Virginia pondered this extra-marital affair. Presumably, Lorna's Abigail had been conceived during one of its 'off' periods. She wondered whether Benny knew yet about these complications and whether, like herself, the police were considering how Eric Simpson and Phyllida Markey felt about them. She tuned back in to Valerie's rather spiteful speculations and wished that she had not let her attention wander.

'. . . Nicky's doing her best to stop Eric offering to bail

him out. Still, he might well be offered Donald's new post now and then it wouldn't be necessary.'

Virginia frantically searched her mind for a question that would produce the name she had missed. 'Was he the only other candidate for the job?'

'The only serious one. If they let him have it, he'll do a much better job than Donald would have done. Morris has never been a front man. He dreamed up ideas in a back room and Donald offered them to the management as his own. Some of the top brass were getting wise to him, though. I think Donald was scared at the interviews. He knew that Morris would be able to explain their future plans more clearly because, after all, they were his brain-children.'

Virginia made sympathetic noises but asked no more. If Benny wanted details of all this he was in a better position than herself to get them. Explaining that her children had to be collected, she excused herself and took her leave.

At home, shelving her problems, she took her usual pleasure in their bedtime routine. The treasures of York had been greatly admired by Declan but simpler enter-tainments and domestic happenings were the highlights of the twins' day. Granny Niamh had organized a race won by Sinead.

'She won at the front,' Michael told his mother, unim-pressed, 'and I won at the back. Grandad said so.

Grandad's friend from next door had visited. His long beard had fascinated Sinead. 'It jiggled when he talked. He asked me how old I was. I told him I was nearly five.'

'She's only just four, and she asked him,' Declan reported, disapprovingly, 'if he'd got nearly to the end of the numbers.'

Virginia smiled. 'Never mind. I don't expect she meant to be rude.'

Michael, as he struggled out of his clothes, remembered that he had another triumph to declare. 'I can tie my shoelaces now, and I used to couldn't.'

'Splendid.' Virginia dropped him into the bath, began

peeling off Sinead's garments and spoke to her elder daughter who had so far contributed nothing. 'Haven't you got anything to tell me?'

Caitlin blinked and snapped out of her reverie. 'I was just wondering,' she remarked, 'why boys don't wear dresses.'

Why indeed? Virginia tried to fix these gems in her memory. Benny would be home with some awkward questions before long but he could always be distracted for a little while with snippets of his children's philosophy.

Mitchell arrived back at headquarters in time, as he had hoped, to conduct his own debriefing. Instead of making a good beginning on this new enquiry, he had had to spend a frustrating day in court. The case in which he was required as a witness had been held over until the afternoon and then thrown out because of a conflict of evidence. However, the station foyer was cool in contrast with the glaring heat outside and in the middle of its early-evening period of calm. The afternoon shoplifters would already have shuffled, some brazenly, some shamefacedly, in and out and the nightly confusion of prostitutes and drunks was not yet cluttering it up.

Mitchell stopped for a word with the desk sergeant, Mark Powers, inevitably addressed as Magic. A note was pushed across the desk towards him. Mitchell picked it up with a nod of acknowledgement and read it. He was used to the sergeant, who was monosyllabic if he spoke at all. 'Did this come from Jennifer Taylor?'

Magic jerked his head in the direction of the stairs and managed three words. 'In your office.'

Clutching Jennifer's note, Mitchell ran up the steps, his good humour completely restored. He found his sergeant sitting in his only comfortable chair, drinking coffee from a soggy paper cup and looking smug.

She grinned at him. 'I didn't get you one. I know you won't drink the stuff out of the machine.'

Mitchell waved the note. 'What's all this?'

'I would have thought it was self-explanatory. There was another metallic-green car involved in another accident last night.'

'So, matey ran his vehicle into something else to account for the damage done to it in Moorside Rise, then abandoned it, possibly to claim it was stolen and collect on the insurance.'

'No, she didn't.'

'She? Look, why not start at the beginning?'

Jennifer made him wait until the paper cup she held was drained. 'It starts with Ginny.'

'This whole affair begins with her. I wish it didn't.'

Jennifer's head jerked up. 'You think she's in danger? That the driver saw her watching him?'

'Or her. That's my most important worry but I doubt that it's very likely. She was behind the wall, under trees. She hadn't switched her lights on and she was wearing darkish clothes. She doesn't think he looked in her direction. He was concentrating on Donald and the road.'

'And he had the women down the street to distract him too. So, why else did you not want Ginny involved?'

Mitchell took a pair of scissors from a drawer and began to hack at tendrils of ivy that were encroaching on to the surface of his desk. 'When I insist that she's a reliable witness whose impression of the driver's intention needs taking seriously, aren't I going to appear just a trifle biased?'

'We all believe her too.'

'Thanks. That's something. I wish to goodness I'd attended this blasted farce as Ginny wanted me to – then I'd have been the witness myself.'

'That would have made you surer? So, what you're actually saying is that you can't decide whether she's right or not.'

Mitchell's expression was offended. 'A police impression would have carried more weight.'

'All yours should have been enough.' Jennifer dodged

the rubber he shied at her and got to her feet. 'Come on, the troops will be gathered.'

They were. The male officers chatted together as they waited. Several of the women were milling round the two new pictures of Donald Markey. One showed him full-length, tall, broad-shouldered but slim. The second was a much-enlarged close-up of the face. The dark brown eyes had long lashes and fine brows like a woman's. Jennifer joined the women and carefully examined the round but lean face. The absurd dimples, together with the thick, close-cropped curly hair, took years away from it. The skin, she thought enviously, looked as though it had tanned at the least gleam of sunlight. She wondered who had supplied these extra pictures.

The officers had fallen silent as their DCI came in. Not all of them shared his hope that this briefing marked the beginning of a murder investigation, but all of them were anxious to know one way or the other.

Mitchell perched on a table in front of the display board to address them. 'Since, unfortunately, there's nothing in yet from the lab, you folk have more to report than I have, so let's get to it. Sergeant Taylor first. What did you get from my wife?'

For once, Jennifer was not ready with her report. No amount of sifting through what she had seen and been told during the day had made sense of it. She had gone to see Virginia, expecting a detailed and lucid account of the incident they were investigating. Ginny had, most uncharacteristically, wasted time in small talk, parried the questions put to her and withheld important information.

She thought over again what Ginny had said. Her friend, Miss Dyson, had 'dropped in'. She wasn't sure exactly what Jennifer required. What nonsense! She had deliberately misunderstood Clement's 'Tell us everything,' and facetiously given details that they all knew were irrelevant. They had discussed the Dyson woman for several minutes before Ginny had admitted that her friend had been at the house earlier. Strangest of all, she had omitted to mention the second road accident and Lorna Dyson's injuries. On other matters, the character of the victim, for example, she had been full and frank.

Jennifer realized that she had hesitated too long and that everyone in the room was staring at her. Hastily, she gave the gist of the information Virginia had seen fit to give her and commented on it briefly. 'Adrian and I were looking for any clues as to why Donald Markey was killed on that particular evening. Your wife heard him mention that he was changing his job. She thinks it's within the same company, so it may or may not have involved moving away in the near future.' Mitchell nodded and made a note.

'Another candidate for this promotion could have been a Morris Tate, who was also a pupil at the school and attending the reunion last night. Mrs Mitchell said that although Valerie Tate, his wife, was in charge of the reception and in evidence all evening, she hardly saw Morris at all.' She glanced at Clement for confirmation. 'Then we wondered about the other headmaster, Maynard's replacement. He was making a flying visit for the occasion.'

Mitchell frowned. 'Why would he want to run Markey over? Would he even have met him except at his interview?'

'A lot of murky stuff can come out in an interview. Anyway, he's yet another old boy. Then there was a Nicky Simpson who left the building at the same time as Ginny. We'd better find out what she was up to, though she'd not have had any too much time to drive round the block and do the deed whilst Ginny was strolling round the building and searching her pockets for her keys.'

'You only need just enough.'

'Ginny thinks that Markey was expecting the car to meet him and walked out when he heard the engine as if the vehicle was going to pick him up.'

'One of the women I spoke to this morning said just the

same thing.' They all turned to Caroline, and Jennifer sent her silent thanks. She had been interrupted before she had had to mention Lorna Dyson. Now she had a little more thinking time – perhaps enough to ring Ginny and find out what was going on.

Caroline briefly summarized the meagre results of the house-to-house questioning in Moorside Rise. Mitchell was philosophical. 'It was as much as I expected. What about your session with Phyllida Markey?'

'It was odd.' There was a pause as they waited for Caroline to be more precise. 'She insisted on seeing me at her own house, without the support of the friends who've taken her in.'

Mitchell grinned. 'I shouldn't read too much into that. I know Val slightly through Ginny. She has a heart of gold but you don't tell her anything you don't want to find on the front of the *Clarion* and small doses of her are enough. Phyllida wouldn't have wanted her there.'

'Right.' Caroline nodded. 'She was very matter of fact. There weren't any tears – in fact, she seemed more pleased to be getting her son home than grieved at losing her husband.'

'You think she was glad to be rid?'

Caroline considered Clement's suggestion. 'Not exactly. I felt she was holding herself in, playing word games with me to distract herself from thinking about it and making an exhibition of herself. I think she'd have been very embarrassed if she'd lost control.'

'How old is the son?'

'He's nine. I suppose he's all she's got now. She'll want him with her, of course – but she looked almost smug when she said she'd sent for him.'

'Maybe his parents had disagreed about sending him away.'

'Yes.' Caroline nodded at Shakila. 'That occurred to me but I didn't feel I could throw that at her today. She was very lady-of-the-manor about letting us look at the house. She forced me to give her a reason – to admit that we were considering a deliberate killing. Her immediate reaction to that was to ask if we thought she'd done it. I told her that we had witnesses to vouch for her being in school all night.'

'That's a bit odd too. I'm sure none of the other people can account for the whole evening. They went off to the loo, took a breather outside to cool off or have a smoke.' Mitchell paused to see if Caroline had anything more. When she shook her head, he thanked her. 'We'll see what the lady has to say when we interview her properly tomorrow. I've one or two other snippets from Ginny. She went to the Tates' house late this afternoon, expecting to find Phyllida Markey there and offer her commiserations. Phyllida being busy with Caroline, Ginny got trapped with Valerie and it turned out to be quite useful.'

Mitchell stood up from the table and rubbed his substantial rear quarters where the corner had dug in. 'Caroline, I want you to talk to Nicky Simpson tomorrow. Try to see her separately from Eric, her husband. Apparently she's been Markey's mistress since schooldays "on and off". According to Val, she's been trying recently to get herself out of the relationship . . .'

'Is he the Eric Simpson who . . .'

Mitchell nodded approvingly at Shakila. He had not known anything about the notorious book himself until Virginia had told him. He felt that the police should have a finger on the pulse of society and knew that most of them, including himself, were slightly out of touch with day-to-day existence. At the end of a long or difficult case, he felt like someone recently returned from a long ocean voyage. Officers knew what criminal activities were going on in which part of town but they missed the cultural points of references that the rest of the world took for granted.

His shift were all waiting for his account to continue and he hastily returned to it. 'Ginny got the impression that the Tates are in some financial trouble and Nicky Simpson is trying to persuade her husband not to help them. She sounds a thoroughly nasty piece. To make things just a shade more complicated, Val Tate confirmed that the new job that Markey had just landed had been expected, at least by the Tates, to be given to Morris. Smithson's been asking a few preliminary questions at the company concerned, Ingalls.'

In answer to Mitchell's nod, the uniformed constable came forward. 'I managed to find a bloke who was a mate of Markey's from way back. Markey's wife was an Oxford student. He met her when the firm was asked to design a telecommunications system for her college. Markey was one of the workmen sent to install it . . .'

Mitchell blinked. 'I thought Ginny heard him say that he'd been a student there himself and that he did the designing.'

Smithson shook his head. 'From what I was told, Markey, at that time, was the one who fixed the screws where somebody else told him, though he did move up to become assistant to one of the designers.'

'So what's the wonderful new job that he and Tate were squabbling about?'

'Being a sort of second-rank rep. Markey was a good front man. Customers were impressed by him and liked him. Ingalls sent somebody who really could explain why the system they were selling would work for a particular buyer and friend Donald tagged along to lay on the charm.'

'He must have laid it on with the Oxford student.'

Smithson shrugged. 'Matey I spoke to said she wasn't much of a catch, except she was rich. She was a mature student, a good few years older than Donald and not much to look at.' He glanced enquiringly at Caroline. 'It wasn't just sour grapes, was it? She's not a dolly bird?'

Caroline turned the injured side of her face away from him. 'Not exactly, but she's an interesting woman.'

There was a pause as they absorbed what for most of them was new information. Mitchell broke it himself. 'Since Valerie Tate knows about the affair between our victim and Nicky Simpson, then it will be common knowledge. To return to Jennifer's question, why last night? Phyllida Markey must have known for years that her husband had a roving eye, but what if Eric Simpson, who isn't much of a socialite, has only just discovered that his wife was one of the harem?'

Jennifer had an objection. 'Ginny said he hardly stirred from his chair. You're probably right about his social life but —'

'He could have left immediately after Ginny did.' Mitchell was growing to like his theory. 'We'll see what Caroline gets from them tomorrow. The other thing that's urgent is looking into this second crash.'

The attention of the assembled officers had been waning as the meeting dragged on. Now it sharply refocused. Mitchell, his expression enigmatic, waved Jennifer forward for a second time. 'Sergeant Taylor somehow forgot to include it in her report. Fortunately she did manage to send me a note about it.'

Red-faced, Jennifer rectified the omission. 'I haven't had a chance to check with Traffic yet, but Adrian and I went to see a Lorna Dyson this afternoon.'

'She's the one who arrived and went home again before the meal?' a uniformed constable asked.

Mitchell beamed. 'So early in the case and someone's actually reading the file!' Smithson muttered darkly and inaudibly. Mitchell transferred the beam to him. 'I didn't quite catch that.'

Smithson was unabashed. 'I said that's the time to quote from the file — early on, when there's not much in it. You can earn your Brownie points quicker.'

Jennifer waited for the sniggers to die away, then gave the only details of this new incident that she knew — its location and its victim's injuries. 'She doesn't know what caused her to hit the tree. She admits to being unwell and very tired.'

'Fell asleep at the wheel?' Clement asked.

'Possibly.'

Mitchell decided they had all had enough. 'Right. Leave her for now till we've got a better picture. Adrian, get on to Traffic and find out all you can, time, witnesses and so on. Get the car brought in.'

Clement was not enthusiastic. 'Now? You want me to go over to Traffic tonight?'

'Unless you can sit on your behind in here and do it by telepathy.' Mitchell released Clement from his glare and turned to address the whole room. 'Just remember that a detective's chief asset is his feet. It's not the piecing together of physical evidence that's going to give us our man, even when they do get around to sending something back from the lab, though it will convict him when we've found him. You're going to walk till you drop tomorrow, asking your questions over and over. Find a recluse insomniac who was walking in Old Lane last night. Go around our own department searching statements for things we've missed. Fill out endless request forms for information. Criminals are caught because of what people tell us – or don't tell us!' His gaze rested on Jennifer long enough to make her uncomfortable. He hoped that would be enough to make her divulge all she knew.

Chapter Four

When Eric Simpson opened his studded oak door to Caroline on Monday morning she was greeted by the smell of freshly ground coffee and the sound of rippling piano notes. She refused his offer to make another brew for her and stood for a few seconds, listening to the music.

'I'm sorry to have spoiled your concert,' she told him as he ushered her into a vast sitting room. 'I'd rather listen to Mozart than do an interview too.'

He seemed unperturbed. 'It's all right. I can hear it again later.' Caroline was relieved. If he'd been listening to the radio he'd have missed his treat and, possibly, been a resentful witness. He closed the door but left the compact disc playing a slightly muffled accompaniment to their conversation. With old-fashioned politeness, he requested a few moments to put away the work he had been engaged on.

As he stowed papers neatly and swiftly in drawers, Caroline examined a postcard-sized silver-framed photograph on a small table. In it, Eric stood behind a woman, presumably his wife, who held a baby on her lap. The picture had obviously been taken some time ago. Eric had been surprisingly attractive. Thick dark hair, long in the fashion of the eighties, framed a thin intelligent face. He was not smiling but there was a glint of humour in his expression. She tried to pin down which feature betrayed it, and failed, then turned to observe her quarry now as he left his desk and gave her his full attention. If he had been a woman, Caroline decided, it would have been said that he had flowered early and faded.

He smiled at her as she replaced the picture. 'The baby wasn't ours, I'm afraid. They never happened to us.' He sat down opposite her and expressed conventional sorrow for Donald Markey's death, adding with more evident sincerity an enquiry after Phyllida. 'I don't know if anyone's told you but Nicolette and I gave the Markeys a lift on Saturday evening. We arrived before they were ready. Phyllida seemed a little *distrait* even then. I've been wondering if she had some sort of premonition of what – well, what happened. Perhaps I'm being fanciful.'

At Caroline's request, Eric reproduced as much of the quartet's odd conversation at the time as he could recall, finishing with a description of Phyllida's rebellious change of clothes.

Caroline made a brief note, then asked her witness to describe Donald Markey in his own terms.

He smiled at her. 'Nothing I can say can transfer my impression of Donald to your mind or imagination. Words I use have associations for me. The same word for you will have different associations. All I can do is give you an inventory and leave you to make of it what you can.'

Caroline blinked as her brain followed this thought to its logical conclusion. Each member of the team would receive this impression which had come first through Eric and then herself. Mentally they would create five different people, none of them Donald Markey. When all their witnesses had added comments, they would end up with a lowest common denominator which would give them a partial and distorted picture of their victim.

She dragged her mind back to her interview. Her tone apologetic, she continued, 'It's not the kind of thing I like asking, but would you describe to me, as you saw it, the relationship between the victim and his wife?'

'It's not the kind of question I like answering.'

Caroline had no difficulty in believing him. 'That makes your opinion the more valuable.'

He acknowledged the compliment with a tight smile. 'I do assure you, there's nothing to Phyllida's discredit.' He paused, still uncomfortable, gathering his thoughts. 'Phyllida understood Donald perfectly. She knew about his philandering, knew he had a physical, animal attraction that women couldn't resist and that he couldn't resist exploiting. He was the obtuse one. He thought that, because she was fat and physically awkward, she was also stupid.'

Eric's hands moved in front of him as though he were manually arranging his words. 'Donald thought she was grateful to him for noticing and then marrying her. "Lifting her off the shelf", he called it on one occasion.'

Abruptly, Eric got up and crossed the room. From a silver tray full of glasses he took two, filled them from a half-full, vacuum-corked bottle of red wine and handed her one. Caroline, who drank abstemiously, failed to recognize the label but thought it looked venerable. She waited for him to make a jocular excuse for this indulgence so early in the day and was glad when he did not. She sipped from her glass, grateful on two counts. The wine would free his tongue and its taste was amazing. She saw that he had brought the bottle with him as he settled back in his chair and continued his analysis.

'I hope I'm wrong but I think Phyllida thinks he married her for her money –'

'It's hers, then?' Caroline was immediately angry with herself for this unnecessary interruption.

Eric ignored it. 'Actually, he didn't, though he very much enjoyed spending it. I think what made him settle for her was that she gave him some stability, a base, an experience of the sort of integrity he was intelligent enough to know he didn't have. He treated her with patronizing fondness, like a family pet, somewhat indulged but needing to be kept in its place. He was always willing to please her, so long as it didn't prove too inconvenient.' He paused to refill his glass.

Caroline put a hand over her own and shook her head. She asked, 'How did Mrs Markey accept this treatment?'

'In a very matter-of-fact fashion. Donald had given her what she wanted.' In response to Caroline's raised eyebrow, he added, 'Zachary.' Caroline was silent, absorbing this detailed and informed account until Eric spoke again. 'A great pity he wasn't twins.'

'Why?'

Eric smiled sadly. 'Because Donald didn't want children. He made sure there weren't any more. That was rather a disaster both for Phyllida and for Zachary. Of course, in some families it works well to have an only child, but Phyllida has invested too much in the boy. It's too much of a responsibility for him . . .'

He stopped speaking as he realized that Caroline was no longer listening to him. A small part of her attention had been on the piano's muffled accompaniment to their conversation. She had been unconscious of it until she was jolted by a slight inaccuracy in a bar she had always had trouble with herself.

There was a brief silence, then she heard the bar again, correctly played but at half speed. It was repeated, a little faster, then faster still. Then the whole section of the sonata was begun again, this time with the tricky phrase safely negotiated. Caroline blinked and became aware that Eric had suspended his account and was waiting for her. 'It's the end of the first sonata, isn't it? The recapitulation of the first movement. It's hard to believe he was only nineteen when he wrote it. Who's playing?'

'It's Nicolette.'

Caroline was astonished. How did this fit in with the picture so far painted by the information in the file about the flighty Mrs Simpson? 'She's very good. Has she . . .? Does she play professionally?'

Eric shook his head. 'Her French grandfather taught her when she was very young. When he died, no one else in her family thought of paying for her lessons to continue. She didn't realize how good she was, so she only grieved a little at the time, both for her grandfather and the break in her musical education. She says she hopes she's kept up the standard she'd reached when he left her.'

Caroline shook her head in wonderment. 'She's a very complex character.'

Eric shrugged and then nodded. 'Yes – if by complex you mean mixed up. She's bilingual and belongs to two cultures but she doesn't see that as an advantage. She doesn't feel she fits in with or belongs to either.'

He waxed eloquent on his wife's problems until a glance at her watch reminded Caroline how long their chat had lasted. Time to be moving if the list on her action sheet was to be worked through. Briefly, she took him through his movements and observations on Saturday evening and noted his equally brief replies.She was unsure whether she had learned anything from this witness that Mitchell would find valuable. She was not at all certain what he had wanted her to find out. She did know that, if she had asked him, she would have received the usual reply – 'Whatever he wants to tell you.'

To signal her imminent departure, she placed the empty glass she had been nursing beside the photograph on the table. Eric Simpson put his own beside it. He had not drunk from it since he had refilled it and she watched as a small dribble of wine ran down the glass and threatened the beautiful waxed surface of the exquisite table. Thanking him for his help and patience, Caroline got up and asked to speak to his wife.

Simpson nodded and led her up the hall to the room from where the music had been coming. Before opening the door, he spoke softly. 'Treat her gently. This is a bereavement for her too.'

As Caroline left, Nicky Simpson sat on the floor in her dining room, hugging her knees and listening as Eric showed their visitor out. DC Jackson had been a revelation to her – police officer and musician seemed a very unusual combination. She had always thought that police officers wore hob-nailed boots and dropped their Hs. This one had come in, congratulated her on her execution of the first Mozart sonata – and without being patronizing. Then she had suggested a way round the technical difficulty of the bars she had had trouble with. Then, she had sat down at the piano and demonstrated.

Nicky tried to imagine what it might have been about the police force that had tempted a girl who had set her sights on being a concert pianist. She had been accepted by the RAM so it couldn't have been lack of talent. DC Jackson said she had wondered if an unacknowledged lack of confidence had been part of her motive. Still, all but the most arrogant performers – and therefore the most insensitive and second-rate – sometimes doubted themselves.

She had also been afraid of the loneliness of success. Nicky could just about understand this. Fame and acclaim might well hinder close friendships in the same way that popularity with men on a purely physical level had hindered her own ability to be warm and concerned about people in general.

After lunch she would try playing that awkward passage with crossed hands as Constable Jackson had suggested and demonstrated.

She was a personable young woman, at least for a detective – not pretty exactly but healthy-looking and appealing. Nicky thought men would be attracted to her. That scar on her face was an obscenity. It looked fairly recent but she behaved as if she was unconscious of it. Certainly it didn't obsess her.

Nicky glanced at her own reflection in the glass door of the bookcase and wondered how she would bear such a mutilation herself. She knew she would think about it all the time – except when she was playing the piano.

She shook her head to clear it. She felt herself to be two people in one body, a musician whom she almost respected and a vain woman, conscious of her shallow life, an English wife and a French granddaughter. It was French to be

– not vain, exactly – but French women were conscious always of the impression they were making on the opposite sex. English women seemed to despise this even while they were fascinated by it. Of course, Englishmen were different from Frenchmen. She should know. She had seduced both.

Now she felt ashamed because she knew she had talent yet lacked the drive to exploit her gift. She would be unable to meet her grandfather's eye if she had to face him today. He would reduce her, make her aware of her triviality. Eric did that to her too, though neither of them did it consciously or deliberately.

The money had changed their lives but it hadn't changed Eric. He was the same wise, kind man as before, glad that he could now afford to be as generous to everybody as he had always been to her. He didn't judge but he wasn't fooled. He didn't shrink from criticizing her, but he took no pleasure in it, was not in the least self-righteous.

People thought she had given Donald the cold shoulder because Eric had got rich, and, indirectly, they were right. But they were wrong in thinking that she was afraid of losing Eric, and consequently the money. It had shown her Eric's worth. She respected his success. She respected even more the way he had dealt with it. He'd increased in stature for her and she'd responded to it. It had changed how she felt about him sexually. The nicer of the two people she was might be the right wife for him.

You couldn't be two people, though. You ended up not being a person at all. It seemed to Nicky that she had never known who she was, only what she wanted and how she was going to get it. And what she wanted now was to find out whether there was a real person inside her to know. She was not sure how to set about it but she knew Eric would help. She wouldn't consult him and make things awkward between them. She would be grateful that he loved her. She would try to see and to be the person he saw when he looked at her, talked to her.

She could not understand now why she had spent two

decades trying to captivate Donald. Had it been even a physical attraction? He hadn't been a better lover. He'd been eager and greedy and her own satisfaction had been merely in her response to his near-perfect body. There was nothing of himself that he had consciously or willingly given her. She was glad to be rid of him. For the first time, she felt a great sorrow for the pain she had caused Eric.

She was not comfortable with sorrow, nor familiar with shame. For the present she responded to them by fishing about in her handbag for Donald's photograph. She felt physically ill as she stared at it. She tore it across with a savage movement, then looked at the two halves. Neither looked like Donald now. She took several deep breaths, then tore the picture into smaller pieces, dropping them into the bin.

Returning to the piano, she put away the Mozart and began to play Eric's favourite Debussy.

Jennifer and Shakila had waved a cheerful farewell to Clement who sat at his desk, snowed under with information about blue/green metallic cars that had recently come to grief. The sun shone brilliantly but the air at this hour was still fresh and cool. Jennifer, whose car was in dock, willingly accepted an invitation to travel in Shakila's aged Renault 4. Comfortable it was not, but its engine ran almost silently and its tall, narrow body nipped easily round more luxurious vehicles. Jennifer made a complimentary remark about it and Shakila nodded. 'Does fifty-odd to the gallon too, even around town. It's not good in the wind, though. It's too high and too light.'

No wind endangered their five-minute journey, and, as they negotiated tall double gates and a curving drive, Jennifer laughed. 'Shouldn't think many of these find their way through here.'

'No, but Eric Simpson comes in his not-very-new Fiesta.' Shakila was not impressed by the scenery. 'The gardens are not very colourful. Why no flowers?'

95

'I think it's very restful, and painting those low walls and the trellises white makes it summery. Anyway, there is a splash of colour over there, round the side.'

Shakila locked her doors and walked over to investigate. A tiny patch of soil, extending for perhaps three square yards and marked off with a brick border, was full of bright blooms, planted higgledy-piggledy with no regard for height or toning hues. 'The boy's,' was her brief comment. She followed Jennifer to the porch and together they entered the hall.

Shakila surveyed the vast stretch of pale carpet, then wiped her shoes assiduously on the mat. 'There's rather a lot of house for two of us to search.'

Jennifer was unperturbed. 'The DI's already done the business side. He took a boxful of papers from the desk last night. He wants to go through them with Sefton.'

'Sefton?'

'These people's financial adviser, whatever that is. Shall we start in the kitchen?'

The room was all orderly serenity, the effect achieved with polished granite work surfaces, limestone floor tiles and cream paint. The litter of small gadgets and cooking implements that gave most kitchens their cheerful, busy atmosphere had been swallowed up by the vast cupboards and nothing had been added for decoration. Silently, the two officers applied themselves to checking Phyllida Markey's meticulous system of housekeeping. Both were soon bored and kept working only by the application of grim self-discipline they needed for so much of their work.

The only item of interest they turned up was a household account book. Jennifer flicked through it, pausing at an entry on the latest page. 'How much do you reckon it costs to run this place?'

Shakila shrugged. 'I couldn't guess in actual figures. A fortune, though.'

'Well, they don't waste it in spoiling the boy.'

Shakila leaned over to read the line indicated by

Jennifer's finger. 'Zak's pocket money . . . £2.00.' Jennifer slipped the book into a plastic bag. 'The sitting room now?'

They opened the next door and went into the huge room. Simple translucent curtains were drawn across the window, letting in the light but providing privacy. From whom? The gardener? Shakila pulled one back slightly and saw that the room overlooked the back garden. The plot was smaller than she had expected and the neighbouring house enjoyed a clear view into it and through the french window. The curtains were necessary, then.

In this room too the predominant colour on walls and chair covers was cream. The carpet was moss green. 'It's like a continuation of the garden,' Shakila observed. Here, though, there were a few imaginative touches. A collection of pastel-coloured blooms was displayed singly in an attractive collection of old glass bottles of various shapes and sizes.

Pictures of the Markeys' son abounded. He appeared to be a small, slight boy with delicate features and wispy fair hair. The dark eyes were long-lashed and, already, the chin was firm. Jennifer laughed. 'He looks like Judith.'

Shakila was surprised. Jennifer's younger daughter had long dark hair and was sturdily built. 'I meant,' Jennifer amended, 'that he looks easy to lead and impossible to drive. Look at that jaw.'

After another period of silent searching, Jennifer waved her hand to indicate her surroundings. 'It's all a bit sterile, isn't it?'

Shakila frowned. 'Sterile seems an odd word to describe somewhere so comfortable. What did you mean?'

'Well, there's nothing personal, apart from these photographs – and I get the feeling that they've only appeared since Saturday night. There aren't any souvenirs, keepsakes, books with things inside, tickets, theatre programmes, library book overdue . . .'

'Perhaps they're upstairs. My brother's house is like that. Everything fit for a guest to see is on the ground floor and all the comfortable clutter is in the bedrooms and the little upstairs sitting room. Let's go and see.' She leapt up the carved staircase two steps at a time.

By the time Jennifer had arrived at a more sedate pace, Shakila had thrown all the landing doors open. 'Is it different up here?' she asked.

'Yes and no. Just look at this.' Shakila led the way into the largest room, which appeared to be Donald Markey's study.

Jennifer grinned. 'I imagine he was given his head in this room.' Crimson walls and velvet curtains made both officers feel claustrophobic in the heat. Shakila glared at a lushly padded swivel chair and a vast desk. 'It's more than a bit over the top. He's probably pinched what was the main bedroom to do his studying. You could measure that desk top in acres.'

Jennifer was amused by her indignation. 'Well, we don't have to stay in here. The CI's given the once-over to this place. What's next door?'

'Zak's room.'

'I shouldn't think we need to spend much time in there.' They went in and Jennifer gave the room a cursory examination. 'Typical rich kid's pad. Judith and Lucy haven't got a fraction of all this stuff between them. Shall we move on? What's left?'

'The library, no less! Do you want to begin in there? Mind if I stay here for a bit?'

Jennifer shrugged. 'Whatever turns you on.' She poked her head round the door and admired the beautiful old wood of the shelves that lined the room. The higher levels held interesting-looking old books on the geology of the area and the leather-bound minutes of the meetings of various societies. She fetched the stepladder from behind the door and began her search. After a while, Shakila joined her. By then Jennifer had reached the shelves lower down with their sets of the complete works of some well established writers. They did not look well thumbed.

'They probably bought 'em by the yard,' Shakila observed. 'Or inherited them from Phyllida's family.'

Doggedly they worked until they had assured themselves that nothing was concealed between any of the pages. Then, with a sigh of relief, Jennifer replaced the stepladder on its hooks behind the door. 'The bedroom?'

'I can't wait.'

It had rather a masculine air, yet Jennifer felt that its furnishing and decoration were Phyllida's choice. There was the same austerity as in the sitting room, again lightened only by flowers. The ones here were so fresh-looking that Phyllida must have bought them since her husband's death. A tribute to him? Her private mark of esteem in their shared room?

After a minute, she rejected the idea. The blooms looked exotic, spiky and striped. There were no leaves and the stems stood in a simple kitchen mug. The bedding was a plum colour with white. The furniture, well polished and venerable, had probably been in the family for generations. Phyllida's family, probably. What she was seeing here did not seem a likely setting for the sort of person Donald Markey was proving to be. She wondered whether, on his marriage, he had joined his wife in her old family home.

It suddenly occurred to her that there had been no sign of either set of parents since Saturday night. Making a mental note to ask about them, she turned to help Shakila search the drawers. They contained nothing more interesting than underwear and clean bedding. On top of the chest that Shakila was examining stood a miniature stacked music centre. She studied the discs in the wall-mounted racks. 'They had jarring tastes.'

'All loud rock music?'

'No. I mean the discs fall into two groups. One of them probably hated everything the other put on and vice versa.'

The drawer below Phyllida's bedside shelf contained jewellery. Jennifer whistled. 'It's all expensive, no costume stuff. Fancy just wrapping it in tissue paper in an old shoe box!'

Shakila leaned over to look, then opened the corresponding drawer on Donald's side. Here were chunky gold chains and heavy signet rings, all in a beautiful, inlaid and velvet-lined wooden box.

As they turned to examine the wardrobes, Shakila sighed. 'I'm working on automatic pilot now.' The clothes were all good quality, Donald's mostly new whilst some of Phyllida's were well worn. No letters, notes or tickets were to be found in any of the pockets or linings. It fell to Shakila to make the only interesting discovery there. In the back corner of Donald's wardrobe floor, pushed into a green wellington boot, was a small, gold-foil wrapped package. The tag read, 'With much love, Nicky, on our anniversary.' She grinned at Jennifer. 'Will I get Brownie points for letting you open it?'

'Yes. Lots.' Jennifer took out a nail file and teased off an abundance of sellotape. A pair of tweezers dealt with the catch of the scarlet leather box.

As the contents were revealed, both women gasped. 'Are those stones real?'

Jennifer's expression was deadpan. 'I'm glad you realize that my familiarity with diamonds means I can always spot a fake. There's a sort of printed certificate thing with this though. Whenever was she going to wear that?'

'And how was she going to explain it?'

Jennifer had decreed a coffee break when their search of the Markeys' house was completed. Shakila had no problem with this instruction from her sergeant but, since it was almost lunchtime, was curious about the reason.

'Think about it. It would have humiliated a woman like Mrs Markey to hide in a corner of her house while we poked around, going through all their things. It would have been awkward for us all if we'd had to let her in as if she were just a visitor, so . . .'

'So that's why you're a sergeant and I'm still a DC.'

'It's also,' Jennifer told her, with a grim smile, 'why Benny's a CI and I'm only a sergeant.'

Shakila was silent, trying to work that out as they scrambled out of the car and approached the door of number 19, Boston Road for the second time that day.

Phyllida greeted them with an enigmatic smile. 'Good morning. Did I frighten the other girl off?'

Jennifer laughed. 'I shouldn't think so. Caroline takes a lot of frightening.'

'So I imagine, if she's come back to the job after what seems to have happened to her on an earlier one.' In silent agreement, the two officers followed Phyllida inside.

In the vast sitting room a small fair-haired boy sat on the carpet in a corner, obviously sulking. He flinched as his mother patted him on the head and suggested that he might play in his room whilst she dealt with 'these ladies'. 'Only for a few minutes, darling. I'll call you down as soon as our business is finished.'

The boy had cheered up when he realized he was being dismissed. Pulling away from the hug she offered him, he departed at speed.

'Mind the stairs, darling. We don't want to find you in a heap at the bottom.' The darling's mother turned to Jennifer. 'Poor lamb. He only arrived quite late last night. His headmaster very kindly drove him home.'

Biting her tongue hard, Jennifer smiled. 'He's probably still tired this morning.'

'Very likely. He's also a little bit cross with me. My mother rang to invite him for the day. He answered the phone before I could get to it. She said to me that it was so that he wouldn't have to meet you and realize how you are looking at things.'

'That was quite sensible.'

'Maybe, but it wasn't the reason for her invitation. She wants to persuade him to go back to that school. It was my father's school. That was how Donald got her on his side

101

about it. It was the only thing he ever did that they approved of.'

'You don't want him to go back?'

Her tone was indignant. 'A child of his age should be with his mother. There's nothing wrong with the local school. He liked it there.'

'So boarding was your husband's idea?'

'Zak's an intelligent nine-year-old. He was beginning to be aware of – well, some of his father's more reprehensible activities.'

'Actually, we were wondering about your parents, yours and your husband's.'

'What about them?' Her tone suggested that Jennifer had questioned their social standing.

'The sergeant meant,' Shakila explained, 'that we were hoping there are family members to support you.'

Phyllida gave them a humourless smile. 'Donald's family never had any time for him. Mine had none for me when I married him. My father died some years ago. My mother moved out of here when Donald moved in. She was slightly more gracious after Zak arrived, especially when he turned out to resemble my father and brother. So, what else do you want me to tell you?'

'Tell us about your husband.'

She considered. 'I haven't prepared a statement so it will be a bit piecemeal. He married me when he was thirty and I was thirty-eight. He died at forty-one which makes me forty-nine. Everyone had theories about it. You've talked to most of our friends so you'll have heard them all. They boil down to my desperation and Donald's destitution and greed –'

'We've spoken to at least one friend,' Jennifer put in, 'who certainly holds neither of those opinions.'

Phyllida disdained to ask for a name but she seemed gratified. 'After that, I always tried to put him first and he always did his best to help me.' After a second, Jennifer realized her witness was not describing a mutual support system. Phyllida had stressed the penultimate and not the final word. She would need to keep her wits about her in her dealings with this lady.

'Donald liked being in charge, telling people what to do. When Zak was at home, he organized the district baby-sitting points system and "did the books" once a month so that he could let everyone know where they stood. He wasn't always kind. When Eric got his TV contract, Donald said the producer was probably repaying Nicky for services rendered.'

Jennifer nodded. 'You're answering my next question.'

'Which is?'

'Had your husband any enemies?'

'We all have people who don't like us, I suppose.' She got up from her armchair and began to pace between it and the window.

'Who didn't like Donald?'

'I imagine the husbands of his mistresses weren't too keen.'

'Any in particular?'

'Apart from Eric I don't know who they were. There was a Jane whose husband they were both wary of but I never knew her surname. She and Nicky were the resident ones. The others were fleeting.'

'You preferred not to know?'

'I just was not interested.' She sat down again and changed the subject slightly. 'I suspect that Donald had the snip as soon as I knew I was pregnant. He was shocked that I was still capable of it. I had to laugh. We had our first quarrel ever when he suggested an abortion and our second when he sent Zak away to school.'

'Couldn't you have stopped him?'

'How?'

'Well, to be blunt, by cutting the purse strings.'

She laughed. 'It wasn't like that.'

'You didn't quarrel over his mistresses?'

She regarded Jennifer quizzically. 'Did you marry Mr Perfect?' When Jennifer coloured, she quickly apologized. '. . . but why should I get angry about Donald's peccadilloes? He didn't live in cloud cuckoo land like Eric and he wasn't everybody's stooge like Morris. He was fond of me and grateful to me. There were none of the fireworks that Nicky could strike off him, but the things he did offer me were constant – no blowing hot and cold.

'I felt safe with him. He was less intelligent than I am. He never surprised me, took me unawares. He was a social animal and I'm not. He had to have a suitable woman on his arm at the sort of places and functions he liked to frequent. I preferred him to take Jane or Nicky to such places than to go there myself where I would have embarrassed us both.

'When my friends are quasi-reluctant in revealing all about our marriage to you and searching for words – only Eric is as articulate as I am – tell them the word they need is realism. Donald and I each asked ourselves what was the best we could realistically expect out of our relationship and settled for that. It didn't make us deliriously happy but it left us content.

'I know some people think he treated me badly but he was often ill at ease with me. I didn't respond to the sort of chat-up lines' – her voice put inverted commas round the expression – 'that his other women friends expected and that was the only conversation he had. He was as kind to me as he knew how to be.'

She fell silent and the silence lengthened. When she spoke again the eloquence had gone. 'I'm sorry to have inflicted all that on you . . . You see, that chapter of my life has closed and now I'm evaluating it, reflecting on it. It's what my mind's full of. If it's any consolation to you, though it was no help to you, putting all that into words has helped me enormously.'

To Shakila's astonishment, Jennifer got up, thanked Mrs Markey for her time and patience, explained that they might have to trouble her again, then led the way out.

Back in the car the DC sought a way to challenge Jennifer's action without calling down fire on her head. She failed. 'What was that all about? What about why she wore those awful clothes at the school do? What about Donald cheating Morris Tate out of a job? What about how the money's been left . . .?' Scared to push her luck any further, Shakila slipped the key into the ignition and began to drive.

Jennifer, in a dangerously patient tone, answered the last question first. 'The CI said we weren't to mention money, beyond accepting anything that was volunteered. He wants to go through the box of gubbins he's taken away and then talk to this Sefton chap.

'As for the rest, in a strange way I felt privileged to have heard that magnificent defence of what, from the outside, seemed a bad marriage. It would have been an insult to follow it up with accusing questions. Benny may understand or he may see it as her way of putting us off our questions until she's prepared her answers. If so, we'll have to have another row.'

Shakila glanced sideways at her sergeant and saw that she was undismayed by this prospect.

A note from Clement was waiting on Mitchell's desk when he returned to his office from the morning briefing in the incident room. It was terse, reflecting the DC's resentment at the small part he had been allowed to play so far in the case. 'Traffic's report on Saturday night's incident in Old Lane. Suspiciously slight damage to a metallic green Mini. Speed of impact estimated at approx. 12 mph. Likely that driver's injuries not caused in this incident. All details so far in file. Adrian.'

Mitchell beamed round the empty room. He'd be lazy and have the file sent up. As he reached for the telephone, it rang. Magic Powers, succinct as usual, delivered his message. 'Old lady from Old Lane.'

Mitchell beamed again. 'Very suitable. Send her up, please.' He liked old ladies. They usually knew all the details he required and, even if they didn't, they were always entertaining.

Mrs Whitaker, ushered in by a particularly attractive special constable, had bowed to the prevailing weather conditions in wearing a pretty summer dress. Her distrust of them was indicated by the addition of a padded anorak, a headscarf and stout walking shoes.

'I came because of your chap,' she announced, settling herself in Mitchell's visitors' chair before he could issue an invitation to be seated. He nodded to the special to stay and take notes, then regarded his witness solemnly. He knew from experience the drill for dealing with visitors like her. The middle was where they liked their stories to begin and prompting them with questions merely held up progress.

'I'd gone upstairs and left the front door open because Marjorie was coming round and he walks in without so much as a by-your-leave. Calls up the stairs, "All right if I steal your TV and video recorder, Ma?" Cheeky young beggar!'

As she paused for breath, Mitchell ventured, 'You're sure he was one of our chaps?'

'Of course I am. Runs past my house on his way to work most mornings, dressed like a garden gnome – or Batman with his cloak missing . . .'

The chap now safely identified, Mitchell let her describe Clement's lecture on proper security. Eventually, he cut in to ask if anything had actually been stolen. She tutted. 'No, o'course not. I haven't come about that. It was about that green car on Saturday. It's been taken away now. More of your chaps, I suppose. P'raps you're not interested but the running chap thought you would be.'

'We certainly are.'

'Well, I think it was an insurance scam. It was an old wreck of a car. I expect she wanted to get something off the insurance chaps to get another, so she drives it dead slow into a tree. Not slow enough, though. I sent my Rodney up there and he says she hurt herself. I hope I'm not getting her into too much trouble, only the running chap thought you'd want to know.'

She paused to remove the headscarf and to wipe beads of perspiration from her face. 'I thought people who came in their own time to give you help would at least be offered a cup of tea.'

Mitchell bit his lip. 'We usually get the business over before we move on to the social part. How do you have your tea?' As his witness beamed and opted for milk and two sugars, Mitchell had second thoughts. He had indulged himself for long enough. There was more to do than hold tea parties in his office, however charmed he might be with his visitor. 'The special constable will take you down to the canteen and get you a bun to go with it.'

'Special, is she? Well then, I can't say you didn't treat me right. Does the canteen have vanilla slices?' She was led away by the highly amused young girl whilst Mitchell now summoned the file. He was sure that Clement would have recorded all the salient points from Mrs Whitaker's account of the 'accident' if only as light relief from the computer and damaged green cars.

The file was still on Mitchell's desk that afternoon when Jennifer and Shakila returned to headquarters. Mitchell described his morning to them. 'I've sent Adrian to talk to the two paramedics who brought Miss Dyson in. I'll check myself on what the lab learned from the car.'

Sending Shakila to return the file, he suggested to Jennifer that they should snatch a pub meal. 'I had a measly corned beef sandwich for lunch and I'm starving.' Shakila departed in high dudgeon with a look that said, 'I know you want to be rid of me.'

The Fleece was crowded but Jennifer decided it was too hot to walk any further. 'That tiny table behind the pillar is free and Mrs Buller will serve us out of turn if you catch her eye. What have you got to say that you didn't want Shakila to hear?'

'I didn't want her to hear us quarrelling.'

'You've read my report on Phyllida Markey by tele-pathy?'

Mitchell blinked. 'You've got a guilty conscience about something else? We'll get that out of the way first, then.'

Feeling less light-hearted about it than she had seemed to Shakila, Jennifer explained why she had cut short the interview with most of their questions unasked. 'She was not just composed; she was completely relaxed, unemo-tional. She seemed detached from what's going on, yet she's efficiently coping with it. All that caused any sign of distress was the boy wanting to go immediately to his grandmother's.'

'You think the victim's only purpose for her was to provide her son with genes to make him handsome and healthy?'

'The irony would be that he resembles his mother.'

'Surely she's intelligent enough to know that physical characteristics aren't all that we inherit.'

'Are we sure about that? Was the nature versus nurture business ever sorted out? Anyway, it was the father who sent him away to school, with his maternal grandmother's support.'

Mitchell frowned. 'Are you suggesting that she could have paid someone a monstrous amount of money to remove the man who was separating her from her son? It would explain why she went to so much trouble to prepare her alibi throughout Saturday evening.'

They considered the question as each of them took a menu from the letter-rack affair on their table. Mitchell scanned his own as he continued speaking. 'She seems to like reminding us that she's a prime suspect, but the fact that she didn't do the deed doesn't mean that she didn't arrange it.'

'We didn't ask her any of the questions you –'

'Doesn't matter. I think, in the circumstances, I'd have done what you did. I'll send someone fatherly like Smith-son to mop up and finish off.' The landlady, having had her eye caught, was hovering in front of them. 'We'll both have whatever's quickest to produce.'

Mrs Buller was used to her police customers and not put out. 'Lasagne then. It just wants spooning on to plates from the tray.'

Jennifer said, with a tight smile, 'You certainly know how to treat a lady.'

Mitchell shrugged. 'Who says I'm paying?'

Feeling rattled, Jennifer returned to her story. 'Shakila thinks she could get the boy to talk. She probably could – she's good with kids.'

'She's good at just about everything – and now the law springs to the defence of stroppy minorities, it's becoming a positive advantage to be female and black.'

'Except in the police.'

'Yes. Maybe she won't go quite all the way.'

An uncomfortable silence began, which Jennifer broke by holding out her left hand. 'Go on, then, slap it. What else have I done wrong?'

Still Mitchell did not speak. Conversations buzzed round them. People got up to replenish glasses. Jennifer picked up her knife and fork and began to eat.

No longer having to meet her gaze loosened Mitchell's tongue. 'Somehow, on this case, you seem to have an agenda that I'm not a party to. It's giving you priorities I don't recognize. Information is being filtered through you and things are being held back. I don't understand what's going on and I'm angry.'

Jennifer continued to chew stolidly. She recognized his degree of perturbation by the fact that his own food was untouched. She swallowed and raised her eyes. 'I –'

His eyes snapped. 'For pity's sake don't tell me you don't know what I mean. You've obviously got a conflict of loyalties. I think you've established a sympathetic relationship with one of the witnesses that's getting in the way of the case. You've never done it before.' Now he sounded bewildered rather than angry.

She put down her cutlery and faced him. 'It's not me who's holding out on you, Benny. Go home and ask your questions there.' She saw it was the last reply he had expected. Leaving his food to congeal, he got up and left the building.

Chapter Five

A pragmatist in most respects, Jennifer continued to eat her pasta as she reflected on her situation. She had been Ginny's friend long enough to appreciate the respect for his work that Benny had always received at home. To leave Benny free she had willingly taken responsibility for their four young children. Benny's support, in theory, was constant, but, in practice, the demands of the job meant that it was frequently offered from a distance. If Ginny was playing a lone hand now she would have a good reason.

Jennifer herself, however, had a job to do. Wearing a detective sergeant's hat, her priority was the investigation. Miserably, she wondered how much their recent exchange had damaged her relationship with her CI.

She had enjoyed working with Mitchell ever since they had found themselves at training college in the same batch of police recruits. They had sometimes walked the beat together. They had progressed to CID almost simultaneously, since when Benny had had the breaks. She admired his work and felt no resentment. She knew that her own marital problems had held back her progress to a certain extent. The Mitchells' marriage had been rock solid from the start and she had never before found a conflict of interest in being Benny's sergeant and Ginny's friend.

Now, unbelievably, Virginia was not being totally open. Jennifer was certain that everything she had said could be believed. The whole truth was being withheld but she had no doubts about Virginia's having given her 'nothing but the truth'. She was determinedly straightforward, often to the point of offensive bluntness. How much information was she keeping back and why? Could Lorna have some hold over her? Jennifer tried and failed to imagine any set of circumstances that her friend would not deal with by straight speaking.

Averting her eyes from the congealed mess on Benny's plate, she got up to do the only thing she knew would be right. Virginia had to know that Jennifer had betrayed her to her husband.

Virginia Mitchell, having delivered her twins to their afternoon session at nursery school, decided to tackle the article commissioned by *Womankind* for which her deadline was only three days away, but it was not to be.

The first telephone call came before she had arranged her prepared notes in order on her desk. Sighing, she picked up the receiver. A torrent of words assailed her ear. 'What's going on, Ginny? Yesterday, two officers came round and questioned me for what felt like hours. The woman's been again just now with more questions.'

Virginia was terse. 'What about?'

'You can't expect me to remember it all, but she obviously thinks I had something to do with . . . well, what happened to Donald. She kept asking how well I knew him.'

'What did you tell her?'

'I didn't dare tell her anything. She'd have thought I was getting back at him for Abby.'

As the half-hysterical recital continued, Virginia realized that the purpose of Lorna's call was to find out what she herself had revealed to the police. 'I haven't said anything.'

'And you won't?'

'Not unless I have to.'

'What do you mean? Why should you have to?' The voice rose higher.

'I can't think of any reason at present why I should

mention your daughter. If at any point I feel it's the right thing to do then I shall have to. That's the best I can do for you.'

'I wish I'd never told you.' Now Lorna was crying.

'I'm beginning to wish the same. The wisest thing would be for you to tell them.' The crying became louder. Virginia cut through the outburst with a crisp instruction: 'Lorna, put the phone down now. Then use it again to ring your doctor. Don't be fobbed off with an appointment in the distant future. Ask for a home visit now.'

'All right.' In desperation, Virginia hung up on the quiet sobbing that followed.

An hour later, the telephone rang again. This time she heard Jennifer's voice. 'Ginny, I haven't much time so I'll get straight to the point. I'm sure you have a reason for the game you're playing. I don't know what it is but it's landed me in bother with Benny. Sorry, but I've told him he needs to discuss it with you.' The line went dead.

Virginia began to clear away her notes. She was in no mood now to produce flippant witticisms about white lies, her brief from her magazine. Why, she asked herself, had she mentioned Lorna to Jennifer at all? Why say that she was missing from the dinner table? Why describe finding and soothing her in the cloakroom? Because it had seemed harmless and sounded co-operative?

No. It was because she was not naturally devious – certainly not to the extent that she could plan to deceive on the spur of the moment. Nor did she want to be. She wondered whether having got herself into this tricky situation had been of any benefit to Lorna at all.

She realized that her championing of Lorna was partly because she didn't really like her. She had always tried to atone for her own prejudice by being particularly obliging to the victims of it. She sincerely believed her to be innocent of Donald Markey's murder. When Lorna had a grievance she had always whinged and grumbled and manipulated, just as she was doing now. She had seldom solved a problem with decisive action.

113

Perhaps she should even have kept her suspicions to herself on Saturday night. Benny was only conducting a murder investigation because of her own suggestion that the driver of the green car had acted deliberately. All the same, she remained quite convinced about this.

When the telephone rang for the third time, she welcomed the distraction. Her brother wanted to know whether Declan would like to have tea with him, followed by an evening of chess. Virginia, who seldom made arrangements for at least her two elder children without consulting them, said, rather shortly, 'Declan will ring back when he gets home from school. He'll be here in a few minutes and so will the twins. It's someone else's turn to do the run, thank goodness. I'm sure he'd love to come but he'll answer for himself. Will you still be at home then?'

'I've just come off the early shift, so, barring some ghastly crisis, I should be here till seven tomorrow morning.'

'Lucky you.'

'Is something wrong, Ginny? You sound a bit – well, aggressive. It usually means –'

'Don't tell me what it means. I don't want to know.'

'Well, I do – want to know what the problem is, I mean.'

Knowing, even before she began, that she would regret it, Virginia asked, 'Do you remember a girl I used to knock around with at school? A hockey-playing type, called Lorna?'

After leaving the Fleece, Mitchell pounded the streets in the centre of the town for more than an hour. How was he going to get his head round the idea that Virginia was not on his side in this investigation? He wished he had Clement's ability to run for extended periods. Running would allow him to put a greater distance between himself and this situation, which he had not had to face since their wedding over nine years ago.

It would relieve his feelings to make a physical attack on this Lorna Dyson who had come between them. He would have to let someone else deal with her. At the moment, though, she was their best bet and he itched to tackle her himself. What would happen between him and Virginia if the woman were arrested, convicted, imprisoned?

How could he explain to Virginia – why did he need to? – the necessity of nailing the guilty person? He could not imagine what she might know about the woman that she was not willing to share with him.

Why hadn't he gone to the stupid reunion with her? Better still, he should have forbidden her to go. He imagined himself doing just that and laughed aloud at the thought of the probable result. A couple approaching him hurriedly crossed the road, then stopped to stare at him from the opposite pavement. He had better take himself in hand. He was only just round the corner from the station now.

His mobile phone rang. Ginny's voice said, 'Found you. No one at headquarters knows where you are.'

She never rang him at work! 'What's wrong? What's happened?'

'Nothing. I just thought I'd do the beef roulade I prac- tised at my cookery class for supper. I don't suppose you've any idea what time –'

'Cook what you like. I'm not hungry.'

'Benny? Are you –?'

He cut the connection. His knees felt weak and the sun, shimmering through the hot afternoon air, was dazzling and disorientating him. Despite what he'd just said, he was not only hungry but ravenous. His lunch had been a joke and he had walked out on the only decent meal the day would offer. Turning the corner and making his way alongside the station's short-stay car park, he saw an aban- doned football in the gutter. Striking it as hard as he could, he watched it travel, hard and low, through the back window of Clement's ancient Astra.

*   *   *

Mitchell turned up marginally late for the evening's debriefing. He knew that Jennifer would be on time as usual and he had no wish to continue his earlier conversation with her. He saw, as he went in, that the feeling was mutual. Jennifer had taken a seat towards the back of the gathering, next to Smithson.

Mitchell apologized for keeping his shift waiting and smiled round at them. 'Thanks to some hard graft, especially from uniforms, all seventy-odd people who attended Maynard's do up at the school have been visited. Half a dozen or so were out and will be chased up tomorrow. Most of what we were told was pretty negative, of course, and everything relevant is in the file. That means all of you getting on to your computers tonight and making sure you're up to date with what we know by morning prayers tomorrow. What isn't there yet, because Adrian's only just got back, is the information we need on Lorna Dyson's injuries.'

He nodded to Clement who stood to attention and concentrated on brevity. 'I spoke to the paramedics who brought her in and the MO who examined her. The whole thing's a mass of inconsistencies. Miss Dyson is claiming that her head struck the windscreen and broke it – but the cuts on her face are fairly minor, not deep enough to cause scarring and certainly too superficial for her head to have demolished the windscreen. The bruising and swelling on her forehead indicate a painful blow but not sufficient to knock her out. She wasn't concussed.'

'Did you have time to get round to the two youngsters who called the ambulance?'

Clement nodded. 'They reported that she was unconscious but they also said they first noticed her because she was waving her arm. The opinion at the hospital is that Miss Dyson's going to swing the lead for as long as she can over this. She's a bit of an actress.'

'But not a very intelligent one. Thank you, Adrian.' Mitchell was annoyed that there had still been no news from the lab about the objects that had been salvaged from the scene in Moorside Rise. Once they had established that Lorna Dyson's car and the one that had struck Donald Markey were the same vehicle, the case would be over. He worked off his irritation on Clement. 'Don't think that lets you off your report.'

Glancing round the room again at all his hearers, he dismissed them with the warning, 'In here at eight thirty sharp.' As they trooped out, he indicated that Clement and the female complement of CID officers should remain behind. Clement, thoroughly disgruntled, asked recklessly, 'Sure you mean me? You don't want me back at my screen checking on green cars?'

Mitchell hastened to placate him. 'And leave me alone with this monstrous regiment of women?' They settled round his desk. 'So, where are we?'

They considered the question in silence for some seconds before Shakila offered, 'Phyllida Markey's the classic suspect. I think she's a dangerous woman.'

Mitchell raised an eyebrow. 'Why?'

Shakila's explanation was less crisp and fluent than her initial comment had been. She was obviously sorting out and analysing her impression as she spoke. 'She's a sort of non-person. She went to Oxford – got a First in English, actually – but it was just to fill some time in. The way she plays around verbally when you try to talk to her proves her intelligence, but, because there's so much family money, she never used it as the basis for any sort of career . . . And her marriage didn't seem to mean much to her.'

Jennifer cut in. 'I wouldn't agree with that, though it was a strange relationship.'

Shakila was not to be put off. 'Anyway, she cares more about the boy than anything or anybody else. He's smothered and he doesn't like it. He was sulking today because he wasn't allowed to escape to his grandmother's house, and he seems to want to go back to his school, the boarding one. He wants to get away from his mother and have

117

some life as a boy rather than as a domestic pet. I'd like to talk to him.'

Her eyes appealed to Mitchell, who asked, 'Did his mother take to you?'

Shakila shook her head. 'I don't know. I left most of the talking to Jennifer and kept a fairly low profile.'

Mitchell gave a shout of laughter. 'Now that I would like to have seen. All right, we'll see if we can fix it.'

Having achieved her object, Shakila subsided. Mitchell collected their attention by lifting from the floor and placing on his desk a large cardboard carton. 'I brought Phyllida Markey's laptop away in this box of tricks. One interesting file in it contained a letter, dated two days before Donald Markey's death. It was to Zachary's headmaster and it announced that she would be removing her son from the school at the end of the summer term. No reason was given, but she thanked the head very prettily for her son's happy stay with them.'

The shift's questions and comments overlapped.

'Wouldn't she need to give more notice?'

'Was it from her rather than both of them?'

'Does that mean that she knew she was going to be free to do as she liked?'

Mitchell beamed at them. 'I printed the letter and put a copy in the file this morning. It supplies the facts. The rest you'll have to work out for yourselves.'

'What about this business of Donald's wallet?' Caroline asked. She hastened to safeguard such colleagues as had failed to read her report. 'I asked his wife, when I saw her for the first time yesterday, if anything unusual had happened recently. She said no at first, but then wanted to know if three months ago was recent enough.'

'So, what happened?' Clement demanded, ignoring his rescue.

'She said that Donald had lost his wallet and all its contents, including his passport, bank cards and all the usual grunge.'

'I don't keep my passport in my wallet,' Mitchell muttered.

'Well, he did and Phyllida said he never mislaid things or forgot things and he was sure it had been in his inside jacket pocket.'

'So, was it ever found?'

Caroline turned back to Mitchell. 'Someone handed it in here at the station. It had been found in that branch of W.H. Smith in the precinct. It had all the documents still there and all the money too.'

Jennifer ventured from her back seat, 'Lucky man. Do we know yet who called Donald out of the school building?'

Mitchell shook his head. 'No joy from O2. The car wheel crushed the phone in Markey's jacket pocket so they can't get anything from it. From their end they can only tell us that the call was made from the telephone box across the road from the main entrance to the school. Eric Simpson remembers the call that Markey took just as people were leaving the supper tables and returning to the hall for the speeches, but he wasn't near enough to hear anything.'

'So, if it was anyone from Maynard's do who rang, they left the school grounds. It was a good time to choose, of course. Everyone was in transit along the corridor past the cloakrooms, lots of folk were probably stopping off for a pee and anyone could have ducked out unnoticed. On the other hand, it doesn't have to be someone who was up at the school – only someone who knew that Markey was and who knew the area.'

'I asked Phyllida . . .' They all turned to Caroline. '. . . who knew that the two of them were going to Heath Lees, apart from their fellow guests. She said she'd think about it, make a list. I haven't had it yet. I'll ring her tomorrow.'

Jennifer said, 'Wasn't there a bit more in Smithson's report on Neville Kyte? He said he'd been standing close to Markey and he'd got the impression the call concerned a business deal of some sort.'

Mitchell himself had only a hazy memory of reading that particular report. When no one else could answer Jennifer's question and no more offerings of any kind seemed likely, he dismissed the four of them, warning them again of the next day's early start. Now he had some time and privacy to try to sort out his situation. Jennifer would hurry home in the hope of seeing her two young daughters before they went to bed. Caroline would be off to cook Cavill's supper or to help with one or other of his musical pursuits. Clement would most likely persuade Shakila to accompany him to the Fleece where they would wrangle happily about who was going to pay for their drinks. This was just an interesting, uncomplicated case to them.

PC Smithson, as well as Sergeant Taylor, had remembered his visit to Neville Kyte and the man's reference to Donald Markey's caller on Saturday night. As his wife settled to watch a film on BBC2, he returned to the dining room where he spread out his notes on that interview carefully so as not to damage the polished surface of the table.

He grinned to himself. Connie wouldn't know what to make of the film, any more than he would himself. However, it was set in Spain where they had recently spent a happy fortnight and he knew she would contentedly relive their holiday and ignore the subtitles. If he were not so hard-pressed he would have watched it with her – but then, perhaps not. She loved having something to tell him.

They were lucky to be as fond of one another now as when they had first met, and the sacrifice he had made to win her had, unexpectedly, provided him with a skill that he had been grateful for throughout his police career. They had met at the local technical college in 1966 when they were both sixteen. Her course was shorthand and typing and his should have been beginners' French. After his first coffee with her in the college cafeteria, he had switched to hers, enduring phlegmatically his friends' derision and his parents' fury.

Connie had even been partly responsible for his choice of career. 'Pity you're not a copper,' she'd remarked, when his shorthand speed reached 140 wpm. 'You'd get down all that the witnesses told you in no time.' He remembered that her father had been interviewed as a witness to a road accident at about that time, which had put the idea into her head, and consequently into his.

It had appealed to him, and she had been quite right. He had kept up the facility and it was still useful now as he was coming up to retirement. Of course, tape recorders made notes unnecessary in official interviews these days, but, out on the job, chatting up small kids in the street, or a nark in the pub over a pint, he was able to record every unwise word verbatim. It made extra work, of course. He had to write up his notebook conventionally each evening, but he'd always been thorough and had never minded taking trouble.

He surveyed his sheets of hieroglyphics. Like most vicars in Smithson's experience, Kyte had had plenty to say, particularly about the Tates with whom he had kept in closest touch. 'Were you a swimmer too?' Smithson had asked. He'd thought it unlikely. The man was tall but without much flesh or muscle. He looked a bit girlish, his teeth and jaw too heavy for the rest of his delicate features, bimbo-blue eyes and fine skin. Rather, Smithson thought, like Steve MacDonald in Connie's *Coronation Street*.

Kyte had shaken his head. 'Not a sportsman of any kind. In fact, I hadn't much in common with Morris. I was just grateful to him.' Smithson had always known by instinct when not to interrupt, and, after a moment, Kyte had continued, 'There was an incident when Morris, Donald and I were in the sixth form. My young cousin, sixteen years old and in the fifth, told me that another boy had forced her to have sex with him. She was a bit naïve and it turned out eventually that things hadn't come to anywhere near the point of actual penetration. I was a bit of a hothead and the boy my cousin accused was the son of one of the staff. The event, such as it was, took place out of school. I borrowed the whip with which the small girl next door spun her wooden top and meted out my own punishment. Rightly or wrongly, I believed that the staff would automatically cover up for a teacher's child.

'When I'd calmed down, I accepted what was a fair punishment for myself – the headmaster's cane applied to the same part of my own anatomy. But for Markey, that would have been the end of it. His version was homosexuality and sadism on my part. Since this was a more salacious explanation than the correct and official one, it became current, at least among such pupils as understood what the words meant.

'The story has dogged me throughout the remainder of my life. In view of the calling I followed it has proved to be a constant stumbling block. In two separate livings a version has reached my bishop's ears and led to embarrassing interviews. I'm sure the incident limited my preferment.'

Smithson knew very little about how the Anglican Church did its business but he thought he had followed Kyte's meaning. He decided he would pluck up courage at the next debriefing. He didn't believe many people had read his report – possibly not even Mitchell. He found that hard to believe, but, if Mitchell did know about it, surely Kyte should have been one of their subjects of discussion at some point.

Smithson thought Mitchell had behaved rather strangely this evening, as though he had had something on his mind. He was fond of all the Mitchells. He hoped that there was nothing wrong at home.

He looked back at Kyte's testimony. The man had said, 'Morris Tate's staunch and continued friendship made at least the rest of my schooldays bearable.'

Smithson had asked what effect this had had on Morris's friendship with Donald. 'They were reputed to be bosom friends but they weren't really. They were just two strong characters in a smallish sixth form. They were both athletic and, between them, the mainstay of school games.' Again, Smithson had waited and been rewarded. 'Both of them declared that they weren't going to university because it was a waste of time. I suspect Donald's reason was that he knew his A levels wouldn't get him there and Morris's that his family needed his wage to help with his numerous younger siblings.'

Smithson had drawn him out on the subject of the Tates who he considered had also been neglected as suspects. He had received only praise for them. 'I think Valerie has a great affection rather than a great love for Morris.' What, thought Smithson, was wrong with that? Just a difference of terminology. 'She married him early, when she briefly blossomed from a schoolgirl dumpiness to a slimness that was the result of a growth spurt. She still has a vivid face and an abundance of beautiful hair, nut-brown and slightly curling, hanging round her shoulders in the not very practical fashion of the day. Once they'd settled for each other and a few of the good things of life, they became what they are now, overweight and middle-aged. They're good sorts, though, both of them. They're still young in mind, good for a crazy plan.'

All this was very interesting, but not what he had set out to check. Ah! Here was the sheet that Smithson had wanted to concentrate on just now. This bit was only brief but it was significant. In longhand, in his official notebook it appeared only as, 'Kyte had the impression that the call to the victim's mobile proposed a business deal. The witness thought this might have been a smokescreen for a meeting with one of his lady friends.'

The hieroglyphics, translated, went into a little more detail. Kyte could not remember verbatim what he had heard. It had been '. . . something like, "Hi, John . . . what sort of deal? . . . I should think I could pop out for a bit. It'll have to be quick, though. I don't want Phyl left here on her own for long . . . OK, soon as I can." Mrs Markey was just in front of me. I don't know her, can't even tell you her first name. He put a hand on her shoulder and said, "Meeting someone in the Rising Sun. Got a deal on. I'll be picked up outside in two or three minutes and dropped off here when I've had a word with this bloke. Will you be all right?" That's as near as I can remember.'

'How did she take that?' Smithson had asked.

'Resignedly. She made no objection, didn't tell him not to be long, but she didn't jump for joy. She said all right, or something equally unworldshaking. Then he wriggled his way towards the foyer. I imagine anyone who overheard took it for granted, as I did, that there was no businessman in the pub and tried to work out which lady was following him.'

Suddenly, Smithson was struck by an idea. Kyte had referred several times to his wife. What had he called her? He scrabbled through his papers again and extracted the one he needed. He was right. Mrs Kyte was called Jane.

Early that evening, several other residents of Cloughton were distracted from their leisure activities by one aspect or another of Mitchell's investigation. Alex Browne, after his sister's startling revelation earlier in the day, had spent much of his evening worrying about it. If there were cracks in even Benny's and Ginny's relationship, he might have doubts about his own with Charlotte.

Something in Ginny's story had rung a bell in his mind. It had rung only faintly though, enough to trouble but not to enlighten him. Something to do with work? He couldn't remember. Was it the story or the name he should concentrate on? He'd type the name into the hospital computer before he started his shift tomorrow. That would mean leaving in time to arrive at six thirty instead of seven! He shuddered at the thought, but the matter was beginning to obsess him and he wanted to deal with it. Having made a firm plan, his mind was willing to put the problem aside and let him enjoy the Eurosport channel.

To his fury, the programme on Australian football he had

planned to watch had been replaced by a recording of a tennis match played earlier in the day. He switched off in disgust and decided to ring Charlotte instead.

After a conversation that did much to restore his good humour, it occurred to him that his fiancée might recognize Ginny's friend's name. He would lose nothing by asking.

'Lorna Dyson?' Charlotte repeated

'I half associate it with a memo or message.'

'At work? You don't mean Laura Dixon, do you? And didn't it say she'd also called herself Lana Dyton?'

Now he remembered. How stupid of the woman to use false names so similar to each other and, possibly, to her own. And, oh Ginny, he asked her silently, as he was thanking Charlotte for jogging his memory, whatever have you got yourself into?

Maurice Tate was in his bedroom, changing from his 'good' office clothes to his 'casual' ones. The terminology was Val's. The only difference, so far as Morris could see, between clothes he wore at home and the ones he went out in was their age and state of dilapidation. Maybe a third difference was that the casuals, bought longer ago, no longer fitted him.

Giving up his struggle with the button on his waistband and trusting the tightness round his trunk to keep his trousers up, he walked round the bed and bent to look at the photograph of the two of them that Val had insisted on having taken on their engagement. He had never been handsome, even at twenty. Interesting-looking? Maybe.

Val had described to her friends his 'quirky attraction'. His red curly hair had been wispy even then but at least it had covered the whole of his head. After school, he had affected a short unruly beard for a while. Val had liked it, told him that young men with whiskers usually looked either bookish or stupid but that he was an exception.

She had persuaded him along to her country dancing

club where she had paraded him shamelessly. He glanced now in the mirror on the wall beside him and ruefully compared what he saw there with the studio photograph. Time had been kinder to Donald.

He had made great sport of their dancing and of the beard. Morris had ignored him, married Val and got on with his life. It had not included children and he had been relieved, after various humiliating tests, to be told that the 'fault', if it could be so called, lay on both sides. His own early life had taught him the grief caused by having more children than you could afford. Val, though family-minded, a great rememberer of birthdays and organizer of family occasions, was not overly maternal.

Morris put the photograph down, pushed the zip of his fly an inch further down, breathed a sigh of relief and reached under the bed for the shoe cleaning box. His 'casual' shoes were clean as he only ever wore them around the house. He knew he was just putting off going downstairs to be overfed whilst he listened to a repetition of what was becoming his wife's constant theme – Donald had always used him spitefully, had poached his girl-friends, had told lies at his interview, stolen Morris's work and consequently his promotion.

Donald had done nothing of the sort. He had lacked Morris's self-confidence, had been jealous of his perman-ent place in the county swimming team, had played soccer well but not to the standard of which he boasted, had been malicious but funny and had never learned how to be content. Morris had applied, against his better judgement, for the job that had been given to Donald. When, in due course, it was readvertised, he had no intention of apply-ing again.

Tonight he was going to tell Val so and burst the bubble in which she saw the two of them living the sort of life that Donald pretended to enjoy. He had to make Val realize that Donald Markey had had very little influence on his own life and career. He was very satisfied with his white collar job in the low to mid-income group because he had an average ability and not a great deal of ambition. They were not destined for the high life, exotic holidays or designer clothes. He was very content with his lot because he had married the woman of his choice and he still loved her in spite of an occasional desire to throttle her.

He hoped that, when she'd listened to all he had to say, she would still love him. He had no real doubts that she would.

Zak Markey sat on the end of his bed. The Winnie the Pooh pyjamas that had been put out for him lay in a crumpled heap on the floor where he had dropped them to show his contempt. He wore one of the plain pairs that had been bought for him when he went away to Haygarth College.

He knew that, when she came in, she would pretend not to notice. She had even come into the bathroom a few minutes ago. As if he couldn't bath himself! Did she think it had been someone's job to do it for him at school? Zak had been mortified.

He stiffened now as he heard her coming upstairs. She would beam at him and then go over and draw his curtains across. She might even fetch one of his old books from the bookcase and want to read it to him.

She did it all! And the book was a Paddington Bear story!

'I grew out of that ages ago. I don't have bedtime stories any more. I can read for myself. We do at school every night till lights out.' He stared at his feet, couldn't meet her eye. She might have started crying and he didn't want to see. He didn't want to make her cry. He just wanted to stop her patting him and breathing over him and calling him darling. He didn't know how he was going to cope now that Dad wasn't here to stop her being a big smothering cushion.

He climbed into bed to get the sheets between them. As he'd known she would, she sat down at his end, facing him, her big bottom pushing up against his knees. 'What would you like then, darling?'

He knew no phrases about biting bullets or grasping nettles but he understood the concept. 'I'd like to go back to school tomorrow.'

Every table in the service station seemed to be full and the man with the tray bearing a cafetière of Douwe Egbert's and a doughnut was obliged to balance it on a narrow shelf surrounding a pillar. He hoped the tray would maintain its equilibrium until, hauling himself up, using both hands, he had managed to achieve a precarious perch on a ridiculously high stool.

Barring this minor inconvenience, he had enjoyed a very satisfactory and successful weekend. Exhausting, though. The new business cards had gone down well. He took one out now and admired it again. First his name, S.B. Sefton, then Financial Adviser, followed by his qualifications, expressed as a row of impressive initials.

He'd let Arlene choose his original cards, grateful that she was willing to help him get established. They had been much too ornate, given the wrong impression completely. Arlene had been invaluable though, lining up her interests with his and playing her role just right. He had intended to take tomorrow as a holiday and celebrate with her the new business the weekend had brought.

When the call from DCI Mitchell had come he had been glad that he hadn't mentioned the treat. Phyllida Markey must have given the police his mobile number. Tonight, he'd have to check through the Markeys' investments and have the documents ready to show them. He could see it was necessary but he could do without it. He felt so tired that he was worried about driving the last thirty miles back to Cloughton. Still, the break in this unpleasant eating place had helped a bit and a wash would hopefully improve matters further. It was a good job he was a morning person and would have his wits about him by nine when this Mitchell required his attendance.

He drank the last dregs of his expensive but reviving coffee and abandoned his distinctly unjammy doughnut, then made for the cloakroom. He'd have to decide how much he needed to tell this chief inspector. In the circumstances, it wouldn't look too good for Phyllida Markey to say that she had called him in in the hope that he could prevent her husband from speculating a little too freely with her capital and spending a too generous share of the interest.

Superintendent John Carroll was rummaging in his freezer, looking for something for his supper. Since his wife had died, he had not so much become domesticated as invented clever ways of managing without the accomplishment of domestication. Learning that his cleaning woman's husband was a retired chef had been a lucky break.

The man had been delighted to turn the experimental cookery that had now become his hobby into a part-time job. The Carroll freezer was kept full, its drawers labelled 'Meals for One', 'With One Guest' and 'Small Dinner Party'. On his part, the retired chef could drink to the same degree as he had when he had been in charge of the kitchen of a small but popular restaurant in Leeds. He could also afford expensive birthday presents for his wife, the superintendent's treasure. A mutually satisfactory arrangement.

Tonight, Carroll was not in the mood to titillate his own palate. His mind was rather taken up with how, the next morning, his DCI was going to receive his directive to scale down their enquiry into Saturday's hit-and-run that had caused the death of his neighbour.

Carroll enjoyed his skirmishes with Mitchell, admired the man's energy, initiative and forthright attitude. On the other hand, intractable was one of the kinder words that sprang to his mind to describe Mitchell's attitude to discipline – or sometimes even the gentlest guidance. He had heard that only his formidable success rate in CID had stopped him being dismissed from every position he had occupied in his progress from police constable to detective chief inspector.

The superintendent sighed, dipped his fingers into the top drawer of the freezer without looking, grabbed a package and closed the door. He stood, absentmindedly holding his frozen supper until mild freezer burn recalled his mind to his evening meal. He dropped the foil-wrapped bundle, sucked his painful fingers and bent to read the label. 'Liver and Onion Casserole with . . .' He read the list of herbs and flavourings and shuddered. Oh, well, one bitter pill to swallow with another.

Detective Sergeant Jennifer Taylor lay on her stomach on her living-room floor, playing Risk with her mother-in-law and her two young daughters. She had no part of her mind to spare for pondering the death of Donald Markey, or, for that matter, any other police concern. This was the first time for a fortnight she had arrived home in time to hear about Lucy's and Judith's school day and to join in their wind-down activities before bed.

The girls were presently co-operating with each other to remove herself and Jane from the board. With that accomplished, they would fight each other to the death. Dark eyes in alert little faces watched every move of the two adults. Long dark hair made coiled patterns on the carpet as they studied the stylized map of the world on the board and worked out strategies of their own.

Till tomorrow morning, Jennifer's CI, the rest of her team, Donald Markey and his family and even her troubled friend Ginny could all go hang.

Boston Road, a few minutes' walk from the Mitchells'

house, was where you bought a property if you required a prestigious address. A car, oddly small and modest in that setting, was parked on the opposite side to and a little beyond number 19.

In it sat a youngish woman whose pretty face was marred by unfortunately large teeth. She had been overcome, suddenly, that evening, by an irresistible urge to catch a glimpse of the real Phyllida Markey. She remained at her observation post as lights came on and curtains were drawn, but no one emerged from number 19. When darkness fell, she drove away.

Mitchell stayed at his desk after dismissing his shift, doggedly clearing his paperwork, until he was sure that all his children would be in bed.

The quarrel between himself and Virginia that evening, like all their disagreements, was short. As always, each said exactly what was meant and neither of them indulged in repetition. Unlike their past spats, however, this one was acrimonious. It was not about a clash of views but about the attitude of each to the other and it scared both of them.

Virginia was angry, her eyes cold, but her voice even. 'It's not difficult to understand. I didn't tell Jennifer about our lunch and about Lorna's accident because I knew exactly what you'd make of it. Don't forget that, before I was a police wife, I served my time as a police daughter. You were going to assume that the accident was her way of accounting for the damage to her car when she ran Donald down –'

'We never fit people up! It's in nobody's interests to get an innocent person convicted. If you do you've still got the villain walking free.'

'Lorna had just come out of hospital. She was shaken and in pain and not in any state to have a fair chance of defending herself. Of course you were going to find out about it. I was just giving her time. I thought she should at

131

least have the rest of the day to pull herself together. I didn't warn her what line you'd take when you did speak to her.'

'You know perfectly well how awkward it makes things for me, your being friendly with someone involved in a current investigation.'

Virginia was unrepentant. 'How could I know on Saturday, when I invited Lorna to Sunday lunch, that there'd be any circumstances to prevent it? Was I supposed to ring her? Say, "Sorry, but my husband suspects you were responsible for last night's hit-and-run so I can't have anything to do with you till you've proved your innocence"? It's now she needs help. I can't ask her to put her problems on hold, keep going till you've got your act together and found your man!'

'Or woman!' Mitchell was shouting. 'When you married a policeman you knew what you were doing – more than most police wives do, as you've just admitted. You knew what I'd have to expect of you.'

'It's not you I'm fighting.' Virginia's voice was still level. 'It's the unyielding, never compromising, insensitive police machine.'

'It works, that machine – and I'm a cog in it.'

'You're so modest.' She gave him the ghost of an impish grin.

Over supper, Mitchell complained, in normal tones, about the untruthful evidence the case was attracting.

Virginia tossed her head. 'Oh, well, there wouldn't be much fun in detective work if all your witnesses spoke the truth. Cases would pass you by and go straight to the courts. The lies are keeping food on our table.'

He eyed her bitterly. 'Since you've been promoted to witness, you'd better see what you can invent.'

He could see he had hurt her. She said quietly, 'I assure you that I've told both you and Jennifer nothing but the truth.' But she didn't meet his eye. They were on new territory.

Chapter Six

In spite of all her defensive arguments, Mitchell knew that his wife did actually feel that she was letting him down. She had done everything she could think of to compensate, taking infinite pains over a passably palatable supper. Afterwards, she had tidied the kitchen. Then, despite the pressing urgency of her magazine commission, she had gone out into the garden and spent an hour in dead-heading the roses and re-edging the lawn.

This morning he had felt unable to face another session of their being barely polite to each other. He had got up soon after dawn, after an almost sleepless night, meaning to leave for the station and breakfast there. When he had come out of the shower and gone down to make coffee he had found her busy scrambling eggs for him.

Clad in a short cotton dressing gown, she moved about the kitchen with the unselfconscious grace that had first captivated him and since kept him in thrall. Now she spoke to him over her shoulder as she stirred. 'I knew you'd prefer to make your own coffee.'

'Do you want some?'

'Please.'

The silly, stilted exchange was embarrassing to both of them. Virginia tried harder, describing some of the children's exploits of the day before.

Mitchell sat in front of his yellow-piled toast, determined to eat without a grimace. The first mouthful startled him into a natural exclamation. 'God, Ginny! That cookery course is doing you some good.'

She smiled, then doggedly pursued her tale. 'Your mother was a bit upset that Michael insisted on watching her get dressed on Sunday.'

Mitchell was surprised. His mother had brought up six children, including four sons, and had encouraged a healthy attitude to all their physical functions. 'What did you say?'

Virginia grinned. 'I told her he was just checking that his mother had the same basic equipment as other women and that she packed it all away in the same sort of containers.'

Mitchell managed a grin of his own. He loved to watch Ginny with her children. She was totally involved with them on their own level but frequently threw him an ironic aside, demonstrating the amused detachment that was woven through her instinctive care for them. It had been the same a year ago when her mother was dying. She could not have nursed Hannah more devotedly, yet she had been constantly amused by the bizarre devices to which they had had to resort to feed, entertain and generally care for her as she suffered the last stages of the horrific disease. This attitude in her daughter had probably kept Hannah sane.

He wondered, suddenly, how much her mother's suffering and death had to do with Ginny's misguided loyalty to her unfortunate friend Lorna. Dare he risk reopening the subject to find out? On reflection, he decided this was not the time. Instead, he thanked her for getting up to cook his meal. Remembering his ungraciousness of the previous day, he promised to ring her as soon as he had any idea of when he would be home again.

She did not stand at the door, as she usually did, to accept and return his hurried parting kiss. He did not pursue her to offer it. He arrived at the station, thoroughly miserable. It was not a state in which he often found himself. He didn't like it. His shift didn't like it either.

By the time they trooped into his office at the appointed time, Mitchell felt as though his working day should be half over. He had arrived whilst the cleaning ladies, in red rubber gloves, were mopping floors round recumbent figures, sometimes three to a cell, amid a stink of stale clothes, drunks' breath and urine. As he began his briefing, he knew that the morning calm would soon arrive as vans delivered prisoners to court. Suddenly he was keenly aware of the solidarity of the community of people in his station and felt grateful for it.

Quickly, he greeted his team and covered the overnight events so far as they concerned CID – yet more computer thefts and the wrongful arrest of a Muslim youth for one of them. To deal with this last item, he selected a PC from the back of the room. He was the right man for the job on two counts: he was Asian and he had proved, so far, to be of little use on the case that currently held Mitchell's interest. He was an interesting new recruit, though, and had shown initiative on previous occasions. He had a whole range of hobbies and skills that he put to the service of his police work. It was rumoured that he could pick any lock in Yorkshire and Mitchell had no wish to hear officially where PC Jain had acquired this accomplishment. The man played a mean game of chess for the Cloughton force and had had published in *Police Review* a series of photographs, in the category 'On the job', with which he had won an award in a national competition. 'One for you, Khalid. You have the background and you have the tact.'

PC Khalid Jain looked suspicious of the compliment. DC Shakila Nazir looked relieved that she had escaped being taken off a murder case to do this awkward and thankless job.

Mitchell knew he had to hurry through this morning's business in time for Sean Sefton's visit at nine. He began on his list of prepared topics, beginning with a reminder that, although their questioning of the people who were around the victim shortly before his death was important, the person who called him away might well have no connection with Heath Lees school. 'We need to dig deeper and wider into Donald Markey's life. Your action sheets today are all directed to that end. We need to keep his wife's goodwill because she's our most useful source of information. At the same time we can't put absolute trust in anything she tells us.'

Caroline raised a hand. 'She's been trying to think of anyone she might have told about the party at the school – people who had no connection with it. Magic gave me a message from her just now. As far as she can remember there was only her mother.'

Mitchell wondered whether this was worth following up. For now, he asked merely, 'What about her in-laws?'

Caroline shook her head. 'Doubt it. They don't speak. Eric Simpson suggested that Phyllida had a premonition about what was going to happen – that that might explain why she seemed preoccupied when he and Nicky collected the pair of them. I can't decide whether he was trying to suggest that she knew exactly –'

'I'm glad someone can believe something bad about him.' They turned to Clement. 'To me he's been coming across as too good to be true, so patient about his poor wife's persistent adultery.'

'Glad to see you've been studying Caroline's report.'

Clement scowled at his CI. 'It made a change from green cars.'

Caroline hurriedly continued her observations. 'Simpson might be a drinker. He offered me wine in the middle of the morning. He kept the bottle beside him and poured more for himself, although he didn't drink the second glass. Oh . . . and he called Donald Markey's death a bereavement for Nicky.'

'Like I said. He's either a saint or a fool.'

Caroline shook her head. 'Or maybe he's playing a very clever game.'

'I expect Nicky does feel bereft. No one else is going to buy her diamond bracelets.' They turned back to Jennifer, who went on, 'The only other woman besides Nicky that Phyllida mentioned was someone called Jane. She professed not to know the surname but she said that both Donald and this Jane seemed wary of Jane's husband.'

Quietly triumphant, PC Smithson stood up. The rest turned to the back of the room to face him. 'There's a report of my interview with Neville Kyte in the file. He's a vicar, as you know, and his wife's called Jane.' He was well satisfied with the ripple of interest his contribution caused and he made a mental note to give Connie her share of the glory when he told her about it.

Watching from his office window, Mitchell saw his visitor drive into the car park in a new Freelander that he coveted. It was precisely eight fifty-seven. Sefton arrived in the station foyer one minute later, so that Mitchell, going down to meet him, shook hands with him at exactly nine o'clock.

For this interview, Mitchell had armed himself, in response to a tip from Shakila, with the help of PC Whitham. Whitham had made a late entry into the force after coming to grief in several attempts to pass his actuarial examinations. If there had been any financial misdoing on the part of either of the Markeys or their adviser, he would have a chance of spotting it.

Sefton was an ordinary, pleasant-looking man, not particularly handsome. The documentation he had brought was neatly and chronologically packed into the different sections of his briefcase. His efficiency underlined his punctuality.

Briefly, without sentimentality, he regretted the painful death of one of his clients and the grief of his wife. Settled in Mitchell's office, he placed papers on the desk with an offer to elucidate the technicalities they contained, either now or later as required. Mitchell thanked him and asked for a short statement on the nature of his work, with particular reference to what he had done on behalf of the Markeys. 'In layman's terms, please,' he added.

Sefton smiled. 'I'm an independent financial adviser. I'm

not trying to be either insulting or amusing when I tell you that means I give independent advice to my clients about their financial affairs. An amazing variety of actual discussions and transactions shelter under that umbrella. I'm a qualified man who deals chiefly with matters relating to life assurance, personal investments and savings.'

'Were you employed by one of the Markeys or both of them together?'

Sefton raised an eyebrow. 'Actually, by both of them separately. I'm not sure whether my behaviour was ethical but it certainly wasn't illegal. Whatever, at the stage when they approached me I was just getting started and needed all the clients I could collect. There has never been a serious conflict of interests between them and I've done my utmost to offer the best solution to every problem either of them has brought me.'

'Have you ever mentioned to one anything about the work you were doing for the other?'

Sefton shook his head. 'Whether they were aware that I represented them both I'm not sure.'

'Can you tell me about your dealings with Mrs Markey first?'

'At the age of twenty-one, Phyllida inherited investments bringing in an income in the region of two hundred thousand pounds a year. The family money came from property dealing going back many generations. Her father diversified into hotels and restaurants – not getting personally involved in the running but backing them for a percentage of the profits. She's never wanted to speculate on her own account. She was well satisfied with how things were – as she should be.'

'So, why did she need you?'

'Because Donald was spending more than he was earning and had some big ideas about wheeling and dealing. She first approached me wanting a tactful way to tie up a lot of capital that had up to then been in both their names.'

'Why did she pick you?'

'Another client recommended me.'

'And Donald?'

'I sent some junk mail to his office, hoping he'd bite.'

'And he did.'

Sefton nodded. 'The first job I did for him was a small life assurance to benefit Phyllida. He made a joke of it – said he didn't mind helping her spend her money but he didn't want to cost her anything when he'd gone.'

'Who's it with?'

'The Pru. It's only for fifteen thousand pounds, well within the underwriting not to require medical evidence. He told me his heart wasn't too good, but for such a small amount no GP report was necessary if the questions on the form are answered positively. Some companies only check when the amount's in excess of fifty thousand. Later, I spent a lot of time telling him horror stories about firms he wanted to buy shares in. It was to Phyllida's advantage but it was genuinely good advice. Donald didn't have a clue what he was doing and he'd have lost a fortune if he hadn't been checked.'

He waved an arm over the desk 'All the details are there. I haven't told Phyllida I've brought you all these documents.' There was an appeal in his voice.

'Neither will I unless it's necessary.' For the first time Mitchell wondered whether there might be a personal relationship between Sefton and his client.

When Sefton spoke again, his tone was sober. 'I've spoken to her very briefly this morning. I was astonished to hear you're treating the incident as murder.'

'Why?'

'Well, assuming financial gain to be the motive –'

'We aren't making any assumptions.'

'Sorry. Obviously it's the first thing to spring to my mind. Anyway, you might find it useful to know that under the current arrangements Donald had very little money for anyone to inherit. Phyllida was making him a very generous allowance but I fixed it so that she kept all the capital in her own hands.'

'So, how could Donald . . .' Mitchell was not quite sure where his question was going.

Sefton grinned. 'She was a soft touch. When he'd disposed of his salary plus his allowance on speculating and reckless spending, she couldn't resist bailing him out.'

Mitchell looked across to PC Whitham who shook his head. 'Nothing for the moment, sir.'

'In that case, Mr Sefton, I've almost finished with you for today. When we've been through these documents you're leaving with us we shall almost certainly need to see you again. I understand you're yet another old boy of Heath Lees.'

He grimaced. 'Not such a satisfied customer as all the folk who turned up last Saturday. I didn't enjoy school and wouldn't have had many happy memories to talk about.'

'So you weren't sorry to have your business trip as an excuse.'

'Too right.'

Mitchell grinned. 'Ducked out of it myself. I had a few sins to live down but that wasn't the reason. I still managed to enjoy myself there – on the whole. I think that one of the guests we've had a word with is a relative of yours, a Mr Eric Simpson. Is he one of your clients too?'

Sefton shrugged. 'He's a cousin a few times removed. I'm sure he's a good sort, but we've hardly ever met. There's a family feud in the generation above us and we found ourselves on different sides of it. When I have met him he's seemed a very private sort of man. I don't think he'd want even the most distant of relatives knowing his business. I can understand that.'

Satisfied for the moment, Mitchell let his witness go. 'You're free, of course, to work and travel as usual. We'd be grateful, though, if you'd let us know if you make any extended trips. We're going to need help when we sort through the gubbins you've brought us.'

Looking a little affronted at this breezy dismissal of his precious documents, Sefton took his leave.

Back from the school run on Tuesday morning, Virginia Mitchell was making a further attempt to be amusing about white lies. She was sure there was a jinx on this article. Just as she was expecting it to do, the telephone rang. She had never been able to ignore it. If she didn't pick up the receiver she would only be distracted by wondering who had wanted to speak to her.

'Ginny? It's Alex.'

'Hi. Look, I've got work to do. Deadline's Thursday.'

'It's about Lorna Dyson.'

Virginia's fingers tightened on the handset. 'Look, can you just forget what I –'

'Well, I could stop interfering, but there are a few things that you ought to know.'

Virginia was puzzled. 'About Lorna? That you can tell me?'

'What does this friend of yours look like?'

'Alex, what's this all about?'

He sighed. 'Does this fit – stocky build, thick dark hair and dark eyes, about five feet two?'

'That could be hundreds of people.'

Nursing had schooled her brother well in patience. There was no suggestion of irritation in his voice as he continued, 'OK. Has she got a large dark brown mole on her midriff, below her left breast?'

Virginia was becoming angry. 'How on earth should I know? Oh . . .' Dim memories stirred of showering after school hockey. 'Yes, she has. I presume she's been your patient.'

'No.'

'You mean . . .'

'That she's one of the shady ladies from my past? No again. Look, can I come round?'

'I think you'd better.' Once again Virginia began clearing away her notes from the table.

The angry red morning sky that had promised a break in the fine, sunny weather had relented and given a bright, warm few hours. Now, however, there were chunks of solid-looking grey cloud overhead, between which the sun still mocked, and intermittent heavy drops fell. Alex sprinted up the Mitchells' short drive to the shelter of the porch.

Virginia let him in and took him into the kitchen. Neither of them seemed to know how to begin the discussion. 'Coffee?' she offered.

'Benny's?' Virginia shook her head but Alex still accepted. Her brother was humouring her! He'd obviously brought news she wouldn't want to hear.

Alex broke the uncomfortable silence. 'Why haven't you told Benny what you've told me?'

'Because he thinks like a policeman.' She waved her hands as, frustratedly, she sought words that would make her brother understand. 'Any sane person imagines that a man with a ladder is a window cleaner or a decorator, but, to Benny, he's a burglar. A young lad hanging around waiting for his friend is sizing up houses. A normal person's "I wonder what that bloke's doing" to Benny is, "What the hell is that bloke up to?" Lorna was upset on Saturday night. She has good reason to be permanently upset and now she's injured as well. Benny thinks she got injured running Donald down and then deliberately coasted her car into a tree to give herself a cover story.'

'What do you think?'

Virginia got up and poured her coffee down the sink. 'I wish I knew. It's ages since I was in close contact with her and I don't know what she's been doing with herself, apart from what I've told you. I don't think the Lorna I mucked about with at school could have killed someone, even with the sort of provocation Donald gave her. I do

142

think that, since the death of her baby, she might have been clinically depressed. What do you think as a nurse? Have you seen depression change a character like that?'

She turned to look at him and was touched to see that he had persevered with his coffee. 'Could you find out all you can about the little girl's condition and whether there really was a possible cure? If, by any chance, this business is pinned on Lorna it would help with her defence.'

'Whoa! You're not talking to a consultant or someone in clinical research. I work in a hospital ward full of geriatrics and terminally ill people. I know a lot about the way they die from natural causes and how to help them do it as comfortably and with as much dignity as possible. Much beyond that and I'm in the same position as you, relying on books and the Internet. Anyway, why do you want to defend her?'

Virginia paused, trying to work out the answer. 'Because I wish I liked her more, and because you've got to do all you can for someone who's had such a rotten deal – and because Benny's not being fair to her.'

'He's acting on the information he has.' Virginia flushed but held her brother's gaze. She could think of nothing more to say. Alex got up and put his cup in the sink. 'The coffee was diabolical. Ginny, what was this woman like when you knew her?'

'In what respect?'

'Was she honest, trustworthy?'

'Yes – to a degree.' Alex waited. 'She never told lies to wriggle out of trouble. In fact she preferred being stroppy. She'd rather announce that she hadn't done her homework than pretend she'd left it at home or lost it, but . . .'

'But what?'

'I've told you how her family always made her feel she wasn't important, so she'd say things to make herself the centre of attention sometimes.'

'Things?'

'Well, she used to say that some TV person, whose name I can't remember now, was her godfather.'

'Did she ever claim she was abused?'

'Sexually abused, you mean? No. She just felt her parents were so involved and concerned with her brother that they'd forgotten she existed. She once told me she wished she'd been the handicapped one. I think she really meant that. Look, Alex, what have you come to say that you can't get started on? I've to pick up the twins from nursery school in an hour and it'll take fifteen minutes to get there.'

He nodded, but fished in his pocket for a notebook before getting started. 'Have you heard of Munchausen's syndrome?'

'Pretending to be ill? Yes, just about.'

'It's an attention-seeking personality disorder, more common than statistics suggest. It gets its name from a German soldier –'

Virginia waved a hand. 'Never mind all that.'

'OK. It's predominantly a female disorder – emotionally immature people with low self-esteem who are dying to be the centre of attention. Sometimes dying is what they do. They go to any lengths, injecting bacteria, injuring themselves, swallowing poisons . . .'

'Sort of super-hypochondriacs?'

'No. Hypochondriacs think they're ill. Munchausen patients know they're not. They're not malingerers either, trying to get out of work, or to get drugs or insurance money. Munchausen patients are in it strictly for attention. They go from city to city, or even to several hospitals within a large metropolitan area. Patients have been discovered with a string of hospital admissions stretching over years. They complain of abdominal pain, chest pain, loss of consciousness, blood in their urine . . .'

'How do they fake that?'

'They don't. They cut themselves and bleed into it. They know the drill. They've usually had an early, genuine experience of a hospital stay and they learn to manipulate the medical care system. Often, they've had a modicum of medical training . . .' Virginia's hard glare stopped him.

144

'So, in case Benny doesn't manage to nail Lorna, you're fitting her up as well.'

Alex dropped his sympathetic approach. 'Shut up and let me finish. Some of these people increase their opportunity to get sympathy by blaming their ailments on someone else, saying their mental problems are caused by persecution and victimization. Almost all of them describe an unhappy, unloved childhood with abusive or neglectful parents.'

Virginia opened her mouth to argue but shut it again as her brother went resolutely on. 'Another variation is Munchausen's by proxy. A mother invents, or even actually causes, symptoms in her child so as to collect sympathy as an anxious and exhausted mother.'

Now Virginia insisted on being heard. 'Are you telling me that there's evidence that Lorna's child died because of something that Lorna did to her? You want to watch what you're saying. You go on a course, learn something new and start looking for it even in a confidential telephone conversation with me.'

'Ginny!' He grabbed her by the upper arm and shook her till she was silent. 'Earlier in the week, at the Infirmary, everyone had to read a print-out of an e-mail that's being circulated to all the hospitals in the county. It was a warning to look out for a Munchausen patient. There was a description of most of the scams she'd tried. She's presented herself under various names, including Lana Dyton and Laura Dixon –'

'It's not necessarily –'

'There was a photograph.' He fished between the pages of the notebook to which he had occasionally referred as he'd told his story, and handed her the picture of her friend that he had photocopied from the one being circulated. She handed it back to him, then sat in silence, her hands covering her face. Alex spoke to the top of her head. 'At least I can tell you she did nothing to harm her child. She never gave birth to a child. She invented the whole thing.'

When his sister made no reply, he pushed back his chair, stood up and consulted his watch. 'I'll collect the twins for you but you'll have to have got yourself together by the time I drop them off. I'll be going on duty at one o'clock and you can't drive to Leeds from here without traffic hold-ups whatever the time of day.'

Virginia lifted a hand in thanks but remained at the table. When Benny heard this tale, he would be even more inclined to believe the worst of Lorna. She remembered a neighbour once trying to arouse their sympathy for his wife's suffering from Seasonal Affective Disorder. When the poor man was safely out of earshot, Benny had given a snort of half amusement, half disgust. 'SAD's the right word for it. Trying to blame the weatherman for all your skiving! Now I've heard it all.'

As far as Virginia was concerned, Lorna's motive for making away with Donald had been disposed of. Since he had never credited her with it, however, her brother's revelations would do Lorna no favours with Benny.

Gazing through his window once more, Mitchell watched Sefton climb into the shiny maroon Freelander that he had parked across the middle of two marked-out spaces. He was reminded that, apart from confessing to being responsible for the damage, he had done nothing about Clement's rear windscreen. As he moved towards the telephone to rectify the matter, it rang. Superintendent Carroll would like a word in his office.

Now what? The super had dropped one or two hints to Mitchell over the last forty-eight hours about the possibility of the driver of their green car being just a drunk or an addict. Whatever or whoever he was, he still had to be found, but Mitchell knew that Carroll was becoming unhappy about the amount of time his team had spent on the personal life of the victim. It could all prove irrelevant.

Mitchell was well aware that his team would probably

have been on Carroll's side in the argument if their witness had not been Virginia. He'd admitted to them – well, some of them – that he felt embarrassed about backing her. Embarrassed, but not uncertain. And he'd been assured that they backed her too. He'd given them the spiel that the super was probably about to give him – told them, if they believed Ginny they must find some supporting evidence and quickly. They were doing their best.

He ran up the stairs and banged on the door, labelled modestly 'John Carroll'. Pleased that his breathing was still perfectly even, he'd heard the quiet invitation to go in. Carroll always spoke to his men like an uncle, but he usually sat behind his desk to do it. He represented rank and, at the moment, Mitchell was his enemy. Inside every superintendent, however pleasant his face and manner, there lurked a dictator. All right, John Carroll was a small one, but, at least at the present moment, Mitchell had no faith that someone so career-orientated would be concerned with the efforts of his men.

Mitchell stared, stony-faced, through the window as the words he expected to hear were spoken. Having given his decision, Carroll proceeded to defend it. 'We've got a country-wide search going on for a smallish green car and our evidence is a paint chip.'

Mitchell ignored the chair his superior officer indicated and continued to stand over him. 'Is it my fault the bloody lab's gone to sleep? You aren't any more eager to get their report than I am!'

'I'll speak to them. Of course we want them to get a move on. And stop talking as if I've asked you to close the book. I merely told you to scale down the enquiry until we have more information to go on. Do you realize how many men in how many authorities are looking for this car? We're going to be very unpopular with the other forces if it turns out to be just a local yob stoned out of his mind.'

Mitchell threw himself into the chair in his fury, then cursed himself for losing the advantage of height. 'I don't believe it was. And neither do you. If Ginny was to be believed yesterday, what makes her impression less convincing today?'

Still Carroll remained patient. 'I haven't changed my attitude to your wife. I said I respected her powers of observation and judgement. I said, if we found any evidence in a preliminary murder enquiry, we'd go full steam ahead – but we've found nothing.'

'Rubbish! I've got a whole list of people who –'

'Who might have been annoyed with or jealous of the victim. It wouldn't take long to find people with a similar attitude towards me – certainly towards you! If someone killed you, I could certainly be accused of having felt murderous.' Now Carroll's voice was becoming dangerously quiet.

Mitchell ignored the danger. 'That's the sort of talk you gave me about the Asian girl and you were wrong that time.'

The superintendent's lips tightened but he remained silent. Mitchell, waiting, realized that his opponent had retreated from the fight. He took a step forward from his chair. 'So, same advice we used to get from bloody Petty then? "Here are your orders, officers. Make a feeble effort with a scaled-down team, so nobody can say you did nothing. If that leaves you with too few resources to do a good job, well, I'm afraid the egg's on your faces."'

Mitchell stormed to the door and slammed it. Outside in the corridor, he wondered whether his standing with his wife would be improved or diminished by the news that he had lost his job.

Shakila had supposed that she would interview Zak Markey in his own home where he would feel comfortable. He had insisted, however, on being brought to the station to have a 'proper' interview. For some reason she had not yet fathomed, Mitchell had seemed displeased by the arrangement. He had hurried Shakila, Phyllida Markey

148

and her son into a lift and up to his office. Then, instead of settling to listen, he had left with a brief, 'Due upstairs.'

Shakila blinked. 'I thought you'd been already this morning.'

He gave her a humourless smile. 'That's right. This time's to apologize.'

Shakila grinned. It was quite likely he meant it literally. She turned back into the room and found chairs for her visitors. Phyllida had agreed to her son's being interviewed provided that she herself was present. Shakila had agreed to her presence on condition that she did not prompt the boy.

Zak was not intimidated. He got up from his chair and walked round the room, examining but not touching. After a while, he turned to Shakila. 'You're black.'

'You're extremely observant.'

'You're being sarcastic, aren't you?'

'Well, you were being rude.'

Zak climbed back into the sanctuary of his chair. 'What I meant was, there aren't many black policemen – or women.'

Shakila nodded and hurried on before his mother could reprove him. She knew that, if she was to learn anything useful, she had to win the boy's confidence and get him to talk freely. To begin with, the subject didn't matter. She saw Phyllida's start of surprise when she asked him, 'If you were given a hundred pounds to spend on anything you liked, what would you buy?'

'Are you going to give it to me?'

'I'm afraid not.'

'So, it's a hypo-thet-ical question?' He stumbled over the word.

Shakila hastened to reassure him. 'If that means that you have to use your imagination, then yes.'

The child nodded, gave the question a moment's consideration, then, with a glint in his eye, announced, 'Jelly.'

'You'd have plenty of money left after that.'

'No I wouldn't. I could get four hundred packets at twenty-five pence from Tesco. I'd keep it all in my bedroom and break pieces off and eat them like sweets. We don't have much jelly at our house. I like all flavours but my favourite is strawberry. Jelly's full of gelatine and it's good for bones and nails.'

So, like his mother, the boy could play verbal games. He hadn't finished with this one. 'If you gave me a hypothetical few thousand pounds, I'd buy a house.'

'You like that word, don't you?'

'Hypothetical, you mean? We had it in English at school.'

Shakila nodded. 'But you've got a beautiful house already.'

'Yes. And I'd take my mother with me. It would be better than where we live now because I'd be in charge. We'd eat what I decided and I'd read my mother a story at bedtime and I'd tell her when to go to bed and I'd go at the same time. When I grow up and I need the house to use for my lady friends, my mother could go back to her old one.'

'I see. I'd like us to stop being hypothetical now and talk about your father. I'm very sorry he died.'

'He didn't die. He was killed by a bad driver.'

'So I hear. You must miss your father very much.'

Zak put his head on one side and thought about it. 'Well, I didn't see him very much but I do miss him. I can't tell you why. At least, not just at the moment.' He glanced significantly towards his mother and was silent for some moments. When he looked up he smiled at Shakila. 'My father had lady friends, you know.'

Shakila saw that Phyllida's face was impassive but she made no attempt to divert her son from the subject he had introduced. 'Does that worry you?' Shakila asked.

'No. Everyone's father at school's the same.'

'Is that so?'

'I suppose a few of them might be making it up so as to be the same as the rest of us.'

Shakila thought it was time to change the subject. 'I said that you were observant, Zak, and you were right about my being sarcastic. I wonder, though, how good you are at recognizing cars. Do you know what colours and makes of cars your parents' friends have?'

'I do if I've seen them. Uncle Eric – he isn't my real uncle – he has an old red Fiesta. Mr Tate has an Astra that's blue. Mr Burgin, my headmaster, has a black Mercedes and he gave me a ride home in it. My father's car is a dark blue Celica. It looks brill from the outside, like a sports car, but, in the back, there's hardly any room for legs.'

'Does anyone have a light green one? Quite a small car?'

Zak screwed up his face to convey deep thought. 'Someone came with my father once to see me at school. Someone called Jane. I told you my father had lady friends. She's one of them.' He would not be drawn any further. Jane was 'ordinary-looking', her car was 'smallish and green but not very light'. Yes, she had talked to him, 'but only about ordinary things', not her job, not where she lived, not what her other name was. Shakila supposed that he had been warned off discussing the lady, particularly in front of his mother.

After another few minutes, she rewarded him with chocolate, thanked his mother for her co-operation and escorted them to their car, all the while wondering how she could possibly arrange to see the boy on his own.

Mitchell sat at his desk and seethed with anger. If the puzzle of Donald Markey's death was going to be resolved he knew it would be by probing into the connections he had had with the people around him. In spite of the embarrassment of Virginia's being the only witness to the death being deliberately caused, and in spite of their being at odds, he trusted her. He solved his cases because he had – well, a nose for them. Not a useful tool in court, nor in defending his point of view to his superior officers. And he wouldn't ever use such an expression in front of his shift. In fact, he felt rather embarrassed within himself, just thinking about it. He'd learned from experience, though, always to follow his nose.

A former detective sergeant, Jerry Hunter, had once justified it for him. 'What you call your nose is really your conscious mind reaping the benefit of what your subconscious has observed and absorbed.' Sometimes, even now, he missed Jerry a great deal – especially when he needed such learned-sounding justification for going his own way against the views of the authorities.

And why had the super had to be out of his office when he'd gone up to make his necessary apology? Mitchell was not sure that he could persuade himself again into accepting the humiliation of Carroll's forgiveness. When they did meet, he would make it very clear that he regretted only losing his temper and not the views he had expressed.

After a while, he got up and vented his feelings in the usual way. Taking a pair of scissors, he cut back to three inches from their roots the strands of ivy that trailed from the pots on his filing cabinet and window sill. He couldn't face lunch with Ginny and he was in no mood to receive a lecture over a pub table from Jennifer. He'd eat in the canteen and find someone there on whom to vent his fury.

As he stomped down the steps, he wondered how far the superintendent was going to demote him. The canteen was the place to find out. If any decision had been taken the gossip would have begun already.

His plate piled high with comforting pastry and chips, he took a seat at a table surrounded by PCs. He needed the balm of their below-stairs attitude, their contempt for official policies devised at the top and for senior officers they considered totally out of touch. They were the noble PCs, feet on the ground, heads full of common sense, getting on with the job, renowned, at least in the canteen, for their instincts. 'Purdy is a real thief taker' and 'Good coppers are born not trained.'

They soon finished their meal, but, after they left, Clement came in and joined him. Mitchell raised an eyebrow at him. 'Want to be out on the job? Find Shakila and go and bring Lorna Dyson in. Leave her on ice for a while and then see what she's got to say for herself.'

To his surprise, the commission did little to raise Clement's spirits. He pushed food around his plate as he asked, 'Where will it get us? She's all wrapped in bandages to collect sympathy. Then you advise her of her rights. It's like saying, "Don't tell me anything, girl. Don't talk to me, I'm trying to put you in jail, you moron."'

Mitchell tasted his canteen coffee, then pushed it away and stood up. 'Do it anyway. It might be my last act of rebellion as a DCI.' Leaving Clement to make of that what he would, he wandered back upstairs. He'd better see what Whitham was making of the Markeys' financial affairs. Later on, he'd maybe cut his throat, if he could find the time.

When he reached his office he found a note on his desk. He wouldn't look at it, wasn't ready to grovel to John Carroll, wasn't prepared to sit with his hands tied whilst a murderer laughed at him. He'd go down and see Whitham and then go and give hell to Lorna Dyson.

His telephone rang. He'd picked up the receiver and barked into it before it occurred to him that it might be Carroll again. It was Magic. 'Note on your desk from the lab.'

Mitchell's sun came out again.

It was a rather more dynamic Mitchell who greeted his team as they filed into his office at the end of the day. Waving the precious lab report, he stood up to address them. 'They found more flakes of paint, in and amongst the bloodstained clothes we sent. They've reassembled the bits of glass as far as they could. Their guess is that they formed part of a headlamp lens and there were enough fragments for them to read the manufacturer's coded markings. Adrian?'

Clement stood up to offer the fruits of his tedious few days with the computer. 'The unit was made by a company called Carello. These components were fitted to Fiat Uno cars in the UK from 1983. The broken plastic moulding was stamped with the letters ONI. The lab guessed that too was the end of an Italian name.' He glanced across at Mitchell. 'The nearest Fiat garage is in Leeds.'

'That's your first port of call tomorrow then. Take one of the Escorts till your window's replaced. Any idea how long –?'

'Lunchtime tomorrow, they said.'

Mitchell nodded. 'Leave the bill in my top drawer.' He was gratified to see that the team looked puzzled. Clement had obviously not spread the story at his expense. He returned to his report. 'The flakes of paint have been compared with the range of Fiat colours available. The top coat colour corresponds with the one Fiat called aquamarine – that sort of pale metallic shade. So, our search has narrowed. Adrian, if you can bear to stay on and see what the computer tells us now, you can have first slot tomorrow and then get off to Leeds.'

'Gee, thanks.' But Clement's face wore a wide beam now that all his key tapping was beginning to produce some useful results.

Jennifer spoke quietly, only to Mitchell. 'That lets the Dyson woman off the hook. She drives a Mini.'

'She did until Saturday night.' He had enjoyed sitting in on Clement's session with this woman who was holding his wife in such thrall. He was certainly glad that the forensic evidence was moving the case along again but frustrated by losing the chance to give Lorna Dyson more uncomfortable interviews and sleepless nights.

What was attracting Ginny to her? Her appearance was unprepossessing, to say the least. Her high colour had been the sort he associated with high blood pressure or drink rather than fresh air. Her almost black eyes had glared at him under heavy brows. Her hair was plentiful but greasy, her jaw strong, almost aggressive, but hung about with a semicircle of flabby flesh. Her manner had been sullen, her unwilling replies to Clement's questions self-pitying. He had interrupted Clement to warn her that wasting police time was a punishable offence, but that had seemed to cause relief rather than fear.

The team was staring at him. He returned to the present and, in as few words as possible, he described the interview and passed on to his next topic. 'I've spent some time this afternoon considering the school's new headmaster, Robert Barnes. Maynard has been asked about him. He was too professional, of course, to give the man a bad press. All he would say was that the staff was getting too inbred and that he'd hoped to be replaced by someone who had never heard of Heath Lees till he read the advertisement for the post. There was no rider about Barnes being such a good candidate that the need for new blood could be disregarded.'

Caroline raised a hand. 'I saw Maynard's wife, Frances. He'd raised doubts about the appointment to her.'

Shakila turned to Caroline to ask, 'What's all this got to do with Donald Markey?'

'Several people have said that Markey, as one of the governors, was going to vote against him. When he was appointed, Barnes knew to expect that friend Donald would make life unpleasant for him.'

Smithson, thankful that he had so recently reread his notes on his Neville Kyte interview, chipped in. 'Kyte's on the board of governors too, representing the Church. Markey accused Barnes of having undue influence by not declaring that one of the other governors is a relative of his wife's. The governor's somebody called Bradley Nuttall and Myrna Barnes was a Nuttall. Markey knew because Kyte let it drop in a casual conversation that he now regrets.'

Mitchell looked up from noting this in his book. 'We left

his local force to interview Barnes. Maybe one of us should go.'

'You're pushing your luck.' Jennifer waited for at least a glare from her CI but was met with only an expression of amiable enquiry. 'I heard we'd been warned off seeing all these folk. I thought we were confined to using the lab's evidence.'

Mitchell's face was deadpan. 'Superintendent Carroll said that we should concentrate on other current problems – at least until the lab produced something to narrow down the scope of our enquiry. I did as he suggested. PC Jain has dealt most tactfully with our wrongful arrest. We've all but pinned the computer thefts on our old friend Shaun Grant who was released from his young offenders' unit three weeks ago. That leaves us free to follow up on this late but welcome help from the white coat brigade. I'll sleep on a decision about Barnes. Get an early night yourselves. Same time in the morning.' They trooped out thankfully.

Mitchell felt almost cheerful as he walked out through the foyer on his way home. Two constables were coming in with the first batch of the evening's prostitutes, spotty, with frazzled hair and very antagonistic. Why, Mitchell wondered, were they referred to as good time girls? They were all streetwise, though, and often funny as they skittered across the polished floor as fast as their four-inch heels allowed them.

Mitchell grinned to himself as he unlocked the car. As he drove home, he tried and failed to anticipate the reception he would be given by Virginia. He had never before experienced this situation between them and so had no idea what might be to come now.

Their actual meeting was eased by the presence of the children. With or without their father, according to the time he arrived home, they had been promised their supper out. Declan and Caitlin were in the middle of a furious argument about whose turn it was to choose the place.

Virginia grinned at Mitchell. 'Since whichever of them

wins will, unfortunately, choose McDonald's, this is an academic exercise.' Without speaking to them she glared at her two eldest and the quarrel ceased.

A vague guilt that he resented overlaid Mitchell's anger, and his unwise lunch still lay heavy. He accompanied his family on the outing but opted out of food and drank only Coke. Virginia gave him a cool glance. 'I'm not sure what I was expecting from you but it certainly wasn't a hunger strike.' For the rest of the meal, he chatted industriously to his children whilst his wife retreated within herself.

Declan gave each of his parents an old-fashioned look. When their offspring were safely in bed, each of them knew that their situation had to be tackled.

Chapter Seven

Mitchell wondered whether the news that Lorna Dyson was no longer suspected of running down Donald Markey would relieve Ginny or whip up her fury to a higher level. He was puzzled. He could think of no reason for it but he sensed that her manner was slightly apologetic. He went into the kitchen to brew coffee and to try to work things out.

When he carried in his tray, the sitting room was full of the kind of music neither of them liked. It was neither solidly classical not cheerfully pop or rock. 'Slithery' was the word that came into his mind. Maybe it was film music – a strange choice for his wife. Violins buzzed at each other like angry insects. He made no comment on it but started to pour the coffee.

After a few moments, Virginia scrambled up from her cushion on the floor and crossed the room to switch the CD off. 'It's from a thing called *The Gadfly.*' Mitchell was pleased to have been right about the insects. 'I was trying to work out what my mother found in it.'

Mitchell nodded. His mother-in-law had been the only musical person in the family, though Declan was promising to be the next one. Hannah had not enthused overmuch about the greater composers but had been very fond of Shostakovitch. They were silent for a while, both thinking back over the last year of Hannah's life, patient and positive as she battled with increasing and, in the end, total paralysis.

Ginny's brother had returned home when things got

really difficult and the two of them had nursed Hannah through those dreadful last months. Mitchell considered again the possibility of a psychological connection between Ginny's devoted care for her mother and her present concern for her unfortunate but self-pitying friend. Perhaps he was fighting not her disloyalty to himself but a stage in her recovery from the trauma of the last two years.

Thankful that the music had stopped, he grinned when Virginia wrinkled her nose at him and said, 'It's truly awful, isn't it?' He nodded, opened his mouth to offer his theory, then, thankfully in time, realized it would not be acceptable to her.

She settled back on to her cushion and introduced the subject of Lorna herself. 'We need to sort out the Lorna business – and without bawling each other out. I needed to be on her side, partly because she'd had such a rotten deal and partly because I don't like her.' She glared at him as he roared with laughter and he sobered up quickly, noting her use of the past tense. Had her attitude to the girl changed?

'If you mean her brother and the attention he got –'

'I don't.' In a few telling words, she related the story Lorna had told her.

As Mitchell listened, he was filled with intense rage. Ginny had been withholding what she believed to be real and vital evidence. With self-control that amazed him, he merely remarked, 'I'd better tell you then, before someone else does, that I've had your friend down at the station for a chunk of the afternoon.' He waited for retribution to fall on him.

Virginia merely announced, 'Alex rang me this morning.'

'For God's sake, Ginny, we've got to get this thrashed out before we bury it again. Chit-chat from your brother can wait.'

'No it can't. Shut up and listen.' She summarized the revelation Alex had brought her in just a few sentences.

Mitchell's anger dissolved. The story, he considered, strengthened his own theory about his wife's condition. It explained what he had been unable to believe. He wanted to touch Ginny, to tell her he understood. He knew from experience, though, that this was not the time, that maybe the time wouldn't come.

Neither of them in so many words apologized for the rift between them. There was, however, a considerable change in the atmosphere and both of them relaxed.

A tap on the door some five minutes later was followed by the entrance of a worried-looking Declan. 'I can't sleep.' He hovered in the doorway until what he saw emboldened him. 'Are you two friends again?'

Virginia nodded, matter-of-factly. 'Yes. Can you go back to sleep now?'

Declan weighed his chances, then came across to settle on the sofa next to his father. 'I could if I had some drinking chocolate and a biscuit.'

Lisa Prentice, demoted from her emergency stint at the Customer Service desk, was back once more behind her reinforced glass screen at her bank counter, dressed in her despised uniform, a navy jacket and skirt and figured silk jabot. What she resented most was the brooch with her name on it, pinned to her lapel and inviting all her customers to report her by name to the manager for every little peccadillo.

She looked up to see how long the queue was and found herself making eye contact with a woman she recognized. The big teeth were still the same. Since it was the end of July, the knitted beret, of course, had gone. Now, the woman – Mrs Barker, was it? – was wearing wide-legged cotton trousers, a white cotton T-shirt and a scarlet sweater, hanging from her shoulders and tied casually at the front by its sleeves.

Lisa refrained from signalling for her next customer and continued her scrutiny. What was it that gave the woman the ability to dress so casually and yet look so elegant? Her feet had varnished toenails and were encased in leather thong sandals. When she turned for a moment to speak to the woman behind her, Lisa saw that her hair was caught loosely at the nape of her neck in a silver hair slide.

An intrepid man at the head of the queue came forward, in spite of the absence of her flashing light. He stood in front of Lisa, blocking her view and bringing her back to an awareness of her responsibilities. She apologized to him but still cast covert glances in the woman's direction as she counted out the notes for his withdrawal. She was intrigued to see the woman deliberately miss her turn and wait, eyeing Lisa, obviously waiting for her to press her button again. The woman acknowledged Lisa's scrutiny with a smile which turned up the corners of her mouth without the lips parting. So, she was self-conscious about those teeth.

Now she was coming over. 'You won't remember me.'

'Oh, but I do. I was filling in for a colleague who had flu when you were in before. Yours was the very first account I'd ever opened.'

The woman raised her eyebrows. 'Really? You were most efficient and seemed to me to be very confident. I'm glad you remember me because I need to explain about paying in this cheque.' Lisa put on a politely interested expression. 'I didn't change my little account to a business one, but I want to pay this into it.' She indicated the cheque again. 'It's a matured insurance policy but it's in my name only and I want to hang on to it.'

She lowered her voice. 'Things aren't going too well, either with the *Evening Post* or with my husband. We're getting to the end with each other and . . . you know?'

The woman shrugged and looked embarrassed and Lisa felt sorry for her. 'Don't worry about the cheque. It sounds as though you have plenty of other things on your mind. I'm really sorry.'

'Thank you. When we've worked through it all, it'll be good to have a bit of cash behind me to make a fresh start.'

Lisa completed the requested transaction. Ah, that was

the name – not Barker but Markey. The cheque was for twenty thousand pounds. Questions might be asked by Mrs Viner if such a large amount went into this account. 'It would help if I could record your plans for the money.'

The woman made a deprecatory gesture. 'I'd need to think about it. It might be enough to start a little business of my own – so I'd not be too dependent on what my solicitor can squeeze out of my husband. I don't want to rush into anything, though, and risk losing it all.'

Suddenly, Lisa felt all beneficence, all powerful. 'That's absolutely fine. Just leave it with me.'

Mitchell whistled as he prepared his person for his return to the station on Wednesday morning. Applying a comb to produce his usual painful neatness, he observed the odd grey hair in the tufts at his temples that he could never tame. He felt slightly indignant but undismayed. Today the sun was shining again, metaphorically at least.

The streets outside were full of summer rain. Mitchell dashed through it from his car to the foyer and greeted a surprised Magic with 'Top o' the mornin',' in his father's best Irish. Arriving in his office, he ruefully surveyed the cropped ivies and gave them a compensatory watering before settling down to read through the small pile of papers on his desk.

The team was glad to observe his change of mood. Jennifer paused to hope that Ginny was equally happy before she settled down to concentrate and Mitchell began to read to them from one of the papers he'd been studying.

'A bit more from the lab. The undercoat sequence on the paint fragments doesn't narrow the field any further but there's a comment on the pristine condition of the surface finish. The car is old but has had remarkable care. There's a further comment on the glass particles collected from the clothes. Most of them are green-tinted. Some have a flat surface and are probably window glass . . . then it gets technical. "There is some correspondence in the refractive index to the glass from the headlamp lens." Blah blah – it boils down to the conclusion that Donald Markey was struck first by the front of the car, below waist level, then hit on the head by the windscreen.'

'Isn't science wonderful? We knew that already. Ginny told us.'

Mitchell nodded to Jennifer. 'It at least underlines that she's a reliable witness.'

'We knew that as well.'

Mitchell accepted this compliment from Caroline, then gave the floor to Clement.

'The Fiat garage in Leeds has been delving into its records –'

'You tried to earn Brownie points by digging the poor manager out last night?'

'If you don't mind, I was in the Cubs, not the Brownies. Anyway, they say the broken plastic moulding was pretty certainly part of the housing of a door-mounted mirror made by a firm called Vitaloni. It was a standard fitting on the Fiat Uno.'

'Right, Adrian. For your first job, can you –'

Clement looked smug. 'Did it as soon as I came in – pulled out every blue or green Fiat Uno and every vehicle without a model name on. Two have been stolen.'

'Only two? We're in luck.'

'Not specially. There aren't many of them still about. One is described as aquamarine, as the manufacturer says, and the other as greenish. The former disappeared from Penzance and the latter from Glasgow.'

'What about times?'

'The Cornish one disappeared last Thursday morning and the other early on Saturday morning, the same day as our incident.'

'They're both long shots. I should think we could rule the Scottish one out.'

But Clement had the bit between his teeth. 'You can

easily drive from Glasgow to here in a day. I'll follow them both up.'

'We can't forget the possibility that the car was not stolen, just used by its owner.'

Clement nodded. 'The owner would be anxious to repair the damage. We'll need to check all the repairs done since Saturday night to all the remaining Unos in the right colour and registered since 1983. Do you think all the local forces will wear that?'

Mitchell grinned. 'I think we'd better ask them ourselves rather than getting the super to arrange it. With luck they'll have done it for us before he gets round to finding out and cancelling. Smithson, how did the victim's wife respond to your fatherly approach?'

Smithson protested. 'The woman's forty-nine. I assure you I hadn't got round to seducing anyone at the tender age of –'

'All right, you needn't reveal all.'

'I felt as if she was interviewing me.'

'Tell me about it!' Caroline put in feelingly.

'She said, when I asked about the rivalry for her husband's promotion . . .' He fished in his chest pocket and produced his notebook, '"I'm surprised you're asking me. What makes you think I was there? Or that either of them confided his interview tactics to me, before or after the event?"' They were used to Smithson's verbatim reports and no longer marvelled at them. 'When I asked her about changing her clothes just before leaving for the party she seemed less self-assured. Said she didn't even know herself. She was uneasy about the whole evening. It wasn't her sort of occasion and that was all she could tell me.'

Mitchell had a sudden whim to meet for himself the woman who had resisted being both managed by Caroline and persuaded by Smithson.

Mitchell had often walked past the Markeys' house and garden and approved of them. Everything was always clean and neat and never marred by dying flower heads. Now, walking through the greenness towards the door, he felt differently. This garden had lost something. It was huge, so there was room for a soothing green retreat with plenty of space left for flowers. These folk could well afford a gardener if they were too lazy to dead-head for themselves.

He rang the bell with difficulty, since he had both arms wrapped round the cardboard carton of documents. Returning them was the ostensible reason for his visit. When Phyllida let him in, he offered to take the box to the office upstairs. She shook her head and indicated the corner below the hall window. He obediently deposited it there.

Shown into the sitting room, he accepted a cup of coffee he didn't want. What he did want was time to absorb the atmosphere of the place and learn as much as he could from the room about the woman who had created it. He wandered round, examining objects and furnishings, looking askance at the weird collection of glass bottles, each with its separate flower. He disapproved too of the photographs, scattered over every surface. Still, he supposed that Phyllida Markey had someone else to do her dusting.

The room satisfied his craving for order but it didn't look very lived in. It had no pictures on the walls. His own sitting room had one wall devoted to the original artwork of his offspring – some of it very original. He had, though, insisted that it should all be slipped into cheap frames and hung up tidily.

To Mitchell's delight, whilst his mother was busy in the kitchen, her son wandered into the room. He had grown a startling amount since Mitchell had last seen him, before he had been sent away to school. The boy stood staring. Mitchell greeted him and waited. Zak was not in the least overawed, offering, for Mitchell's information, 'You're Declan's father.'

Mitchell had carefully read Shakila's report on her conversation with the boy. He'd admired her technique. She'd asked what seemed like irrelevant questions about spending imaginary money and been given more information about the way his mother stifled him than direct questions would have produced.

He cudgelled his brain for a similarly off-beat approach. He had always considered himself good with children. He should be. He had enough practice at home. 'Declan wants me to buy him a chameleon as a pet,' he volunteered, hoping something useful would transpire, though not quite seeing how.

Zak wrinkled his nose. 'That's an insect, isn't it? What on earth does he want one of those for?'

Why indeed? Mitchell had had no great hopes that the subject would link up with his enquiry. Perhaps Shakila was successful because she believed that she would get what she wanted, had faith in herself.

Zak's thoughts too had apparently turned to Shakila. 'Did you send that black police lady? She said I was rude.'

'And were you?'

'Yes.' It was a statement of fact, offered with neither pride nor contrition. 'Why do the police keep coming?'

'Because we're trying to find out who was driving the car that . . .' Mitchell hesitated, trying to find the least distressing way of completing the sentence.

'That knocked my father down and killed him,' the boy offered helpfully. 'Well, we don't know. It would be better if you asked somebody else. I was telling the black lady about my father's lady friends.'

'Really?'

'She didn't ask me about my mother's boyfriends.' He paused suggestively.

Mitchell, after a hard struggle, resisted the temptation and confined himself to a nod. 'Right.'

Zak wandered over to a table, took a pack of cards from his pocket and began to spread them, face downwards. Mitchell recognized the box and the game. It could last for ever and it was Caitlin's usual ploy, as bedtime approached, to spread out her own pack and beg to be allowed, 'just to finish this game'.

Phyllida Markey appeared with a tray. She seemed displeased at the sight of her son in the company of the DCI but relaxed when she saw the game spread in front of them. With a sly wink at Mitchell, the boy hurriedly launched into a garbled explanation of the rules. His mother dismissed him to his room with the bribe of a game later in the day, before settling Mitchell into one of the huge cream armchairs. It allowed his broad, muscle-bound person the room to be comfortable. She sat opposite to him and waited in silence.

Mitchell commiserated with her as a neighbour, mentioning a rugby match in which both he and Donald Markey had once played and commenting on the slight friendship between their sons. In return, she thanked him for Virginia's visit, of which he had been unaware.

He had planned his introductory remarks and questions for this interview very carefully. The Markeys' bank had been reluctant to co-operate with their investigation. Mitchell knew that it was unlikely that his superintendent would put his weight behind the request. Indeed, he would be horrified if he knew that Mitchell had made his wholesale confiscation of papers from the Markeys' office. He wondered if the contents of the carton represented all their financial affairs and whether Lloyds was the only bank where either of the Markeys held accounts. The records he had found and that Sefton had produced so readily might not be giving them the whole picture. He grinned to himself. Perhaps he would be able to delight Clement with some more computer work.

Mitchell began with a few innocuous questions which PC Whitham had already answered but which he hoped would set his witness at her ease. Phyllida herself raised the subject of Donald's insurance policy on his own life. Mitchell listened carefully, then casually remarked, 'Our financial wizard wondered why it was taken out with the Prudential when all your other –'

Phyllida anticipated the rest of the question. 'Donald didn't want this first little approach to his own financial adviser to be part of my family package. Sean suggested someone. He usually works with Virgin, apparently, and could get Donald a good deal with them – not special terms exactly, but smooth running and a favourable attitude.'

'You knew your husband had consulted Sefton then?'

She nodded. 'Donald was very proud of having discovered him. He was continually telling me what he had learned and how quickly. He even claimed to have taught Sean a trick or two of his own. Sean indulged him – was very good at managing him by flattery.'

'Did your husband realize that you too –'

'Of course not. Actually, he did very little work for me. Once I'd explained my dilemma, he didn't charge me for keeping an eye on Donald's affairs. He said he was making enough from him. My husband hadn't been brought up having spare money. I didn't want to patronize him but I didn't want him to learn the hard way.'

'So, Sefton guided Mr Markey through the insurance maze and they went on from there.'

'Actually Sean did all the transactions for the policy without either of us. When the forms arrived, Donald was away on a course and I was in bed with flu. He took in all the documents they wanted to see, filled in the forms for us and so on. Donald and I just signed – after having him talk us through things, of course.' She smiled. 'He organized the filing system upstairs. I shall leave him to put back all that stuff you've dumped in the hall.'

She had seemed so willingly co-operative and informative that Mitchell was shocked when she added, 'I presume, at some point, that you will explain to me how all this interest in our financial affairs is going to help you find the driver of that green car.'

He was saved for the immediate moment from replying

by the reappearance of Zak, demanding his lunch. Mitchell was politely dismissed and he escaped thankfully towards the front door. Zak shook hands with him, saying goodbye very formally. Then, with a malicious grin, he added, 'It didn't matter about the black lady not asking because my mother doesn't have boyfriends.'

Phyllida looked from Mitchell to her son, gave the former a single nod and opened the door. Mitchell made a hasty departure. To try to explain would only have been to make the situation worse. He drove his car along the road, round the corner and into his own drive. There, he sat and thought over what he had learned. He had a feeling that he had missed something. Sefton had been helpful enough the previous morning. How much more pressure could he put on him to reveal all? It might be useful too to ring both the insurance companies Phyllida had mentioned, though he was not sure what he was looking for from any of these people.

He cheered up as he realized that he might, after all, have persuaded young Zak to contribute an idea. His mother had looked less than comfortable at the boy's denial of her putative, illicit love life. Zak had merely seemed triumphant at having embarrassed both adults. Perhaps Caroline would be the best person to sniff out any extraneous men in the new widow's life. Hadn't she felt that Eric Simpson might have more to reveal? She could start asking her questions there.

Caroline was glad of an opportunity to return to the Simpsons' house. She was fairly sure that Eric had not been the driver of the car that Clement was still zealously seeking, though his alibi was not quite as watertight as Phyllida Markey's. He would have been a set piece in the school hall, taken for granted, but, she imagined, conspicuous by his absence. Like a picture that no one bothered to look at that was missed when somebody took it down from the wall.

The garden smelt fresh and earthy after the morning rain which had stopped only a short while ago. Now the sun reflected dazzlingly from the granite chips in the surface of the drive and from drops of water cradled in leaves and petals. Before she rang the doorbell, Caroline paused to admire an extravagance of yellow lupins.

This time, it was Nicky Simpson who opened the door to her. Caroline followed her up the hall, mentally rehearsing the questions she wanted the couple to answer. On her first visit here, armed only with the information gleaned from Saturday night's preliminary questions, she had expected to dislike them. In the file notes, Nicky had come over as predatory and greedy and Eric as weak. On meeting them, she had found that she liked both of them and hoped neither of them proved to be implicated in Donald Markey's death.

Nicky offered her a choice of sitting-room chairs, then settled herself opposite Caroline. There was no sign of Eric. The room reflected his innate preference for elegant simplicity, though it was marred by Nicky's little peccadilloes. They were small but significant and interfered with Caroline's enjoyment of the cool pastels. She was particularly offended by a cushion with a fussy pleated frill, an illustration of Eric's tolerance and indulgence.

Caroline blinked when, observing her visitor's attention to it, Nicky remarked, 'That cushion offends me more each time I see it, but Eric chose it, bless him.' Caroline reminded herself that Nicky was French. Her remark had been revealing. It had also sounded nervous. Time to cash in.

She pulled from her pocket a smallish, oblong leather case. She opened it, her eyes on her interviewee. Nicky looked convincingly puzzled, then shocked, as Caroline allowed the gold and diamond bracelet to hang from her finger and thumb, catching the light and dazzling them both. 'Do you recognize this?'

Nicky looked for a long moment, then nodded, not

meeting the DC's eye. Caroline waited a full twenty seconds before Nicky asked, 'Did he buy it for me?'

Caroline didn't pretend to misunderstand. 'Yes, but since he obviously hadn't handed it over, it now belongs to Phyllida.'

Nicky tore her eyes away from the stones, went over to the window and seemed to gaze at a point in the middle of the lawn. Without turning, she asked, 'Can't it just go back to the shop without Phyl knowing?'

Caroline had been asking herself the same question. She didn't answer it. Instead she said, her tone making the words an invitation rather than a command, 'Tell me about it.'

'He bought it from Beckham's in Leeds, I imagine. That was where we saw it.'

'How long ago?'

Nicky came back to her chair and tucked her feet up on it. 'About a fortnight. We only met by chance. At least, that was what I thought at the time.' Caroline raised a questioning eyebrow, showing close attention without interrupting the flow. 'I had a hospital appointment, just routine, nothing serious. I mentioned it to Donald as my excuse for refusing an invitation to have lunch with him. He knows I always spoil myself after going to the Infirmary – with coffee and cake at Betty's.

'He came in with another man who soon left and then Donald came over to my table. He asked me if I could spare the time to help him choose a present for his goddaughter. I was surprised he had one. I couldn't see him taking that sort of interest in a child – or associating with churchy people who'd give their child a christening. Anyway, we went to Beckham's and bought a charm bracelet. Pretty thing – a silver chain and the dangling bits were all ballerinas. He said the girl was ballet mad. He let me pick it and didn't show much interest. In fact, neither did the saleswoman. She was very casual. I think now that he'd set me up and the shop knew about it. We began looking at other things – all the stock was gorgeous – and then the saleswoman was much more chatty.'

Nicky grinned and rearranged herself in the chair. 'I bet he took the charm bracelet back and that the goddaughter doesn't exist. They wouldn't mind doing the paperwork, considering the profit they must have made on that.' She waved towards the leather box in which the treasure was now safely shut away.

'So you know what it cost?' Nicky nodded but didn't mention the amount. Caroline was unperturbed but also undeceived. 'Surely you realized what was going on?'

She coloured. 'Why should I? It's not my birthday till December.'

Having been given the information she needed, Caroline was happy to change the subject. 'Your husband believes Phyllida was very tolerant of her husband's womanizing.' She saw that Nicky was rather affronted by the expression.

'There wasn't much she could do about it. She knew I wasn't interested in him any more.'

'But he was in you?'

'Yes.'

'Did Phyllida ever show any sign that she was paying him back in his own coin?'

Nicky laughed. 'Who'd want to be the man?' Caroline watched her remember that she was not talking now to ever-understanding, ever-excusing Eric. She blushed furiously and her question hung in the air between them. 'I need to make a mental apology to Phyl but not to you.' Her tone was belligerent.

'True.'

'Anyway, the sort of man Phyl respects – and she wouldn't have any sort of relationship with one she didn't – wouldn't have affairs.'

'And do you think she respected Donald?'

'No, but in her own funny way she loved him. She wouldn't have done anything to hurt him.'

When Caroline asked to speak to Eric she was told he

was writing. Caroline could hear faint strains of music coming from upstairs. 'It sounds as though he's taking a break and, important though his publisher's deadline is, I think he'd agree that a police investigation takes precedence.' Nicky gave in and allowed Caroline to go upstairs and announce herself.

Halfway up, she recognized the sound of Dire Straits. Mark Knopfer was asking, 'Why worry?' Caroline had a sizeable collection of rock music of her own and admired the group. Of what skulduggery could she suspect a Dire Straits fan?

As she reached the top of the stairs she could hear that the singer was being accompanied by a rhythmic drone, its pitch varying by little more than a semitone. It took her several seconds to realize that Eric was singing along with Mr Knopfer and she warmed to the man more strongly than before. He was unaware of the absurdity of the sound he was making because he had become lost in the sentiment of the song, or else mesmerized by the soothing regularity of the melody. And, maybe, to his ears, he was reproducing the tune. He had made himself vulnerable because he had responded to the stimulus of the music, like a cat that rolled on its back when its stomach was tickled.

It reminded her of a time long ago when she had sat in the front row of a choir many miles from Cloughton. Her father had sat in the row behind, bawling his heart out, occasionally sharp but usually flat. Her bones had seemed to melt as she listened, her musicality offended but her affection for him daring anyone to comment. It was as though he had lost a protective skin so that a breath of criticism would injure him physically.

She waited until the song was over before she rapped on the study door, then apologized for disturbing him. He waved her to a chair, making no excuse for his own performance, merely observing, 'A bit of a change from Mozart.' After a few seconds' pause, he added, 'I'm glad you're here, I want to make a confession and you're the one officer who might understand.'

PC Khalid Jain was out of uniform and clad in the sort of jeans and sweatshirt that would give him the street cred he needed tonight. He was sitting on the wall that surrounded the car park of the Fleece, admiring the scenery. Behind him the land dropped until it disappeared into the smoky haze that was Cloughton, only the odd church spire, mill building and three tower blocks showing sharply above the fug caused by the working day.

PC Jain preferred the scene in front of him. In the field alongside the pub, sorrel and buttercups stippled the green with red and yellow. In the little pub garden to his left the beds were colourful and the flagstones decorated with an intricate shadow pattern as the sun began to drop behind a leafless tree strangled by ivy.

Half his attention was reserved for two youths, one black and tall, the other white, small and slight, who, having made their flashy motor bike secure, approached the door to the bar. Unobtrusively, Jain slipped in behind them. The Asian youth he knew slightly. At Mitchell's command and to his own chagrin he had grovelled and apologized to him for an arrest that, in his own opinion, had been fully justified, though insufficiently backed by the kind of evidence the court would accept. The smaller, blond youth he knew very well indeed.

When the two, pints in hand, were safely occupied with the gaming machines in the corner, Jain risked crossing to the bar to buy his own drink. He remained there to consume it, a quarter turned away from the counter, so that the youths were still visible out of the corner of his eye. He would find a seat if and when the boys settled at a table.

For now, it suited him that they should play their games and drink freely. By the time they tired of the trivial entertainment their tongues would be flowing freely too and he'd see what he could learn from their indiscreet chatter. He had no intention of bringing up the matter of under-age drinking. For now it was irrelevant. He knew that circumstances dictated the decisions of every street copper. Whether he took action on an untaxed car or a stone through a window would depend on his workload, on what the law-abiding locals expected and on how near it was to the end of his shift. Or, in this case, how much he could learn about a more serious offence by ignoring a misdemeanour.

Tonight he was concentrating on stolen computers, though, if either of the lads drank more than another half, which they certainly would, he'd make sure they didn't go home on the bike outside. He took a deep swig from his glass, checked the boys again, then let his thoughts wander. He was quite enjoying his secondment to Mitchell's team and was amused by the DCI's desperate attempts to turn Donald Markey's hit-and-run into a full-blown murder enquiry. It was interesting to work for this officer about whom rumour was rife, favourable to him or not according to whether the speaker liked his punches pulled. Mitchell did not. Jain liked him, on the whole. He was human, fair – and a loose cannon: an unusual combination.

Jain considered whether he liked the idea of being permanently transferred to CID and decided he did not. He enjoyed his ordinary work, knew and loved his patch and felt a slight contempt for the plain-clothes men. He made an exception of Clement who, on his daily run, had made himself as familiar with Cloughton's backstreets as he was himself. They both knew where the potential high-crime areas were – that isolated all-night petrol station on the Bradford road, the poorly lit parking lot behind Crossley Heath library, the disused warehouse up the hill from the bus station . . .

They were also both on first name terms with many of the local petty criminals – thieves, minor drug dealers, prozzies. It was why he was here now, where he knew young Shaun Grant, three weeks out of jug, would be commiserating with Javed Khan on his unfortunate arrest and probably claiming the credit for his subsequent release. Tonight they'd be enjoying the force's discomfiture along with their ale. Jain intended to have the last laugh, however many off-duty hours it cost him.

Ah, they were tiring of their electronic games. They would not have had much appeal for Shaun, who had known how to cheat them since he was eight. Jain ordered himself another pint as the lads settled themselves at the smallest table in the dark corner in front of the door to the cloakrooms. It was usually the last one to be taken. Excellent. Now, at the right moment he could slip into the end one of the three adjoining bays and possibly hear some of their conversation. That was, provided no one switched on the TV.

Shaun had taken the chair facing the wall, probably for his own protection. That suited Jain. Khan was facing him, but probably would not recognize him in civvies. Even when its wearer was apologizing, people tended to look at the uniform rather than the face. So far the boys were talking football. Jain was disgusted. Wasn't the cricket season short enough without stealing its thunder in July? After a while, he began to think the two young villains had recognized him. Their argument was not heated enough to be genuine and he had never, in the past, found that Shaun took any interest in the game.

The sole occupant of the next bay emerged to replenish his glass. His back view seemed vaguely familiar and, when the man turned with his brimming pint, Jain recognized him. He put down his own glass and was wondering whether to make himself known when both men were distracted by the entry of a striking-looking woman. She made her way towards them and disappeared from Jain's view, presumably seating herself beside his acquaintance. 'Surprise!' he heard her announce.

Her welcome was less enthusiastic than she seemed to expect. The conversation was conducted in angry whispers. Jain listened, intrigued, feeling thankful for a quiet

176

midweek evening, warm and pleasant enough to keep the majority of noisy drinkers outside even at nine thirty.

'What the hell are you doing here?'

'Waiting for somebody to buy me a drink.'

'Do you have to be so bloody stupid?'

'I'm bloody thirsty. I've been talking all day, saying what you told me, going where you told me –'

'Move further over, right into the corner!'

The tone changed from angry to hurt. 'You didn't tell me not to come.'

'I thought your own bloody common sense would tell you. How on earth did you know that I'd be in here?'

Jain cursed a group of newcomers, standing in the doorway and shouting to their companions outside to hurry themselves. When they had retired with their pints to the billiard room, the conversation on the other side of the screen was still in progress. The woman was getting angry. 'I have work of my own to do. I can't just walk –'

'You could have applied for some leave.'

'You could have given me some warning. It's all right for you, working for yourself. You can go where you like when you like.' The woman's voice was rising.

He hastened to soothe her. 'All right, I know. You're here now. What shall I get you?'

'Gin.'

'What? Why?'

'Because I'm sick of being your slave, always doing what you expect me to do . . .'

Questions, ideas, even a theory or two were beginning to form in Jain's head. He grabbed his notebook and jotted down the gist of the exchange. There was another thing he could do, but he'd have to be quick. An influx of customers from outside had surrounded the bar making queuing necessary. Good. He took out the tiny camera he kept permanently about his person and walked over to a nearby couple who happened to be his neighbours.

He gave them a broad wink and explained, in a voice loud enough for the woman to hear, 'I'm making a composite picture for the pub wall – you know, customers enjoying themselves. Give me a big smile, please.' The woman in the bay behind him looked up, startled by the flash, and he pressed the shutter again before she could either turn or object. He moved on quickly. While he was about it, he might as well have a picture of Shaun Grant passing on his trade secrets to his newest recruit.

DC Shakila Nazir, having spent six months creating her minimalist flat, had recognized its sterility and sold it. Three months ago, she had bought a stone-built, mid-terrace house with four tiny rooms, one of them halved to accommodate a shower. She loved it and was enjoying herself exploring its location in detail.

This morning, with her car in a nearby garage suffering its MOT, she stood, waiting for the bus that would take her into town, and surveyed what was now her main shopping street. It contained three public houses and a useful variety of fast food outlets – fish and chips, Indian, Chinese and the traditional corner caff offering variations on pastry and chips and dark tan-coloured tea served in thick pint mugs. She had sampled them all and found fault only with the last.

The bus queue was encroaching on the forecourt of the only remaining general store, which opened eighteen hours a day. This morning, as always, it was being patronized by a selection of black and white children, the younger strictly shepherded by the older, exchanging sweaty coins for a breakfast of Kit Kat bars and cans of Coke.

Shakila saluted them, then fell to analysing her lack of enthusiasm for the day ahead. One concern was that her beloved Renault 4, canary yellow decorated with rust, would be found beyond cure. Financially, it would be slightly inconvenient to replace it just now, but she cared less about the money than about losing an old friend and having to get used to a new one. Another cause for irrita-

178

tion was that, yesterday, her DCI had had the opportunity she had wanted for herself of a few minutes alone with Zak Markey. She was sure that she could have got him to say more than he had told Mitchell.

The bus lumbered round the corner. The children stopped terrorizing the shop assistant and made to hurl themselves on to it in front of the queue. Without comment, the waiting adults watched Shakila line them up and wait until their elders, though not necessarily their betters, were aboard. With no resentment, the children clambered up the stair. She made to follow them and continue her supervision and the driver, more grateful than the queue, offered her free transport whenever he was on duty. She laughed and began to plan her day in a better frame of mind.

Finding herself the first to arrive in the incident room, she examined the noticeboard for new additions until Mitchell joined her. Since he seemed to be in a good mood, she tackled him with a point that had been bothering her. 'Sir, are we conducting a murder enquiry or not?'

Mitchell winked, put his finger to his lips and spoke in a melodramatic whisper. 'I am. Superintendent Carroll isn't. You lot are just doing as you're told.' He abandoned the whisper. 'So far as the powers that be and the media are concerned, this is an accidental death, though we do have permission to throw the book at this driver for his recklessness and for not stopping.

'We're still being left to get on unsupervised thanks to Adrian making headway with tracing the car. Eventually, the super thinks his putative drunk will be picked up, will make his feeble excuses in court and be given six months! Then, he'll be a very good boy and only have to serve three. That's what we flog our guts out for.'

'So, what's your plan?' Mitchell glowered but Shakila remembered the bus driver's admiration and pressed on. 'We're doing as we're told. You're doing the telling. We want to know what you're thinking. In fact, we need to know.'

179

'All right.'

'All right what?'

'I'll tell you what I'm thinking, but not twice. You'll have to wait till the others arrive. Anything else, constable?'

Shakila grinned. 'Yes. What's a putative drunk?'

'One that only exists in the super's head – and that's the last unprofessional remark you're getting this morning.' He began to arrange papers on his desk.

Shakila got out her pocketbook and went over her own notes. Neither of them looked up until the room was full and the clock on the wall registered the half-hour.

Mitchell stood and greeted his officers. They saw his half smile and waited for something out of the ordinary. 'I have received a request – no, a demand – to know the exact nature of the current investigation. I can't speak for my bosses, but I'd like to make it clear to all of you that I'm looking for a murderer. I believe someone wanted Markey dead and I'm going to find that someone. Carroll doesn't agree with me. If you do as your action sheets tell you, it leaves you out on the same limb where I am, which makes the tree a bit unsteady. It means you're having to choose which boss to obey. If anyone's uncomfortable with that they'll have to say. No hard feelings. Naturally, I'll carry the can for the rest of you. If I'm wrong, you'll fall with me but I'll make sure you fall soft.'

The room was silent, so that Smithson's slightly asthmatic breathing was evident. When no one spoke, Mitchell continued. 'The evidence that is all I have to support my conviction came from my own wife and I feel a little uncomfortable about that –'

Jennifer was the only one who dared interrupt. 'We've already dealt with that.'

'Thank you. The situation means that any other business that is sent our way has to be dealt with promptly and successfully. That will be our chief defence against criticism. Do you all understand where you are now?'

'I think you're saying,' Caroline summarized for them, 'that we get on with the day's business and, if we should happen to find ourselves anywhere near the places our action sheets mention, and if we have a spare moment, we can do what's on them in passing.'

Satisfied, Mitchell perched on the corner of his desk and beamed round. 'I'm glad I've made myself so clear. Now, go back in your minds to last Saturday night. Someone we haven't identified yet calls Donald Markey out of school between nine thirty and ten. That person or an accomplice is waiting for Donald to position himself at the particular place in the road where he makes a good target. It's almost dark – I think the timing of the call was not by the clock but by the degree of light – and the driver is expecting, going up that back road, not to be closely observed. He knows that the official car park is at the front of the school and he won't be expecting Ginny to be tucked into that little space by the bins. He probably doesn't notice her.

'He might have calculated that the odd garden in Moorside Rise will still be in use but most of them have overgrown hedges. It must be a facer for him when he sees the women sitting out on the pavement. So, why doesn't he abort his plan?'

They considered, then Jennifer suggested, 'Because he's already stolen the car.'

'Because a failed attempt would make Donald suspicious and more difficult to set up the next time?' Mitchell nodded approval of Shakila's theory.

PC Smithson added, 'He's already psyched up for it, acting like an automaton by then. He can't help completing what he's planned.'

'All right. Keep that scene in your minds till this whole enquiry is over.' Suddenly, Mitchell's tone changed. 'Where's Jain?'

A uniformed officer called out, 'He had a late night, sir.' Mitchell glowered until the man added, 'He's left an account of it on your desk, sir, and he's in hospital this morning. Got his foot run over by Shaun Grant's motor bike.'

Mitchell blinked, then turned to Clement. 'Any further on with the cars?'

Clement stood up. 'Yes and no. The Cornwall Fiat has been found on a cliff top. It's undamaged. The local force reckons it was joyriders who pushed it there when it ran out of petrol.'

'What about the Glasgow one?'

Clement shook his head. 'Nothing yet.'

'All right.' Mitchell reached for their action sheets. Taking the hint, his officers filed out, collecting their programmes for the day as they left. He indicated to his CID team and Smithson to remain behind. 'I'm sure you've all been using the file for your bedtime reading. Let's hear your random thoughts and questions.' When no one stirred, he went on, 'No, not all at once. Form an orderly queue, please.'

Smithson raised a hand. 'The little boy, Zak. Was he just making mischief or was he really giving you a hint that his mother had a gentleman friend?'

Mitchell was glad that somebody else had raised the question he had been asking himself. 'Caroline, you've seen a fair amount of her. What do you think? Might she have something going with Sefton?'

Caroline shook her head. 'No, it's Eric Simpson.'

'What makes you think that?'

Caroline grinned. 'Having him tell me about it gave me the idea.'

'So, what's happening between them?'

Caroline shrugged. 'I don't know how much he was playing it down – or even making it up. He was looking for Nicky one day. They'd made an arrangement to meet. It wasn't important to Nicky so she'd forgotten and didn't turn up. He tried the Markeys because he knew she'd been with them earlier. Phyllida suspected that she was out somewhere with Donald. Uncharacteristically, she burst into tears. She said she was upset for Eric as much as herself. They talked, got hungry and went to an out-of-town restaurant for a meal together. They continued to see

182

each other, alone together, not often but over a long period. Neither, according to Eric, wanted to give up their own partner.'

'Was it a physical relationship?'

'I got the impression it was but I didn't ask specifically and he didn't say.'

'When was this? Last night?' She nodded. 'So, why is he telling us now?'

'Because of what Zak said to you, of course. Phyllida was very worried. She wasn't angry with the child, just concerned that it was on his mind. She saw what he said as his attempt to defend her.'

'I saw it as his chance to get his own back on her.'

'For what?'

'All manner of things – embarrassing him in front of his friends, treating him like a baby, taking him away from his school . . .'

'Well, whichever, Eric thought it better to confess than to be found out.'

Mitchell looked resigned. 'Put it in your report and we'll all meditate on it.'

Clement raised another matter. 'Phyllida Markey said her mother knew she and Donald would be up at the school. She disapproved of their marriage, didn't she?' Objections came thick and fast.

'He'd have known her voice, surely. She wouldn't have been able to lure him out.'

'It might depend on what she told him.'

'Whatever it was, he'd hardly have responded to her by pretending to arrange a slightly off-colour business deal.'

Clement subsided and Smithson spoke up. 'Why did you think, sir, that the Markeys had more bank accounts than we know about?'

'The bracelet, of course.' Shakila realized that the question had not been addressed to her and fell silent, waiting for a reprimand.

Mitchell merely nodded. 'I showed it to Phyllida as a seeming afterthought, when she thought I'd finished with her. It startled her. She said she'd never seen it before and I believed her. She had no problem in guessing why I'd brought it or where we might have found it. She admitted that, if she'd known it was there, she'd have taken it away. Now that Caroline's persuaded Nicky Simpson to tell us where it was bought, we don't have the tricky problem of getting it authenticated at the force's expense without the super finding out.'

The door opened behind him. Shakila, who was facing it, grabbed her action from the desk. 'Right, sir. First to Computer World and then to Shaun Grant's mother. Do you want the report at lunchtime or at evening prayers?'

Smiles at Shakila's quick wits were hastily concealed and the team left, with the exception of Clement, who had received John Carroll's nod to remain. It was to him that the superintendent handed the slip of paper he had brought.

Clement examined it as Carroll spoke to Mitchell. 'Clement's Glasgow car has been found – in Glasgow.'

Mitchell turned to his DC to commiserate, but saw he seemed quite pleased with his lot. Clement deferred to the superintendent, who explained. 'Your officer is looking too cheerful. The car was picked up on a housing estate on the outskirts of Glasgow. It is drivable but it has damage which is consistent with the hit-and-run incident we are investigating. That's good as far as it goes. The local force is doing the forensic tests for us, which is very generous, considering the brief we gave them.' He gave Mitchell a hard look. 'Let's be thankful for the milk of human kindness, eh?'

He turned, and Clement rushed to open the door for him before following him out to begin on Mitchell's plans for his morning. Mitchell heard the beginning of the lecture Clement was receiving. 'You realize, of course, that the idea that an unidentified fingerprint can be stuck into a computer and compared with all the prints on file is a myth . . .'

The voice grew fainter and Mitchell returned to his

musings on the diamond bracelet. Without asking Phyllida Markey the amount of her husband's allowance, he had gained the impression that it did not cater for presents costing several thousand pounds. Why spend so much? Had Markey really loved Nicky Simpson, been so desperate to get her back? He had plenty of motivation for opening a secret account. Apart from spending on his women, he must have been irked by having to go cap in hand to his wife for pocket money.

Where had the extra money come from? Possibly one of his investments had come up trumps. He could just have been lucky at the races. He'd have cashed in in a big way if he'd been reckless as well as lucky. Mitchell was sure Sefton knew something about it. There were almost certainly some facts that he had not disclosed and possibly others that he didn't know about. How could he make the man less discreet? Perhaps he should try him with a woman officer. He'd see what Jennifer came back with. In the meantime, he'd see if he himself could discover in which bank, if any, Donald Markey had been squirrelling away his winnings.

Chapter Eight

Having read the cryptic note from Jain that Magic had sent up to his office, Mitchell was tempted to make his hospital visit straightaway. Before he could decide on his immediate priorities, however, a further call from Magic announced the presence downstairs of 'an insurance chap, wants to talk about Markey.'

Mitchell felt a prickle of excitement. He had suspected, from the moment that the extent of Phyllida Markey's fortune became clear, that the motive for this killing was financial.

As the 'chap' was being escorted to his office, Jennifer appeared. 'I've been to –'

'Yes, I know. I sent you there. Anything exciting?' She shook her head. 'Well, this might be. Grab a chair and butt in when you feel led.'

The visitor arrived, brought by a civilian assistant who was sent off for refreshments. He wore highly polished shoes, a good suit, shirt and tie, but he was shrunken inside them. His features were gaunt and Mitchell suspected that his neatly combed hair was a wig. He offered both officers a firm handshake and took the chair he was given.

'Gordon Abson. I'm from the Norwich Union offices in Hill Street.' The voice was not shaky, but the man had to pause between phrases to draw more breath. His face was intelligent, his manner anxious. 'I've come because I noticed something unusual when I was checking the files this morning, before paying out on a claim. After I'd consulted a colleague, we both thought you should know about it. I should have noticed before. It's part of my responsibility to keep the cross-database up to date.'

Mitchell realized that, if he wanted to understand what he was being told, he would have to stay with the explanation, step by step. If he lost track he would miss the point that the man was painfully trying to make. 'Cross-database?' he asked.

His visitor smiled. 'There are in the region of a hundred brands of insurance available in this country at present, run by perhaps fifty independent companies. The lower tier brands are underwritten by the main companies – they come under our umbrella – but practise under their own separate names.'

'I see.' Mitchell acknowledged the coffee tray the girl brought in and busied himself pouring until Mr Abson was breathing more easily again. When the man was ready, he continued his account. 'Three different people have been doing my job in the last six months. The first retired. He was succeeded by a lady whose husband left her and she moved to York where her family lived. That left us in confusion. I took over as a temporary measure, but I have cancer and will have to retire before long. And, besides all this, we've been having the computers out.'

Jennifer grinned. 'Sounds painful.'

'Well, you know what I mean.' Mitchell was not sure that he did, but something important had brought this sick and worried man to his office and he'd wait to see what it was.

Abson had paused to settle his breathing again. Mitchell tried to prompt him out of his excuses and bring him back to the point. 'You said you'd noticed something unusual.'

Having justified his delay in noticing it, he became businesslike again. 'I saw that someone had taken out two small policies on the same life.'

'Is that not allowed?'

'I suppose it's allowable, but there doesn't seem much

point in it. It would be more sensible, for the same result, to pay a larger premium for one bigger pay-off.'

Jennifer was thinking furiously as she replaced her cup on the tray. 'Were they both Norwich Union policies, or was one of them for a brand name under your – umbrella, I think you said?'

'The latter. Maybe the insurer was not aware of the connection. Now, the insurance business is very suspicious. We're not fond of the unusual. Naturally, all our clients are hoping to get something from us and some of them are quite unscrupulous about it. So, the first thing I did was ring a friend who works for AXA. I found that they had a policy there, taken out by the same insurer and on the same life.' Mitchell flashed Jennifer a glance that he hoped she would take as a warning against mentioning the Markeys at this point. 'That's still not illegal, nor against either of the companies' rules.'

'Was the insurer hedging his bets, making sure he hit the jackpot even if one of his companies went bust?'

'I'm afraid we didn't think anything so charitable as that. However, my first consideration was the death certificate. It stated that the death was accidental and so I had been instructed to check the policy and then pay out the contracted amount.'

'Yes?'

'As I've said, I consulted a colleague about the whole matter. Mrs Kyte told me that you had questioned her and her husband because he had attended the function at the school that evening. She said that you seemed to be treating the accident as a suspicious death. I was very surprised because I had seen nothing about it in the local paper beyond a brief mention of the unfortunate incident.'

It suddenly occurred to Mitchell that the superintendent's attitude to this investigation had at least protected them from being hassled by the press. He smiled at his witness. 'I believe we're all talking about the hit-and-run incident that killed Donald Markey.'

188

'So, you are looking into the possibility of a crime having been committed.'

Mitchell took this speech to be a comment, not a question and continued, 'And your colleague, Mrs Kyte – would she be Jane Kyte, wife of the Reverend Neville Kyte, the incumbent of St Margaret's Church?' Abson nodded. 'Was the payment made?'

'That's it, you see. We don't know whether . . .'

Mitchell did see. 'What I'd like you to do, Mr Abson, is to ring your client and describe all the awkward circumstances you've mentioned to me – the painful computer operation and your changes of personnel. Give him the impression that the money will be paid when the little glitches have been sorted out, but don't, on any account, pay him anything. Meanwhile, you could help us a great deal with some technical information. First, though, I insist that you have a short rest.'

'But I have to get back.'

'Your employers won't make any bones about your absence if I make your excuses.' But Mitchell suspected that what was worrying the man was what his employers might think of his being at the police station at all. 'I promise to tell them that it was me who called you in.'

When Mitchell rang Cloughton Royal Infirmary to enquire after Constable Jain and request permission to visit him, he was not too surprised to hear that, with the doctor's grudging permission, Mr Jain was on his way home in a taxi. He would not only walk again, but would be getting around, in a fashion, very soon. If he was Mr Jain's employer, the redoubtable sister commanded, he was not to suggest that getting around meant getting back to work.

Mitchell decided that there would not be much wrong with Jain's tongue and that the cryptic note he had received from him required an explanation. He therefore rang Jain's home number, but received no reply. The mystery was soon solved by a message from the desk sergeant. Constable Jain had just presented himself, on crutches. He was wanting to know if the DCI would mind coming to meet him downstairs.

Mitchell made a rapid mental survey of the ground floor and decided there was nowhere hospitable enough for an invalid. Sudden inspiration struck. 'Magic, there used to be a wheelchair at the back . . .'

'Still there.'

'Can you send someone –'

'Go myself. Shift's over in four minutes.'

'Thanks. Tell Jain I'll wheel him up myself.'

Ten minutes later, true to his word, Mitchell was pushing a sadly ancient and wheezy invalid carriage towards the lift to the accompaniment of ironic cheers and concerned enquiries from whomever they passed.

Having negotiated the lift and reached his office, Mitchell parked the chair and went over to his desk to retrieve Jain's missive. Then, he stood, holding the scruffy piece of paper in one hand, regarding his constable solemnly. 'I heard that you'd left a report on my desk. I can't find it.'

Jain blinked. 'It's in your hand, sir.'

Mitchell placed the offending document back on his desk and read from it. '"Spent four hours in the Fleece, Wednesday evening – in the furtherance of my duties, naturally. Verbal report to follow and pics in due course."' Mitchell let ten seconds pass before adding, 'Perhaps you'd like to give me your definition of "report".' Jain waited, trying to gauge the DCI's mood. 'I take it you won't be claiming those four hours as overtime, or putting the pints you consumed on your expenses sheet.'

Jain decided that, in spite of what he considered his coup, he had better conduct himself more according to protocol. 'I'll write the report, first chance I get, sir.'

Mitchell grinned. 'I'll make do with the verbal one you promised me for now. I've heard that your foot's going to mend. How painful is it?'

Jain scowled. 'Take no notice of the quacks. I can get on with the job in a fashion and I've got enough painkillers to make away with myself and those two villains.'

'Don't do anything to them till we've got the Markey family sorted out. I can only deal with one murder case at a time. You promised me some pictures. Been painting for me, have you? I didn't realize we had an artist in the ranks.'

'I'm not –'

'I think you are, actually. I saw your "On the Job" entry in the *Review*. I don't know much about the technical aspects of photography but I was impressed. You caught the urgency and boredom, the fear, even our smug satisfaction when we're ordering the public about.' Jain stared at his feet and Mitchell felt his embarrassment with him. He recognized himself in the lad, and knew he had had more practice in defending himself when he'd spoken out of turn than in accepting a compliment graciously. 'Well, let's hear about this self-appointed vigil in the Fleece then.' He came to sit in an armchair opposite the constable.

Jain leaned back cautiously in his conveyance and fished in his top pocket for his notebook. With its help, he gave Mitchell an account of what he had seen and heard the previous evening, pleased with the rapt attention it received. 'Young Grant was definitely rattled when I flashed the camera in his face. He jumped up and deliberately tried to make me drop it, hoping he could stamp on it "by accident". It was on a cord round my neck, as always when I'm using it, so no harm was done. I could see the pair of them trying to remember what they'd been talking about all night. I realized I'd been wrong about them having sussed me.'

'And what had they? Talked about, I mean.'

Jain shook his head. 'Not a lot to interest us, but Khan made an offer to "join in on Friday night".'

'Details?'

'None. Shaun refused him. He said, "They might still be watching you," but that was all.'

191

Mitchell nodded. 'And your other customer? Who was the woman – his significant other or a professional partner or colleague that he doesn't treat very well?'

'She said she had work of her own.'

'Well, maybe they each had a separate list of clients. He's obviously the boss, though. Seems to have pulled her off her own duties to run around helping him with his.'

Jain shook his head. 'I don't think it sounded like that. I don't think they even work together. She was furious because he could work for himself, was a free agent. It suggested that she would have a different job with regular hours. He told her she should have taken some leave. If he was her boss that wouldn't have made sense. Anyway, does that matter? We've no reason to think his quarrel with some strange woman has much to do with his dealings with Donald Markey.'

'If you really think that, why did you bother coming to me with all this?' Mitchell was tight-lipped. 'Anything that happens to anyone connected to Donald Markey matters. You say you've got a picture of this woman?'

'I haven't developed it yet. I'll do it as soon as I get home.'

'Don't do anything the hospital told you not to. Can you develop a film sitting down? We can always get it done in the police lab.'

Jain was adamant. 'No sweat. I'll get some lunch and then do it this afternoon. Bring it in as soon as it's done. And I might as well bring in one of our light-fingered friends while I'm about it.'

'Right, then. So, if the woman's not his employee or colleague, then she's got to be his girlfriend, fiancée, live-in partner or whatever.'

Jain paused, trying to project himself back to the scene. 'What would fit in with my impression, sir, is that she used to have some sort of romantic association with him and has been demoted to just being his errand girl. I definitely didn't get the feeling that the work she did to earn a living was for him. She hoped he'd be pleased to see her and she was upset when he wasn't. Towards the end of the evening, it got noisier and I only heard the odd phrase. Two things I noted, though. In one little lull I caught something about her risking her job.'

'Perhaps she's taken time off before for him.'

Jain nodded. 'The last thing I've noted is an accusation from her to him. "You'll end up marrying this one."'

'An accusation? It could just have been a prediction.'

'It was in the tone she used. I think that might be the reason why she turned up, to see whether she looked like losing him to some other woman – and also why he was put out when he saw her.'

'He didn't address her by name?'

'I didn't catch it if he did. He wasn't just surprised to see her, he was horrified. He didn't want anyone else to see her, shoved her into the far corner of the bay.' Jain scowled impatiently. 'Why can't we just pull him in and ask him?'

'Not yet. Get your pictures done, keep your eyes open and we'll wait . . .' He overrode the objection Jain opened his mouth to make. '. . . till we've got enough leverage to persuade him to tell us all about it. My job's on the line over this, so don't argue. Meantime, once your studio portraits are fit for the high standard of the noticeboard in the incident room, maybe someone can find out what Shaun Grant has lined up for himself on Friday night. If little friend Khan was miffed at his snub, maybe he'll want to tell us what a bad boy he nearly fell under the influence of.'

Jain laughed. 'I shouldn't be surprised if I misheard that bit of conversation, sir, and Javed puts me right. What really happened was that Shaun was trying to lead him astray and get him involved, but he bravely resisted.'

Mitchell said, his face solemn, 'And, if that's the case, you'll have the pleasure of offering him another apology.'

The man sought by Mr Abson and, subsequently, by Mitchell's team had finished the part of his business that had been keeping him in Cloughton. Now, the quicker he was out of the town, in fact as far from it as he could conveniently travel, the better. Swiftly, he loaded his car with most of the objects from his rented accommodation that held any value for him.

He had realized some time ago that, when it was time to go, he would have to leave in a hurry. His preparations had been half completed before that time arrived and he was soon finished. He had been careful to show no outward sign of undue haste and now drove his vehicle at a sedate pace towards the end of the street. He turned left towards the station and the centre of town although his first destination lay in the opposite direction. He was more than halfway to Bradford before he took the Leeds road.

No need to drive right to the centre, thank goodness. She'd better be ready when he got there. Better not have had second thoughts about taking a sickie and getting her packing done. She'd better not want to take much with her either. He was not sure yet what exactly he had in mind for her in the long term. Or in the short term, come to that. It might not be necessary for her to bring anything at all.

He saw, to his annoyance, that her car was parked outside the front of her house. He parked behind it and marched to the door. He knew she had been watching for him, had seen him arrive, but she let him ring the bell. She didn't answer it. Didn't answer until he leaned against it and its sound was continuous.

By the time she opened the door he was very angry. She could see that. Her voice broke as she told him, 'I'm not coming with you. You can't come in.'

He pushed roughly past her, then pulled her away from the door, slamming it. 'Get your coat on and come just as you are. If you've packed nothing then you're taking nothing. Into the car, now!'

She didn't trust her voice to utter another refusal but she sat down on a hall chair. He slapped her face hard, then stood back to allow her to do as he had told her. Her eyes watered as she stood up. She sniffled and felt for a handkerchief. Suddenly, she stepped sideways, kicked the chair towards him and ran down the hall towards the cloakroom.

With the chair to negotiate, he failed to reach it before she had flung herself in and locked the door. As he debated his next move, he heard her voice. 'Mr Dickinson, can you and Tom come round right now? My boyfriend's hitting me.'

He doubted whether she had her mobile phone on her person but he dared not take the risk. He slammed out of the house, flung himself into the car and drove off, scattering the gravel on the newly surfaced road.

'So, we see, forming before our eyes,' Mitchell was declaiming, melodramatically, 'an insurance scam. Mr Abson kindly explained to us exactly how it might work. The super has played into our villain's hands. If it had been known from the start that this was murder, then the company itself would have investigated, of course, and not paid out till what Mr Abson calls the proposer was proved to be whiter than white. There's no delay with payment if there's no suspicion. Once the policy and the death certificate are produced, it's plain sailing.'

'So he'll already have collected on at least some of the policies? That means he'll have scarpered by now.'

'Not so fast.' Mitchell waved a hand at Clement. 'Mr Abson's company is withholding for the time being because of what I've just explained to you. If our villain has tried his game with other companies, they might have come up with the goods already.'

Caroline was puzzled. 'How did he get round the medical examination?'

'No problem, apparently. For a very small dividend, there's what's called a free medical limit. He just has to find out what it is and take out a policy for slightly less.'

'So what did Mr Abson consider a very small amount?'

'It varies between twenty and fifty thousand pounds. For a payout below that, the insured person doesn't need to provide any medical evidence, not even a report from his GP. If all the questions are answered positively, the company won't check on the proposal form. The fraudster signs it himself and no one can check up on the signature because they've nothing to compare it with. The free limit gets smaller as the age of the assured person gets higher, but Donald Markey was only forty-one.'

Clement whistled. 'So, assuming an average take of thirty-five thousand and maybe ten policies, someone gets a nice little windfall.'

'Sounds easy,' Jennifer put in. 'I'm surprised more people don't try it.'

'Probably more than we realize do.'

There was silence as they all looked for loopholes.

'Don't you have to prove identity when you take out a policy?'

'Yes, but you can do it with just a driving licence or a marriage certificate. He wouldn't use a passport. That has a photograph.'

'Wouldn't the companies get suspicious if they were asked a lot of questions about this free medical limit?'

'They might be suspicious about people with incurable diseases, but they must have been prepared to take that risk when they introduced the exemption. In any case, matey could get all the information he needed from the junk mail these places send out through the post. It's all available on the Internet as well.'

Jennifer, ever cautious, put a temporary halt to the excitement. 'Well, we all know what we suspect, but what have we got so far that we can prove?'

'Three policies have been taken out on Donald Markey's life besides the one his wife admits to – probably, let's say possibly, more.'

Clement grinned at Caroline and answered in the same

vein. 'Donald Markey was killed last week – probably, let's say possibly, deliberately.'

Mitchell waited but no one produced any more established facts. 'All right. How are we going to prove what we suspect? Let's have some comments and theories.'

Caroline caught his eye. 'Didn't Phyllida Markey say that Donald lost his wallet?'

'That's right. When we asked her if anything unusual had happened that was all she came up with. You're suggesting that that was when the policies were taken out?'

Caroline, busily riffling through the pages of her pocket book, ignored Jennifer's question. 'Here it is. It had his driving licence in it, and his passport which couldn't be used.'

'Don't driving licences have pictures now?'

'Yes, but Donald's probably had his for twenty years or more. I think . . .' Caroline stopped speaking as Shakila, who had so far remained uncharacteristically silent, leapt up in her chair.

'Whatever is our customer going to do with all his cheques? He can't trot along to his usual bank and pay them in there. They'll all be in Phyllida's name. Do we think she's involved? Why bother when she's got more money already than she can spend? Someone using her name, when he'd finished trailing round all the insurance companies, would have to go round again, opening a different new account for paying in each cheque.'

Mitchell grinned at her. 'What about all the ID needed for that?'

'It would only need to be "borrowed" for a day. And it would have to be a woman doing this part at least to pay in cheques made out to Markey's supposed wife.'

They looked at each other, and then at Mitchell who was beaming. 'If Jain were here, he'd tell you he'd seen her. What's more, he's taken a photograph of her.'

They all turned to him. Shakila asked the question. 'So which of them is it?'

Mitchell shrugged. 'He's developing the picture this afternoon.'

'But doesn't he know . . .?'

'As he pointed out to me himself, with not a little resentment, he hasn't been sent to any of the women we've been taking a particular interest in. We'll have to wait till he's finished. He'll ring then and I'll send someone round. You'll have to be patient till then . . . Did I say something amusing?' They straightened their faces. 'So, back to what we suspect.'

'That John Sefton's our man.'

'Sean.' Clement looked puzzled. 'Sean Sefton, not John.'

'Sorry. I must have misheard.' Clement reddened as he realized that he had also let his DCI know that he had not read at least some of the reports in the file.

Mitchell, however, was concerned with another matter. 'My God! So did Neville Kyte. We have to get him. Go back to that phone call, the one that fetched Markey out of school. Our clerical friend heard it. Remember? He thought that Donald was quick-witted enough to pretend it was a business call when it was actually a woman. I've never had the impression that Donald was so devious. He seems to have been pretty brazen about his women. So, it really was a business call – or, at least, a hoax one. Like you, Adrian, Kyte misheard Sean for John. Not that it really matters now. We'd all got round to Sefton already. Nobody else had such easy and unquestioned access to all the Markeys' paperwork.'

'It might,' Jennifer observed, 'make a great deal of difference in court. So, now it's *cherchez la femme*.' She looked across at Mitchell. 'Any more orders for tonight?'

'Just one for Adrian. The rest of you go home and think. Back here at eight and you won't be let in unless you can produce at least one good idea.'

Clement lingered as bidden, wondering what he had to do and unsure whether to feel privileged or resentful.

He cheered up when Mitchell asked, 'Are you running tonight?'

'I was planning to.'

'Splendid. Can you run on a course that takes you very frequently round Sefton's flat?'

Feeling it to be a great sacrifice, Clement offered, 'Would you prefer me to park outside it?'

Mitchell shook his head. 'I'll be doing that.'

'Wouldn't it be safer to bring him in now?'

'Yes, but it might be more interesting to follow him, you if he's on foot and me if he's driving. Make sure you've got your cell phone with you.' He was interrupted by his desk phone. Jain's pictures were ready. 'I'll send someone else for them. I want to be on this job as from now. Sefton's about to scarper. He's precious few reasons left for hanging around here.'

At first, Clement enjoyed his run around an area with which he had been intending to become more familiar. Sefton's district, once smart and prosperous, was coming down in the world. In the dusk there was a faint air of menace on the roads. The pavements were litter-strewn and he knew that mugging incidents were increasing. He had been surprised to learn that the prosperous-seeming Sefton was renting here. As he ran along the district's shopping street, he noticed a man look over his shoulder before drawing money from the cash dispenser outside the bank.

Two hours later, he had become as knowledgeable about his surroundings as he felt he would ever need to be. As he turned, for the fifteenth time, on his tedious circuit into Sefton's street he was hoping that his DCI would share his boredom sufficiently to call a halt to what seemed now a pointless proceeding.

As he passed Mitchell's car this time, the passenger door opened and he was invited in. The pair had very little to show for their vigil. No one had arrived at the house.

Several people had left, but none, in however clever a disguise, could have been Sefton.

Sweating profusely, but with his breathing even, Clement asked, 'Sure you want me in unshowered?'

'I've smelt worse in the cells on a Friday night.'

'What were you hoping? That the lady friend would turn up again in spite of her frosty welcome last night?'

Mitchell shrugged. 'Or that he'd lead us to her.'

'Maybe she's there already.'

'What, in the dark? Are there any lights at the back of the building?'

Clement shook his head. 'Not at his windows. There's a door, though. Why are we only watching the front?'

'We're watching the back.' Clement remembered the scruffy youth kicking a ball against a wall in the back lane. 'Shall we go visiting then?' Clement made no move. 'Wake up! What are you dreaming about?'

Clement wiped his beaded forehead with a damp arm. 'I'm wondering why uniforms can't do this obbo, rather than a DCI.'

'Simple. The powers that be don't think there's a case to answer and uniforms won't work for the love of it like you.'

'So, you've got another willing stooge round the back?'

'Not to say willing, but he owes me. For the rest, it's just me and you, chum.'

Not displeased with this answer, Clement reached for the door handle, sending waves of sweat-laden air to engulf his DCI. Mitchell wrinkled his nose. 'Your urgent need of a bathroom can be our excuse for calling.'

They walked to the door of number 9 and rang the bell to Flat 2. 'That means the first floor, I suppose.'

Clement had done his homework this time. 'He has the whole of the first floor. There's a young couple with an infant below and students in separate rooms on top. You realize that, if they're in, we'll probably be dragging them out of bed?'

'Excellent.' Mitchell rubbed his hands. When a second assault on the bell produced no answer, he tried the door. It opened on to a square lobby, part of what must once have been an imposing entrance hall. A door to their left led, presumably, to the ground-floor flat. Looking up the stairwell they could see a similar lobby on the floor above. They trod uncarpeted stairs to reach it.

The bell here produced no result. Mitchell knocked, knocked harder, finally hammered. The door remained closed but the angry ground-floor resident appeared below to remonstrate. When Mitchell heard the thin wail of what his expert ears judged to be a toddler, rather than a small baby, he felt compunction.

He produced his warrant card. Clement, expecting to hear him make a spirited defence of his right to do his job, was surprised at his humble apology. 'My twins are just four now, but their toddling days are recent enough for me to realize the trouble we've caused you.'

Now the young woman was putty in his hands. 'Never mind. At least I've only one. You'll not raise Sean, though. He's not there.'

'Do you know where he is or whether he'll be long?'

'Not really. He was loading some stuff into his car this afternoon. Said he was off on a business trip and wouldn't be back for a while.'

The two officers exchanged rueful glances. Clement asked, 'Is there anyone else here who'd know?'

'I can't say for certain, but I doubt it.' The wails below redoubled. 'I'll have to go and settle him. If you can wait a few minutes, I might be able to help you.' She regarded Clement's brief shorts and vest with some amusement. His skin, as they stood on the draughty landing, was goosepimpled. 'You look chilly. I'll make a hot drink if you like.'

Gratefully, they followed her downstairs and into her own territory. The child had left his bed and was sobbing in the hall. She picked him up but the wailing began again.

Mitchell held out his arms. 'If we look cold, you look exhausted. Give him here and you put the kettle on.'

She demurred. 'He's at the clingy stage, roars at strangers.'

Mitchell reached for the boy and began playing a game with his fingers. In seconds, his face still wet, the child was trying to copy him. The woman's jaw dropped. Clement's dropped lower. When the mother arrived with the promised refreshment the child was asleep in Mitchell's arms.

His reward was meagre. Sefton, said Mrs Brownlow, had driven along the road in the direction of the middle of town.

'You think he might have been going to the station?'

'I doubt it. He couldn't have carried all the stuff he had in the car.'

'He was on his own?'

She nodded. 'Come to think of it, though, the front passenger seat was empty. He'd crammed all the clutter of stuff into the boot and on to the back seat. Maybe he was picking someone else up.'

Mitchell took out Jain's picture and handed it across, being careful not to disturb the sleeping boy. 'Have you seen this woman before?'

She gave it her full attention. 'Yes, just the once, yesterday afternoon. She came here looking for Sean but he was out. She came down here to ask. I told her, wherever he spent his day, he spent most evenings having a quiet pint in the Fleece. Actually, she asked me if he had a girlfriend. I told her it was none of my business. I thought she might be a reporter. Is she?'

'Why did you think that?'

'Well, I've seen that man here sometimes – the one who was mown down in that terrible accident on Saturday . . .'

They took their leave a few minutes later, their sensible witness having declared that she had nothing else to tell that would be of any use to them. Clement handed over a card with the incident room number and the usual request. 'If you do think of anything else that might help us . . .'

'Yes, I'll ring the number. What if there's a way you could help me?'

'Do you have a problem?'

'Often.' She glanced down at her son, now gently snuffling on her own lap, then across at Mitchell. 'And you seem to have the perfect answer to it.'

Having dispatched Clement to make himself clean and fragrant, Mitchell rang his wife. She sounded long-suffering and spoke against a background of cheering and excited shouting. 'Whatever's going on?'

'Some foreign football match. Alex has arrived to watch it here because his TV's on the blink. It's only just started too. There'll be another hour of it at least.'

'Splendid. He can listen out for the kids and you can meet me in the Fleece.' He anticipated her objection to his suggested venue. 'It's Sefton's local. I think he's gone farther afield but I'm living in hopes that his lady might not have realized that yet.' Quickly he brought her up to date with his day's discoveries.

A quarter of an hour later they were sharing a table from where Mitchell could see the door of the lounge bar. Virginia was showing a lively interest in the progress of the case. 'Let me have a look at Sefton's woman then.' Mitchell handed over the photograph which Smithson had picked up from Jain's house and delivered to Mitchell's car as he kept his watch. She examined it closely. 'Well, this rules out Val, not that she was a likely candidate.'

'Smithson says it's not Jane Kyte. She wasn't likely either. She'd be aware of the possibilities of a scam like this but she'd hardly involve her own company and she was the one who encouraged Mr Abson to come to us.'

'Is there no national database for insurance policies?'

'Apparently not. According to Mr Abson, some countries have one. That leaves Nicky Simpson or someone else who, as far as we're concerned, has only just come on the scene. We'll know whether Mrs Simpson can be left out as well as soon as I've shown that picture to Caroline. I'm not disturbing her tonight. I don't think the Simpsons will want to absond before morning.'

Virginia picked up the photograph again. 'She's a lovely woman, apart from the horsy teeth. She's attractive even with them. It's odd that one arrangement of the standard set of features should be so much more pleasing than another, usually by general consent, though I suppose it's often by media persuasion too.'

Mitchell groaned. 'For Pete's sake don't go all philosophical. I want some practical suggestions.'

She ignored him. 'It's the same really in any aesthetic area, the arrangement of words and musical notes, or of features in a painting, the movements in a dance . . .' She stopped as her husband got up from the table in response to the call for last orders.

When he returned, bearing a pint of bitter and a half of lager, he brought an ultimatum. 'Put all that stuff about arranging things in your next article and forget about it for tonight.' He held her glass aloft and put it on the table in front of her only when she gave the required promise.

She pushed it aside, then asked, 'So, have I got this right? Sefton deals with each company himself, negotiates as if for Phyllida and gets his female accomplice to sign all the proposal forms. Then he applies for copies of the death certificate, still on Phyllida's behalf, presents them and the policies and collects the cheques. What's on the death certificate, by the way?'

'As from Monday, the super, in his wisdom, decreed accidental death.'

Virginia nodded. 'Right. His accomplice, with stolen documents which are returned before Phyllida misses them –'

'If she did miss them he could always make some excuse for having needed them. Phyllida didn't take a close interest in what was going on.'

204

'Right again. The accomplice opens a series of new accounts and pays in the cheques. What then?'

'How do you mean?'

'Well, the money is still in the name of Markey. The only way I can think of that she could get it out would be using the cards she's been given at a cash dispenser. What can you take out – two fifty pounds a day? Someone might well be on to them before they'd taken it all, especially if one of the banks got suspicious about the steady stream of withdrawals.'

'They'll try to take it out as soon as it's available – almost certainly by a cheque for the whole amount to an account abroad. She'll probably have some story ready about it.'

'So, what are you doing about that?'

Mitchell took a long draught from his tankard. 'About the accounts, nothing until tomorrow. About Sefton's chances of getting at them – well, I've put a stop on his passport and put out an alert for him in as many places as I can think of.'

'On whose authority?'

Mitchell looked mulish. 'I can do it on my own authority for forty-eight hours.'

'Well, whatever trouble you've stirred up for yourself with your immediate boss, I think you're right in casting your net wide to find Sefton now. He sounds to have taken far too much luggage to have gone on a day trip to Cleethorpes. I'm not surprised to hear you've found he's a villain.'

'Why do you say that? He seemed a pleasant enough chap to me.'

'Geoff Maynard didn't like him. Maynard has always looked for the best in the worst villains and found something to like – even in you, Benny. There must have been something basically amiss about Sefton, even at school, that he became aware of. It'll be interesting to ask him. So, how soon are you intending to take all this to John Carroll? Before the arrest? After the trial?'

'I'm debating between tonight and tomorrow morning.'

'Make it tomorrow then. He'll be in a better frame of mind and it gives me time to add powdered Mogadon to your breakfast coffee. What else have you planned for tomorrow?'

'A long sleep if you have anything to do with it. If I survive my interview with the super and my breakfast, I shall ring all the banks in the phone book to ask about accounts in the name of Phyllida Margaret Markey. Then I shall find out which branches were used and which personnel carried out the transactions. Then I shall send several people, certainly including Shakila, to speak to those people and show them the photograph. An odd detail about our much sought lady from each of them and we might have a useful collection of information to begin a search for her.'

'And ditto with all the building societies, I suppose.'

'I'll leave Clement on that. Finding out exactly what Sefton's little haul amounts to should keep him off my back for a while. Drink up. Your brother will think we've left him those kids to bring up single-handed.'

Mitchell's dreams were pleasant on Thursday night. In them he entered his superintendent's office and, in triumph, threw down the evidence, some of it admittedly circumstantial, that a murder had been committed. John Carroll offered unreserved congratulations to his DCI for finding the killer in spite of his own unremitting opposition to the investigation.

Mitchell's subconscious mind had conveniently woken him before he had had to admit that the man he set out to arrest had left the town for parts unknown. Over breakfast on Friday morning, he alternately planned how he would enjoy his triumph in reality and berated himself for not arresting Sefton immediately after that first talk with Gordon Abson.

Forty minutes later, as he tapped on Carroll's door, he had a change of heart. Maybe he would do better to take

206

the approach Ginny had advised 'The first thing I'd casually mention,' she'd remarked, as she burned the toast, 'would be that he was in court all day yesterday and not available for consultation.' This suddenly seemed good advice. He wondered how she had known where the super had been yesterday and decided she must have been talking to Jennifer.

He took a deep breath and opened the door. The superintendent was seated behind his desk. So, it was to be a formal interview. He tried to contain the smug smile that kept twitching his lips. 'Whilst you were in court, sir, there were a few developments.'

'So the grapevine tells me.' Carroll's expression was grave rather than unfriendly. He remained silent. The initiative was with Mitchell.

'We had a visit, sir, from a clerk, or whatever his title, from the Norwich Union office in Hill Street . . .' Mitchell gave a fairly honest description of his team's labours, stressing the necessity to follow up swiftly the new information provided by Gordon Abson and by PC Jain. 'We thought it was virtually certain that, in the circumstances, you would have sanctioned what we did.'

The superintendent heard him out, then observed, with a tight smile, 'You think, possibly, that, given your head, you'd have pre-empted any payout by arresting Mr Sefton on a murder charge.'

With a superhuman effort, Mitchell managed not to agree with this supposition. 'If the papers had been screaming murder, sir, Sefton would have known none of the companies would pay up. He'd have gone underground sooner. I don't think there would have been sufficient grounds for an arrest before yesterday.'

He suspected that it took a similar superhuman effort on the part of his superintendent to refrain from saying, 'When did that stop you?'

Mitchell continued, 'If you can spare the time, sir, I think the best way to bring you up to date with the details would be for you to attend the briefing. There'll be reports coming in that I haven't heard myself.'

Carroll laughed. 'I was coming anyway, but it's nice to be invited.' Mitchell got up to leave. His superintendent let him reach the door. 'And, Benny . . .'

'Sir?'

'Someone, I suspect either your sergeant or your wife, gave you some very good advice before you came in here.'

Mitchell had enjoyed his morning meeting with his team. They had been feeling the superintendent's breath hot on the backs of their necks and working out how much of their reports they could present without giving evidence of their DCI's disobedience. All had been sweetness and harmony, with the exception of plaintive mutterings from Smithson who had spent the previous day researching all Valerie Tate's refused invitations.

He had cheered up when Mitchell sent him to telephone a witness who had seen a damaged Fiat Uno being driven through Gretna. Clement was now busy trying to trace all the investments that had been made in Donald Markey's life and demise.

Shakila and Jennifer were dealing with the several less significant matters that had arisen overnight, his sergeant accepting her lot with more grace than his DC. Mitchell had saved for himself the marathon trawl through the list of banks and building societies that Sefton's accomplice might have approached about opening a new account. He felt more thankful than he had expected to be doing it with his superintendent's authority.

Towards the end of the morning, John Carroll knocked on Mitchell's office door, waiting to be invited before entering. His conscience now clear, Mitchell waited for whatever he had to say.

The superintendent remained in the doorway. 'You

look like a hungry man. Shall we have a spot of lunch downstairs?'

Mitchell grinned to himself. He had decided to grab a sandwich at his desk but going to the canteen in this exalted company would quickly empty the tables and get rid of the queue that made a hot meal so time-consuming. Carroll regularly, though not frequently, ate with his 'men'. The women objected to his terminology and the men to what they considered his patronizing tone. They had not become comfortable with having him on their territory, though the canteen culture grudgingly admitted him to be 'something approaching human – for a plain-clothes super, at any rate'.

Mitchell got himself outside a generous meal as he reported on his morning. 'Twelve places have had accounts opened in the name of Phyllida Margaret Markey in the last four months. Lloyds said, as I knew they would, that Mrs Markey had had three different accounts with them ever since she came to Cloughton thirty-two years ago. Sefton began handling some of her affairs three years ago and more or less all of her husband's two years before that. He wouldn't go into more details over the phone.'

'I'm not surprised. What he said was more than I'd have expected.'

'He did take the precaution of ringing me back and asking for me by title.' Mitchell put down his knife and fork and regarded Carroll resentfully. His plate had been heaped as high with greasy food as Mitchell's own, yet there was not a spare ounce of flesh on the man.

'Any news of a sighting?' Mitchell shook his head. 'Does Jain have a picture of him too?'

Another shake. 'Jain was hoping the woman wouldn't tell him she'd carelessly let him take hers.'

'So what are you going to do now?'

'Check on Sefton. Where and when has he lived in Cloughton? What family has he, here or elsewhere? What properties does he own, here or anywhere else? Who's his doctor? – and so on.'

'The flat?'

'Rented, and only since last January.'

'Right. I'll let you get on with it then.' Conforming with the request on the poster on the wall, Carroll began to scrape and then stack his and Mitchell's crockery on the trolley.

'You're wasting your time, mate,' Mitchell told him silently. 'They won't like you any better for being humble.'

Returning to his office, Mitchell found Shakila waiting in the corridor outside. He opened his door for her and waved her to a chair. 'Just give me a minute to look at my messages.' He picked up the three slips of paper on his desk but his telephone rang before he could read any of them.

Shakila listened in unashamedly. Mitchell answered guardedly to frustrate her. When he put the receiver down he was grinning broadly. 'Shakila, you're in the right place at the right time yet again. You're going to a small branch of Barclay's in Leeds.' He scribbled an address on a page of his notebook and tore it out for her. 'Ask for a Miss Lisa Prentice.'

Shakila caught his excitement. 'What do I want from her?'

'Anything you can persuade her to tell you. She opened an account for the second Phyllida Markey in March this year. We're looking for a woman. Your witness is a woman. You're a woman. How the hell can a man tell you what she noticed and knows?'

The manager of the Barclay's branch which employed Lisa Prentice did his best to charm Shakila, offering her all assistance and giving her a tiny office in which to speak to his counter clerk. Neither woman was deceived.

'Don't keep me longer than you have to,' the girl begged, nervously, as she examined the photograph

210

Shakila produced. 'He's all sweetness to you but he's annoyed that I'm off the counter, especially as I might have involved the bank in some shady business we might be blamed for. Yes, that's her.' She handed the picture back.

'It'll take as long as it takes, I'm afraid, but I won't spin it out. Just tell me exactly what went on between you and this woman.'

Lisa swallowed, prepared herself to begin her account, then looked up anxiously. 'Has she really got herself into serious bother? She's got enough problems as it is, without me dropping her in it.'

'What trouble?'

Lisa repeated the story of the woman's divorce and her need to have money of her own. Before she had finished, she fell silent, watching Shakila's expression. 'She was stringing me along, wasn't she? She was laundering money? Well, that's my job finished.'

Shakila shook her head. 'I doubt it. She must be a clever customer. She's pulled the same trick in several other banks.'

'I'm not sure that's going to help.'

'We could play on how Barclay's helped to stop her. After all, you're the only one to remember her.'

The girl looked slightly less worried. 'She really took me in. I was really sorry for her.'

'And bent the rules for her?'

'Only very slightly, if at all.'

'OK. Let's think about why you remember her. As my boss pointed out, women notice things about another woman that a man would miss.'

Lisa's face lit up. 'I know what you mean. I thought about her a lot after both times I dealt with her. I envied her. She's one of those women who always looks right.'

Shakila grinned. 'My sergeant's another. She could come to work in an old blanket and make you wish you'd got one like it. Then you realize you'd only look as though you were wrapped in a blanket!'

'Yes. On the train, on the way home that day, I was

211

trying to work out how she did it. It wasn't clothes, but everything else was right. Her nails were filed and varnished. Her hair looked as though she'd done nothing with it but it still looked right. You need a good cut – and the right kind of hair – for that. When she came the second time, she was very tanned but I think it might have been fake. She wasn't all that young and the sun would have made old skin dry. It wasn't a home job, though. Not a sign of a darker patch or a streak. And her make-up was so subtle you wondered whether it was there. You can't get that effect with cheap stuff. I think now that she probably wore casual gear – you know, to . . .'

'Throw the rest into relief?' The girl nodded doubtfully, obviously not knowing the expression.

'I think she might be a beautician. Then she could get it all done on the cheap and she'd know all the tricks.'

'But you said –'

'Yes, but *you* said she was telling a load of lies.'

Halfway through the afternoon, Mitchell answered his phone yet again. 'Sir, I've found her.'

'Found the Prentice woman?'

'The second Mrs Markey. She's called Arlene Asquith.'

'Are you certain? How did you do that?'

'By booking seventeen facials.'

212

Chapter Nine

'Keep me up to date with every development,' Carroll had said. Mitchell obediently picked up the phone. He had hardly moved from his desk today, spent hours with the telephone receiver to his ear, yet he felt involved and in control of the case.

'Sir, we've found her – the woman in the photograph. Actually, to give credit where it's due, Shakila found her. With the help of a strapping young PC that Leeds have lent us for the journey, they're bringing her in. Shall I wait for you before I start questioning her?'

'I think this is your show, Benny. Just let me know how much further on we are when you've done with her.'

Mitchell decided that he too could make a sacrifice. 'I reckon the women'll get more out of her than a bloke. How about Jennifer and Shakila for an example of out of the frying pan into the fire?'

'Or Morton's fork, perhaps?'

'Who's what?' Mitchell replaced the receiver.

Arlene Asquith had not spoken a word since she had entered the station. The interview, if it could be so called, had so far lasted ten minutes. She had not confirmed that she understood her rights, nor indicated either in the negative or the affirmative whether she wished to be legally represented.

Jennifer was now calmly making a shopping list on the back page of her notebook. Shakila merely stared at a point between Miss Asquith's eyes. After some further time, she remarked conversationally, 'Your lipstick's smudged.'

'I don't wear lipst . . .' The woman's expression was murderous.

In the same tone, Shakila said, 'Now you've started, you may as well go on.'

Miss Asquith thought about it, then shrugged. 'All right. Why am I here? What exactly are you accusing me of?'

Patiently Jennifer set the tape recorder going again, went through the procedures required by PACE, then sat back, leaving the questioning to her DC.

Shakila began by answering the question she had already been asked. In layman's terms, she told Arlene Asquith that she had been arrested on suspicion of money laundering and being an accessory to a murder. There was another long silence. Jennifer sighed and reached to turn the tape off again. Shakila's gesture indicated she should sit back in her chair.

Arlene Asquith turned to the DC. 'Will things go better for me if I tell you all about it?'

'It certainly won't do you any harm.'

Resentfully and apparently inconsequentially, she said, 'He hit me!'

Shakila's tone was laconic. 'He hit Donald Markey. You came off better than he did.'

'Big deal. He's not going to get away with slapping me around.'

'Fine. Tell us all about it, as you were suggesting, and there'll be a lot more he won't get away with.'

She made a sound, halfway between a laugh and a sob. 'He was going to marry me to keep me quiet. Now he wants to marry her to save himself the trouble of doing all this again.'

'To marry Phyllida Markey, you mean?'

'Who else?'

'I know. You have to be specific for the tape.'

She nodded. 'I meant that Phyllida Markey has enough money to satisfy even Sean. He'd be able to spend all the time without taking so many risks. I'm a risk to him now. I'm learning to look both ways when I'm crossing the road.'

Having served her purpose of getting the witness into a frame of mind to talk, Shakila sat back and let Jennifer take her through the story, most of which the team had already pieced together. The pair had met when Miss Asquith's first business was about to go into liquidation and her house sold to pay her debts. Desperate to avoid returning to her parents' house, she had first agreed to help him and later moved in with him.

'Did you realize how he intended to come by the money you were to make available to him?'

'Not when I first agreed and was given a small advance. I did after Mr Markey died.'

Her share in the proceeds of the scam had not been great and she had taken a job in what had used to be a rival salon to be able to leave Sefton's flat and rent her own. 'Sean wasn't keen on me moving out. He'd realized I wasn't just his puppet and wanted me where he could keep an eye on me.'

'Not in the Fleece, though.'

'No. That was what made him decide I was a loose cannon and plan to move me away from here. I wasn't prepared to be taken over and refused to go. Then, as I told you, he hit me.'

Jennifer nodded. 'You won't be surprised to hear that our first priority is to find him. Have you any idea where –'

'I wish I knew myself. I wasn't joking when I said I daren't cross a road.'

'OK. Let's try another way. Tell me everything you know about him – even things you think we wouldn't have the slightest interest in.'

Miss Asquith looked nonplussed but did her best. 'He doesn't seem to have any family – not that he talks about, anyway.' There was another long silence that she broke herself when she saw Jennifer's impatient expression. 'I'm

215

not messing you about now. I just don't know what to say.'

'Where did you live for the time that you were together?'

'In a flat in Leeds but he sold that. He moved to Cloughton and started working for the Markeys. He owns a place up in Scotland somewhere but I've no idea where. He mentioned it right at the beginning when I was doing everything he wanted. I asked him what we'd do and he said we could go there. He was very vague and I wasn't encouraged to press.'

Jennifer paused, wondering how much of what she was hearing could be believed. Shakila took the opportunity to butt in. 'Did you notice anything at all unusual about him, apart from the illegal way he makes a living?'

Miss Asquith frowned. 'I think he has another name.'

'A second forename?'

'No, a completely different one.'

'What makes you think that?'

'Twice I've seen letters in his wallet addressed to a . . . Mr McKenzie, I think it was. The address was a Scottish one. I suppose it might have been the property he told me about.'

'Can you remember any part of it?'

The witness wrinkled her nose as she thought. 'Does Dufftown make any sense? That's what's coming back to me. Is it a real place?'

Neither officer knew. Jennifer asked, 'Does Sefton know you saw these letters?'

'We never talked about it. I shouldn't think so. Was that helpful?'

'I think it might be.'

'Good. Does it earn me a lift back to Leeds?'

'You aren't going to Leeds, I'm afraid. At the moment you aren't going anywhere.'

The murderous look came back and Miss Asquith's lips made a thin straight line. Shakila thought that she would

216

have rather more trouble getting her witness to break her silence this time.

DC Caroline Jackson returned to the station after completing her day of mundane duties which had included an interview with the mother of Shaun Grant. No other member of the shift was to be found, but a note, left on her desk by Clement, explained the situation briefly. A search in Dufftown, made by the Grampian police, had produced a Kenneth J. McKenzie, or, at least, Sean Sefton masquerading under that name. He was at that moment being escorted back to Cloughton.

It was the usual time for debriefing but no one appeared to take it, so Caroline wandered downstairs to consult Magic. As always, he knew exactly what was happening and answered her question in his inimitable manner. 'Pub at eight thirty.'

'Which one?'

'Fleece. Ours.' Caroline understood. In a town where the industry had centred round wool since the time when its inhabitants had lived in wooden huts, there was an abundance of public houses with signs that depicted cartoon sheep, sweet, clean, sentimental sheep and evil-looking rams. The informal discussion, replacing the debriefing, would be in the station's local, where the sign displayed a woolly ball with a surprised-looking face. It was not, Caroline had long ago decided, an impressionist design – just a very bad painting.

She glanced at her watch. There would still be time to go home to have tea with Cavill if she snatched a quick coffee in the canteen. There she heard a more detailed, though possibly garbled version of the day's events. The news and the coffee, dire but stimulating, jointly provided her with a better idea as to how she should spend the intervening time.

The back room in the station's particular Fleece was saved

for the force's almost exclusive use. Officers met there so frequently, and the liquor flowed so freely, that the landlady was willing. Caroline found her colleagues sitting round two sides of the table in the corner, comfortably sprawled on velvet-covered bench seats.

She grabbed a stool and placed it opposite Mitchell. Clement, who had leapt up when she entered, returned to place a brimming glass in front of her. She nodded her thanks.

Mitchell eyed her with mock severity. 'You're late.'

'I've been busy.'

'Get anywhere with Mrs Grant?'

'I listened to a list of Shaun's virtues and two conflicting alibis. You'd almost have thought she loved him. Oh, and I've been making some phone calls.' She picked up her glass and made them wait till her throat, dry from so much talking, was well lubricated before continuing. 'To some insurance companies. Not all of them were still functioning. Good line to work in – they go home for tea.'

'Go on!'

Caroline gave Mitchell a hard look and decided that he was not quite sober. 'Both the Pru and AXA found in their records a policy paid out upon the death of a Kenneth James McKenzie. It was four years ago. Cause of death – a road accident. He was insured with each of the companies for a sum just below their free medical limit . . .'

There was a clamour.

'So, he got away with that one . . .'

'And pinched the poor bloke's documents to set himself up with a new identity in Scotland . . .'

'And bought this property in Dufftown in that name . . .'

Everyone but Mitchell looked excited. 'But I promised Ginny I'd take a day off tomorrow.'

Shakila spoke for them all. 'Who needs you? We'll sort out the rest of it between us.'

Epilogue

Khalid Jain still had no wish to join CID, but he had begun to feel the stirrings of ambition. He was studying at present for his sergeant's examinations. He still loved his patch, but now he also loved a little red-haired police cadet and therefore must begin to make his way in the world.

If he progressed far enough up the police ladder not to have a beat to walk, he'd have to be like Clement and run round it in his own time. His foot was healing nicely now. Perhaps he'd see what sort of a shot he could make at running quite soon.

Nicky Simpson, found guilty of nothing more than self-indulgence, adultery and manipulation of others for her own convenience, had not been required to appear in court.

Under the stern supervision of Cavill Jackson she was studying piano and music theory. Under her own sterner eye, she was studying how to be a better wife.

Since it was obviously what he wanted, Phyllida Markey had sent her son back to his beloved Haygarth College. Her house in Cloughton had been bought by a company of men whose sect made them remarkable – in that area at any rate – for their shaved heads and bright orange robes. The neighbours were suspicious of their quiet behaviour and their signs on the outer wall, written in an unrecognizable script.

219

Phyllida, oblivious of her former neighbours' disapproval, had moved to Sheffield, from where Zak could come home each weekend. It seemed a fair compromise. She had not given the Simpsons her new address.

The Tates had also moved house. Having been eventually convinced by his wife that his employers were exploiting him, Morris had become a partner in Valerie's desktop publishing business which was beginning to flourish. They lived now in a flat over their office premises in the shopping street patronized by Shakila Nazir. Occasionally, they all met in a queue for fast food and tried to remember where they had met before.

Virginia Mitchell picked up the one letter that constituted that morning's post. It was addressed to herself in writing that she recognized and her heart sank. Head on was the only way she knew to deal with an unpleasant task She opened the envelope and sat on the bottom stair to read the seven sheets it contained.

Dear Ginny,
I have three reasons for writing. The first is, of course, to apologize – for everything. The second is to try to explain. The third is to ask you to do something for me.

Her spirits falling, Virginia read on.

So, I'm very sorry for all the trouble I caused you and for trying to deceive you. I know that, if I return to the resentments of my childhood, you might stop reading, but I must touch on it briefly. I wasn't ever abused, either physically or sexually. Nor was I physically neglected. You knew me in those days. I was well fed and as well dressed as the rest of you, but, as you know, I felt that my parents were distant and not affectionate.

Even when my brother was away at his residential school, all the conversation was about how he was getting on, whether there was any improvement, when could he next come home. I used to wonder if they remembered that they'd ever had a daughter. They didn't even trust me to do anything for Colin. It was as if I wasn't there.

One of my few pleasant memories from that time was having my appendix out when I was sixteen, just after leaving school. In the hospital, a nurse would come in to me each morning, plump up the pillows and say, 'How are you today, Lorna?' It was just little things like that, asking if you had any pain or how your night had been. I felt that no one had ever felt so much concern about me before.

When I was discharged, I looked for a job. I didn't have many options, having messed up my GCSEs. I worked at a bakery and in a shoeshop and nearly died of boredom. Then I went to work in a hotel where I could live in, make a new start without life revolving round Colin. It wasn't much fun, cleaning up after a lot of ungrateful people and being expected to act cheerful twenty-four hours a day.

One day, in desperation, I pretended I had a terrible pain in my head and the manager sent me to the nearest hospital. I was the centre of attention again and had X-rays and scans but when they mentioned surgery I was scared. I didn't want them making a hole in my head and I said the pain was improving. I knew what I'd done was wrong, but I had to do it again.

I left the hotel and started a college course, picking up the exams I needed quickly. Then I started my nursing training. At least that bit of the story I told you was true. I did qualify eventually, but my studies were held up by further spells in hospital. Nobody seemed to suspect what I was doing. I added blood to my urine specimens and deliberately caused myself a series of 'accidents'.

Once, when I was working on the wards, I injected myself with bacteria from a patient and ended up in ICU. That time I was really scared that I might die.

I didn't always succeed in convincing the doctors and sometimes people who had begun by treating me very kindly could turn very nasty indeed when they realized what I was up to. One surgeon stormed up to my bed in front of all the other patients and ordered me to get out. At two hospitals, the staff took pictures of me to warn others to look out for me.

Usually, though, I ran away when people got suspicious. Once I still had stitches in and I had to take them out myself. That was no big deal for a nurse, of course. Once, up north, I was arrested, charged with stealing food and lodging from the hospital. My parents rallied round and helped me settle out of court.

You'll be wondering why I never made a genuine request for psychological help.

Virginia was asking herself just the same question. She had decided that, maybe, as well as appreciating the attention, Lorna was enjoying the game. She was tempted to throw the letter in the bin without finishing it. Did she care what sort of mess Lorna had made of her life and did she really want to get involved with her again? Impatiently, she screwed up the remaining sheets, but then could not bring herself to destroy them unread.

If someone had said, 'I know what you're doing but I don't know why,' I might have done that, but I was always approached in a confrontational way. I suppose doctors don't like being taken for fools, having people manipulate them, wasting their time and making them seem incompetent. I never intended to make doctors look stupid. I just wanted to be in hospital.

Now that I'm seeing Dr Fielding, I can see all the harm

I was doing. Sapping health care resources and denying myself the treatment I really needed. It's wonderful to be in a consistent relationship with a single caring doctor who's giving me insight into my motivation. I've ended my deceptions now because I don't need them. He asked me simple obvious questions that I ought to have asked myself – such as, did it ever occur to me that my parents' motive in keeping me from helping to care for my brother was that they didn't want his problems to spoil my life? They were trying to leave me free to benefit from my education and enjoy my friends. He agrees that they were wrong but not that their intentions were. I'm going to have to apologize to them too.

If you're still reading, Ginny, and haven't thrown my maunderings in the bin, let me tell you that I have a reason for inflicting them on you. I'm not just trying to justify the way I've behaved. Please read on.

The other day, I was in the waiting room before my appointment with Dr Fielding. Like all the other patients, I was passing the time by leafing through some magazines. To my surprise, I came across two articles written by you. One was about telling white lies and it really made me laugh. The other was about nursing your mother and that made me cry – cry inside at any rate.

Ginny, will you please write something about me? Not to collect sympathy for me and not mentioning me by name, but about people like me. I want other people with this disorder to know what I've learned. I thought I was hurting no one but myself and that I could stop what I was doing any time I wanted. It worked out differently though. It's inevitable that others are affected and I couldn't stop by my own willpower.

Through the therapy I've discovered that there are better ways to meet my need to be cared for. I used to think my tricks were the answer but they only caused more problems and solved nothing.

Thankfully, Virginia saw Lorna's signature at the bottom of the page. She heard Benny call from the dining room that her toast and coffee were cold. She went through and dropped the letter beside his plate. 'I should start halfway down page six. The rest is Lorna being self-indulgent.'

Mitchell read from where his wife's finger pointed, then looked up without the exasperated expression she had expected. 'That would be an interesting job for you. You might offer it to one of the broadsheets.'

Virginia grinned. 'The broadsheets have started to use their common sense at last. You can read the *Indy* now without needing a table top or arms like a gorilla's. Seriously, though, I'm not going to do it.'

'Why ever not?'

'Because my immediate reaction was the same as yours – that Lorna's story was something I could use to achieve my own ends. It should be written for Lorna's sake, and for people like her, as she says.' She looked at Mitchell, appealing for the right advice, not sure what she wanted to hear.

Mitchell knew his reply had to be carefully considered and couched in just the right terms. He thought he'd got it right. 'Bollocks!' he said.